Hidden

Mountain

(The Dominguez Adventures Volume II)

Sammy Sutton

Special Thanks

To Dr. Neely and his team at Barnes Jewish Hospital at Washington University in St. Louis, without you this book would have never reached the public. I will forever be thankful for the attention and care everyone gave and continues to give me upon each visit to your facility. Not only did you remove the threat, but you restored my quality of life. After only four months Hidden Mountain is complete.

ISBN-10:0985770902

E-Book ISBN-13:978-0-9857709-0-7

Disclaimer

Hidden Mountain *is a work of fiction. All events are products of the author's imagination. Any similarities to real people or situations are purely coincidental.*

This novel is dedicated to Eva L. Rehnquist. Your guidance and enthusiasm about **Hidden Mountain** gave me the courage to return to what I love.

Cover image by William Kenney.

Chapter 1

"The secret of a good memory is attention, and attention to a subject depends upon our interest in it. We rarely forget that which has made a deep impression on our minds."
Tyron Edwards

It's hard to say when I actually met Amanda. My first awareness of her came while I was in a state, not quite consistent with reality. Nevertheless, it was real to me, the man, but I am a scientist, therefore with reluctance, I will admit, I met Amanda in this accepted dimension at a Las Vegas High-Stakes poker game.

I am an anthropologist, more specifically, an archeological anthropologist. I study, analyze, and hypothesize man's relationship with, his environment, fellow man, and minutia he develops. It is by no accident that I said man, not woman, because I have yet to understand the female species.

My specialization is ancient man, and antiquities. I am well versed in several ancient languages. Convenient to my discovery at the Mountain, I am considered an expert in the area of Paleo-Hebrew pictogram translation. In other words, I study the behaviors of those who are now, dead. There is no doubt that I am far more knowledgeable about the long departed, than the current living. I accept this as a prevalent element of personal truth.

The University of New Mexico is home to my professional allegiance. Even though, I have not taught regular classes there in over a decade, I still play an intricate role in the Department of Anthropology. I give lectures when I'm stateside, and advise graduate students. More importantly to the administration, my work appeals to the departments endowments governing board. None of this should shadow the fact that I am an ardent fan of the UNM basketball Lobos.

I would be remiss if, I didn't mention the fact that I do not fit the common stereotype associated with my area of expertise. I am a Miami born Cuban-American with Jewish roots, recently coined by pop-culture as Jewban. For fifteen years I was estranged from my immigrant father, and had very few visits with my mother, and seven siblings. My Pop is a retired Miami Judge, whom has returned to the family law firm. By all accounts, I come from an extraordinarily successful family.

Pop always demanded excellence, and I always seem to disappoint his expectations. My other siblings conformed and specialized in law and finance, the family's customary line of work. In my father's harsh words, my career as an anthropologist, by design was unconventional and therefore equated with being a hippie. He claimed it was an excuse for educated grown-ups to roll around with one another in the dirt, and then, have the audacity to pretend it was a profession. Thanks to Amanda, my Pop and I have reconciled, and the man actually seems to respect me and my career.

It would be pure negligence not to revisit the events of that one particular day when my entire existence changed. I intended for the only aberrant activity to be a test drive in my new sports car, which I affectionately call, Raven. My taking a trip to Hidden Mountain was anything, but unusual. I couldn't begin to calculate the number of trips I made down New Mexico's interstate 25 from Santa Fe to Los Lunas. From the beginning, the Mountain has intrigued me, drawing me back time after time.

Hidden Mountain is one of America's most unique mysteries. It is a treasure trove of seemingly misplaced archaic evidence. If the area did not disturb so many ingrained beliefs, it would be considered a fantastical expose' of the era coinciding with the Israeli reigns of King David and his son King Solomon.

At a glance, from across the New Mexico landscape, Hidden Mountain is less than conspicuous; the summit only stands about 1800 feet above sea-level, and spans approximately twenty-two acres. The Mountain is covered in stilt, and ancient volcanic rock. The sparse vegetation is congruent to the area with an assortment of sage, cacti, and Amanda's favorite prickly pears.

Unintentionally, I'm sure; our civilization has added a couple of sardonic elements to the surroundings in the form of railroad tracks, and a landfill. The area is blockaded by a fence, and the general public must receive written permission to enter the premises. I am a common visitor; therefore I am afforded carte blanche entry.

On the way up the mountainside, a large Decalogue stone stands with inscriptions dating back to around 1000 B.C. The authenticity became a legal battle in the 1980's. A trial spawned, and ultimately, the inscriptions received verification. The Ten Commandments on the stone are ancient Paleo-Hebrew, and are the same as appear in Exodus, Chapter twenty.

An aerial view of the Summit provides unmistakable proof as to the presence of an ancient Hebrew campsite. The imprint of the landscape perfectly matches its counterparts in the Middle East. It has preternaturally been left undisturbed leaving virtually no room for doubt as to the validity of the comparison.

I was enjoying the hike and looking forward to my inevitable moments of speculation on the summit. The trip to the Mountain like all the others before it was status quo; at least until the second the earth collapsed under my feet, and I plunged into a pit within the ancient inactive volcano. I don't remember the actual journey downward. I do recall the moments after my descent. The images are strange, but vivid. Granted, more than one possible explanation exists for the polarizing evolution of events.

In the midst of a dry mist, from a deafening silence an ancient man appeared. He communicated with me, but without the need for words; it would be later before I would understand his revelations. In a flash, the archaic man dissolved out of existence, only to be replaced by a woman, whose gemstone eyes both frightened and intrigued me. Her faceted gaze pierced through my chest, to wrap around my soul. I wanted to touch her; the need was so strong, my body cried out in pain for the longing. I understood her telepathic message, but I couldn't then, nor could I now, translate it into a language any man could understand. An enormous pain ravaged through my gut as she faded into the cloudy abyss.

My torture continued as I was teleported through a vacuumed tunnel, back to this common reality, a place, I was not sure I wanted to be.

I spent the next few minutes rolling around on the cold hard rock within the dead volcano in utter anguish from the physical pain and the misery of my soul from being wrenched away from the welcoming vision before me. The pain of my body was compounded by the greatest moment of disgusting self-pity, I had ever known. In my darkest moment of abasement, I groped for the familiar and, I reached out for my glasses; but instead felt the familiar texture of an ancient animal skin. Searching with one hand for my elusive glasses, I kept one hand on the skin just in case it too decided to disappear. In disbelief I stroked the surface, and put on my recovered glasses, and fumbled for a flashlight.

Yes indeed, it was a bundle of scrolls and once illuminated and unfurled the true depth of its value was discovered for it was authored by none other than King Solomon. I emerged from the bowels of the volcano with a mission to find the woman in my hallucination, understand the intentions of the ancient King, and discover the rightful home for the treasures.

I found the woman, and the hold she has on my soul is the only reason I am still here. The adventures we have shared were only the first steps on a path we must follow in order to share the King's journey and find out what the end may hold.

Later during a return visit to the Mountain Amanda found the final scrolls. By this time, I had discovered, translated, and analyzed thousands of artifacts. Many possessed a prophetic undertone. My job as an anthropologist required I make conjectures about the meaning. Prior to finding King Solomon's Scrolls, I avoided the seductive temptation of linking archaic meaning to modern society, at least in any significant way.

Solomon's Scrolls were different. Despite the cabalistic nature of the message, it was clear the advice was meant for the present population. OPERA's explicit violent communication towards me supported my assumption.

After I authenticated the relics, Amanda and I put King Solomon's trustworthiness to the test. After all, The Scrolls were the most solid proof supporting his existence. Written off by many, his reputation had suffered brutal assault in recent years.

We worked for hours compiling a collection of ancient references to the popular King. Practically every culture in existence during his reign referred to him. Myth or reality; accurate or exaggerated; the King was an ancient rock star.

The eerie omen among the warnings garnered my attention. The Cosmos was about to emerge into an all-out war. Without protection, the Earth and the human race would be nothing more than pulverized collateral damage.

According to Solomon, twelve open nexus' existed around the planet. The thirteenth, not yet activated, was an imperative piece of the synergistic energy puzzle. The increased power would strengthen the protective magnetic field.

Complicating matters, opening the thirteenth gate demanded a Chosen One from each of the thirteen Tribes. Identifying this group would require me to test science, and ultimately disturb the beliefs of many.

At the same time, the mystical message tested Amanda and I personally. Humankind's relationship with one another as well as nature was an inescapable part of the King's journey. We were not excused from his lessons. For in the abyss of so-called coincidence, we were forced to face the wrath of our demons.

The nearing convergent cycles sparked my fears. The sun, the moon, and the earth would line-up forming The Galactic Alignment and end the 26, 000 year cycle. No one on Earth knew the impending results of the anomaly.

According to the ancients, the 13,000 year cycle hiding Isis would also end, soon. The spawning would trigger the beginning of a violent birthing cycle in the Cosmos, and once again, the beloved Isis would be unveiled to earth's inhabitants.

The night sky would light up for a 1000 years creating a

magnificent spectacle for all to experience. The question weighing heavy on me was; could Earth's magnetic field protect us from the nuclear fireworks in the Heavens?

The wise King Solomon saw the escalating energy as a problem. If the energy penetrated, the waning magnetic barrier would dissolve anything it contacted, and radiation would contaminate the rest. The thirteenth gate had to be opened to create the additional force field.

Signs of escalation were already in progress. The rising level of energy from the heightening Solar Cycle was already creating pockets of disaster. Our technological lifestyle was becoming a target of the constant threat.

Chapter 2

"The beginnings and endings of all human undertakings are untidy."
John Galsworthy

In a matter of days, my life as a dedicated archeological anthropologist had emanated into a world engulfed by secrets, risks, and espionage. Amanda's peculiar entrance into my once sterile intellectual world created nothing less than the perfect dichotomy. Hell, she was a dichotomy. Amanda's unusual radiance intrigued me from the beginning. She is both benevolent and alluring to this day, this often confuses me.

More importantly, at this particular point, I was obsessed with her mystery. At first, I believed her to be incredibly intelligent, but indecisive, perhaps even slightly off-center. In Miami, the events compelled me to draw a different conclusion. Somehow, the illogical became cryptic. Her demureness took on a new meaning.

Now here I am; recovering at my parent's expansive Miami home as a result of OPERA's henchmen having hurled me into a near oblivion that could only be described as death's doorstep. Operation Political Empowerment Reform Alliance, better known as OPERA is a powerful organization operating within obscure shadows of the United States Government, for reasons, not yet clear to me, they want King Solomon's Scrolls.

Finding Amanda and seeing her is my only thought. Trying to get out of bed made me realize just how weak I was.

Someone must have been posted out in the hallway to listen for movement, for soon after giving up getting out of bed on my own, Marc, my younger brother came into the room.

"Hey sleepyhead, finally decide to rejoin the living?"

I nodded, for trying to move my mouth had already proven painful. My tongue felt like it was wrapped in barbed wire and stapled for good effect.

"I know you have questions, and I will try to tell you all I know."

I mumbled and tried to say Amanda's name. I needed to know she was okay. Marc must have understood for he told me what I needed to know.

"Amanda is fine. Better than you anyway. Her injuries were slight and she doctored herself with the most amazing collection of little bottles and packs of flowers."

His words gave me a small token of relief, but I needed to see her with my own eyes.

"You are pretty banged up, but nothing lethal. Your mouth is going to take some time to heal. Pop says it's just the swelling and small cuts that he hopes do not get infected. Of course if they do-you might find it hard to be lovey-dovey with the flame haired beauty down the hall." I am quite sure Pop did not add that last part.

Once more I tried to rise from the bed, and Marc pushed me back down. "If you need the bathroom, just say so and I will bring that little pitcher Nydia left for you to use."

The image of indignity that picture brought to mind was enough for me to gain the strength I needed to push up on the side of the bed. The effort cost me greatly since I could only use one arm; the other was in a sling.

"Okay Antonio, I get the message. Just give me a minute to get Ramon. Your carcass weighs too much for me to get down the hallway on my own."

Funny man, I knew I was larger than my brothers, but hard work on dig sites gave my large frame the extra muscle I needed for my work. I could hear Marc laughing and the sounds of Ramon joining him as they neared the door. I am so glad my family gets such entertainment from my pain. Grimacing with sarcasm does not have quite the same effect as being able to say it; but it felt good anyway.

***

Barely able to move, I shuffled slowly along the hallway with assistance from my younger brother Marc on my left, and my brother-in-law Ramon on the right. I was determined to reach Amanda, to see for myself that she was fairing as well as they told me.

My thoughts became focused on Amanda when we entered the room.

I could see my appearance shocked her, but the joy on her face quickly replaced the shock. She rushed to my side and just the feel of her next to me gave me strength.

When I tried to speak, my mouth felt as if it was on fire, and

Amanda immediately began giving orders.

"Marc, Ramon, take Antonio into the bath, and I will bring something to help his pain." Amanda hurried to that infernal case of hers and began digging for God only knows what!

Marc and Ramon helped me into the bath and sat me down on the closed commode. I tried to mumble thanks. But it sounded and felt like I was speaking through crushed glass, and I soon gave up the effort.

Marc patted my shoulder, and Ramon said; "How about I get a pen and paper and you write what you want to say?" I nodded gratefully.

I made the mistake of looking in the mirror across from me, and my eyes widened at the sight. No wonder everyone was concerned, I looked as if I had gone 10 rounds with Hulk Hogan and lost!

Amanda came in with a small bottle; she smiled at me and set it down beside the sink. I tried to speak, and she patted me on my head and smoothed my curls. With all this patting I was beginning to feel like a sick dog. I watched Amanda fill a small glass with water and add a few drops of amber liquid from the bottle.

Amanda called Marc to help me stand beside the sink. Then she told me; "Antonio just swish this around inside your mouth, a small amount at a time. Do not swallow it."

With Marc propping me up on one side, I managed to take the small glass in one hand and raise it to my lips. I sniffed the contents, but the odor was flowery and slightly nice. Smelled sort of like spicy honey, I like Honey its sweet. I took a small sip and swished it around in my mouth. At first it was nice and then my mouth caught on fire, some of it went down my throat and I gagged; and did what came naturally, I spewed the amber colored water all over the mirror in front of me. Amanda was pounding my back and Marc was laughing. All I could do was wheeze as the effects of the medicine wore off.

I turned and looked at Amanda accusingly; "It was just a little Calendula powder and Tea Tree Oil." She replied defensively. "I told you not to swallow it."

Pushing the glass back to my mouth, Amanda insisted I finish the treatment. I closed my mouth and shook my head no. Marc was laughing again, and I pushed him with my hip.

"Drink it Antonio, stop being a baby!" Amanda had that obstinate look on her face, and I knew I would never hear the end of it from Marc if I wimped out now.

Sighing, just like the put-upon poor man I felt like-I swished and spit over and over until the foul brew was gone. My eyes were watering by the end and knew I was acting like a child when I tilted sideways out of feigned weakness and spit the last mouthful right on Marc's shoes.

Marc's exclamation of disgust almost made it worthwhile when he let go and I really did tilt all the way over and ended up on the floor.

"Damn-it Antonio, I'm sorry. No I'm not. You did that on

purpose!" Marc was still laughing while he helped me up. Amanda was now giving him the look, and I felt better already. My mouth did feel less painful, and I experimented with moving my tongue around and sighed with relief when I discovered the foul brew had rinsed out most of the glass.

My relief ended shortly after when Amanda said I had to repeat the process every two hours the rest of the day.

Marc called Ramon and the two of them helped me back into the bedroom. They were going to take me back down the hall, but I insisted with the aid of the small notebook and pen Ramon had brought, that I would stay here with Amanda.

"Of course you are staying here, we have been apart too long." Amanda's sweet compliance made me feel so loved. Marc and Ramon carefully assisted me in lying back on the soft bed where soon I hoped my love would join me.

"After all, I need to be sure you are taking care of your mouth and I have a few deep massage tricks that while painful, will help you get over that awkward step and make your arm feel better." I frantically wrote a note to Ramon and shoved it at him.

"Do not leave me here. Take me back to the small room. She is going to torture me when you leave." Both of my male compatriots read the note and looked at me with their brows raised, and then Ramon crumpled the note and threw it away. Both of them turned to look at Amanda; and I knew what they were seeing. A titan haired beauty with small hands and a petite body; how much harm could she do?

"Sorry brother, but you're on your own." They left me there to my fate; what kind of brothers were they? Petulantly I drew the covers over my shoulders, and vowed to ignore everybody for the rest of the day.

A soft knock at the door announced the arrival of my sister Nydia.

"Antonio, I made some tea, just the way you like it."

Okay, maybe not everybody. My sister Nydia was sweet and kind and she loved me, no matter how stupid I acted. Besides she made great tea. Don't get me wrong, while Nydia was a truly good woman, you have to remember the Judge was her father and she inherited half of her genes from him; and sometimes there was no hiding the fact that she was truly his daughter!

I mumbled my now familiar version of thank you, and Amanda fluffed the pillows behind me so I could sit up and drink the tea.

I watched Nydia and Amanda chat for a while, and had to smile. While both were beautiful, tiny women, well-educated and well spoken; there the comparison stopped. Nydia was the consummate wife and mother with a streak of stubbornness and loyalty to her family. She was well educated and well spoken, but she used her charms in subtle ways that kept my brother in-law wrapped around her fingers. She kept her hands in projects that promoted his career and allowed her to be a moving force without ever allowing people to realize she was there behind the scenes; like a chess master.

On the other hand, my Amanda; she was a virtual silent dynamo. Never letting anyone too close she moved through life with a purpose, towards a goal that not even I knew the full story of yet. But I knew we would soon have to breach that wall she built around herself and get to those secrets she guarded so fiercely. If Nydia was a chess master, Amanda was the one who wrote the book of the rules.

As the women's voices washed over me, I began to doze off and the last thing I remember is the touch of Amanda's hands as she gently gripped my face and kissed my forehead. Her voice was soft as she murmured; "Sleep my love, and I will wake you in a couple of hours." That jolted me for a moment as my peaceful drift into sleep was interrupted by the reminder of torture to come! Yet, not even that was enough to stop my weary body from claiming sleep.

Chapter 3

"It is sometimes an appropriate response to reality to go insane."
— *Philip K. Dick*

The next day, I awoke to the sound of Jose's voice. "Antonio, you need to wake up for a while." The sound of my brother's voice jarred me back from a dream world where Amanda was fading away before my eyes-looking towards the door, my brother's form was murky...I tried to focus. "Jose'?" I was glad that my mouth seemed to have improved enough for me to be understood. "Glasses," I couldn't see a thing without them. Jose moved to the nightstand and placed my glasses in my hand.

My brother Jose', the oldest son was and always will be a younger version of my Pop. Always the attorney; he never wasted words he laid out the agenda, and stated the obvious. "Antonio, you need to wake up, we're about to receive information from a very reliable source, and you should be present." With that cryptic message, Jose turned and left us alone.

The sound of the closing door aroused Amanda; sleepily she asked; "Is something wrong?" She rolled her daunting eyes at me when I chuckled.

"Nothing love, just an invitation from Jose." Unlike the long days before, my voice was once more understandable.

Waking fully, Amanda sat up and hugged my neck. Her excitement bounced through the tones in her voice. "Antonio, I am so thrilled you are able to talk."

"Well it certainly is an improvement over yesterday when I could not speak and just had to listen." I responded with a faked tone of hurt. Despite the fact that I'm not a kid, Amanda brings out a much younger version of me. I loved to tease her, but sometimes I forget that she can't always tell when I am teasing or serious. Since Amanda immediately pulled away and looked contrite, I could not hold onto my faked demeanor of hurt feelings.

"Come here honey." I said in my best imitation of Rickey Ricardo. She smiled and placed her sweet lips against mine. I didn't mind the pain. Our eyes met for one entranced moment. Her speckled tanzanite eyes remain my kryptonite.

I pleaded with her to lock the door. Amanda rose from the bed, and moved gracefully across the floor. She turned the knob into the lock position. I watched her return, my anticipation building. She floated back to me like an angel in flight. I raised my uninjured arm to her, but she reached for the other.

With a quick inspection she turned my arm over and moved it up and down. She explained. "We need to remove these bandages, so you can shower. When you are finished, I will put some fresh ones on these wounds." Her voice was beautifully normal this morning-only she wasn't uttering the romantic words I had been hoping for! What in the hell, that wasn't at all what I had in mind. What happened to my temptress? This woman was a replica of a military nurse calling out orders; brush your teeth, shower, and don't forget to shave.

I still looked like hell, my body was bruised and blue, but in reality, the wounds were mostly superficial. As painful as they were to the touch, they weren't threatening. Amanda went to open the door, but I thought differently. If I wasn't to have the romantic, sensual interlude I was imagining, then I would have some answers to some tough questions-or force Amanda to respond honestly another way.

"Amanda, come here, bring your train case," I ordered. In recent days during the morning hours Amanda approached the day with exuberance. This was in stark contrast to the pasty pale cranky woman she became by the afternoon and evening hours. I understood Amanda had allergies and sensitivities that had a history of developing out of control. After all, Amanda was a Levite her affliction was genetic dating back to the time of Solomon. The sensitivities of the Levite Priests proved to be a lifesaving adversity in ancient Israel.

She kept her supplies in a black train case along with her witchy brews she used in her so-called herbal remedies that I often called voodoo. This train case was an unreasonably protected possession and I intended to find out why.

"Antonio, honestly we do not have time for that right now." I turned to face her to make sure she heard me.

"I understand exactly how much time we have. I need to

check a couple of things." She delivered the case, turned, and walked away from me.

I assessed the contents, and removed several items. My obtrusion angered her, "Why are you suddenly so interested in my train case?"

"Amanda calm down, I'm simply taking an inventory of your supplies." Her secrets began to annoy me.

Her skin turned a brilliant red. "I will have you know, I am perfectly capable of taking care of my own supplies." Her haughty, brusque reply should have been more than enough to warn off a smart man. Apparently I am not that smart.

"Amanda, stop acting as if I'm invading your space. If we are going to be partners, this private little world of yours is over, get it? Sit down and shut up."

"How dare you, Antonio? That is a horribly ugly thing to say." Her skin was hot with fury.

"Honey sometimes, you don't play fair, and that's ugly too."

"Fine, Antonio... Maybe you should find someone who plays more fairly."

My frustration quickly turned to anger. "See? Right there, Amanda, there you go. You'll do or say anything to keep me out of this box. What does this son-of-a-bitch represent to you? To me - it's a tool to save a certain person's life... However, I know for you, it's much different."

I threw the contents back into the case.

"Amanda, forget it. Go get José for me." Baffled and

furious, I was determined to win this battle. Her medications were running low, and she damn well knew it. I had watched her self-medicate on several occasions since our arrival in Miami. Prior to that I had only witnessed her consuming a variety of herbs and supplements.

Shortly, Amanda returned with Jose, and the two stepped inside. "José, come help me." Her peevish expression sent the anger wrenching from within me. José's forehead wrinkled.

"Help me to Pop's study, and listen to me José, I mean this." Jose was very adept at saying a great deal with a single raised brow, and right now his silence was filled with questions. But smart brother that he is he acknowledged my unusual anger, yet he remained silent and only nodded.

"Take this case, and under no circumstances do you let go of it. Do you hear me?"

"Antonio?" He questioned me.

"Damn it, José, trust me."

Amanda paced. "Antonio, you are acting as evil as them."

Her harsh statement struck me as ridiculous. "Yeah, it is real damned evil to want someone to live. I must be Satan."

Gripping the case, Jose' helped me onto my feet. My gait was slow, but showed much improvement.

"Antonio, that is private!"

"No, Amanda, it used to be private. Live with it."

Amanda changed her voice from demanding to persuasive and silky; "Antonio, if you knew how much this hurts me right now, you would not do this."

Being the evil one I responded accordingly; "Bull Amanda, I'm evil, of course I'd do it."

We walked down the hall, away from her. Amanda was not giving up easily, and I knew our conversation was not over, as she yelled from where she stood;

"Antonio, you have no right to do this!"

"Do you think that is going to stop me?!"

Her tone became strangely calm. "Antonio, this is not working, I need to go home."

I shook my head at her utter overreaction. "Honey, you're stuck here. You might as well get used to it."

"You cannot keep me from going home."

Under the spell of my intense anger, I stopped José and hobbled around to make sure she understood me. "I'm not stopping you, remember the bad guys? They don't care that you're upset about the secrets in your little train case. They want what you know. They're the ones that'll keep you here, Princess."

She yelled louder now with heavy accents, "Do not ever call me princess!"

"Don't act like one – Princess!"

"I had no idea you could act in such an evil way!"

I laughed. I couldn't help it.

"Come on, José."

Now, we had successfully stirred, my Pop, the Judge. He

stuck his head out of his study and demanded; "Antonio, what in the hell are you doing to her?"

I snapped; "Pop, stay out of it."

My father was clearly stunned. The retired Judge was not accustomed to being given orders. José shot a telling look to our father, and did that eyebrow thing again-since he had learned it from Pop, I guess he knew what it meant.

"Fine, Antonio. I hope you enjoy violating my privacy!" Amanda yelled from the hallway; and then proceeded to slam the bedroom door.

"God, José… That stung…" I pretended to shrug it off, and we went into Pop's office.

"José, lock the doors."

Pop asked, "What is going on, Antonio? She sounds completely devastated."

"Pop, you'll see. I need to sit at your desk." I informed, as they obliged my request.

"I need a pen and paper." I opened the box and removed everything and started writing all of the label information on the sheet of paper.

José asked, "Are you going to tell us what this is all about?"

"Let me stress this point - I think you sense a distinct properness to this woman. Right now, even within your presence, she would sooner walk in here naked than have us look in this case. In fact, she just said it. In her eyes, I'm violating her."

Pop stood, speechless.

José asked, "Why? What's up with that?"

"I don't know, José. I tried to get her to deal with it in her own time. I thought, with time she would trust me enough that we would work through it together. José, she is suffering from sporadic bouts of illness. Truthfully, I'm not sure what is going on, it isn't exactly like any allergic reaction I've ever seen. Hell, I really don't know what she's treating, but I've seen her do it a couple of times.

It is almost as if she is not the same woman I first knew. Amanda is quick on her feet, funny, smart and dedicated to her own strengths. Now she's irrational at times, ill, can't hold onto her thoughts, and steadily getting worse. Amanda would never screech or embarrass herself or anyone else, but here she is self-medicating… something, and I do not know why.

José spoke his mind. "Amanda is a smart woman; Antonio, you're overreacting."
The Judge remained quiet; his years in the courtroom always left him with an interesting perspective.

"Sometimes, she's jumpy for no apparent reason." I took a deep breath, the moment I finished the phrase I realized it sounded as if I doubted her. My own personal admission made me nauseated. In the presence of my father and brother, I had to move on, and get away from my ludicrous Freudian slip. Maybe, I needed to convince myself.

"In her mind, she is capable enough, and she has learned to

compensate. Hell, one night in Vegas she kicked a guy's ass, while I watched from the pavement; because he had just laid me out."

Pop and José both laughed, their laughter helped calm me. Even for me, this was pretty funny.

"I knew you would find it tremendously entertaining. Especially, once I told you I was out of the game. It was plenty humiliating."

The men were clearly amused, and my less than flattering precocious statement seemed to disappear in the humor.

"But back to the point, her being is surrounded by these odd anomalies that she wished did not exist. Something makes me think despite her persona she is dying to talk about it. I operated virtually alone, for years. I don't harbor anywhere near the amount of issues she has about complete privacy. Her monsters are real.

Now, pay attention. When our research arrives, take notice, the woman maneuvers the subject with remarkable speed, depth, and relevance and a vast expertise.

Once, I got into her computer for the same reason I'm doing this to her today. I found a damn hard drive full of research papers on a variety of subjects. I'm talking, dissertation quality. In fact, more eloquent and extensive than the majority I've read. I tried to correlate a theme among the subjects, but the commonality was not there.

I continued to ramble without direction about the woman I

had fallen in love with; books are sacred to her, beyond anything you can imagine. One time, I did get her to admit that books brought out her passion. As she cried and yelled, something about it - 'was prison'. She screamed through her tears, 'the books saved me! The books saved my mind'.

At the same time, when I inquired to gain more information, she refused to speak of it, and behaved as if she was embarrassed to have let her guard down."

Pop and José appeared well beyond perplexed.

"Watch Pop, when you want us to go over something intellectual, she'll somehow blow out of here like a hurricane. You know why?"

Pop shook his head.

"She wants neither the credit, nor the opportunity to reveal it's her discovery. Yesterday, while we were resting Amanda claimed she shared some 'epic' with you and José regarding the Natives and New Mexico. Frankly, I didn't believe she would do that. I'm still skeptical that she would ever reveal her actual knowledge. If she did, then the previous trauma obviously brought her defenses down."

Pop chimed in, "You know son, she did discuss a great deal, but obviously she knew more. The premise of the conversation wasn't to provide us with knowledge or history, but to enlighten us about you. She was responding to a statement she overheard me make while you were being treated at the Emergency Center. Her explanation required she insert some of her coveted facts.

Antonio, she wanted us to understand you, and your ties to New Mexico and the Natives. She spared nothing to achieve that for you."

I couldn't imagine what she explained, but I would make it a point to find out later. I went on, "I see that basically my theory still stands. As crazy as it sounds, she covets knowledge. I'm deeply touched that she allows me into her world at all, and I'm damn sure, I'm the only one there." Calming down now, I beseeched my family for assistance; "I'm open to your insight."

They both shook their heads. Feeling even more alone in my dilemma fostered by Amanda's actions, I looked down at the desk at the list I had compiled.

"José, I think it's a good time to get these medications stockpiled for her. Perhaps, a physician can give us some erudition. I'll need you to take care of it. I think we need a 90 day supply."

"Absolutely, I agree. I'll handle it all, Antonio, immediately." José never flinched to help when truly needed.

He glanced at my father before speaking his mind; "I hate to remind you, but there's a woman back there that saved your life yesterday, and as we speak, she's contemplating your death. What are you going to do?"

Trying to collect my thoughts my hand slid across the soft lining. Stumbling for words, I stared at the open case. I raised my head; "Could you two give me a few moments alone to finish my inventory? I could really use a Brandy Pop, I like the brand you keep in the Cigar room better than the one you have in here."

Both men shared an expression of puzzle, and although reluctant granted my request.

As soon as the door closed, I slid my fingers behind the slight opening in the silky fabric lining of Amanda's now infamous train case. I slipped the cool metal between my two fingers and removed the small listening device. Anxious, I shuffled through the items in the drawer of my father's desk, and took out a brass letter opener. Acting in haste, I popped the tiny back off of the device and separated the components, then stuffed it inside my pocket. Just as I closed the desk, Pop and Jose returned.

I latched the case and shoved it across the desk in the direction of my brother.

"I have what I need, take her the damn case. I'm gonna play some hardball with her." My mind was set.

"You want me to take her case back, and that's it?"

"Yes, maybe she doesn't trust anybody else, maybe she never has. No doubt, it's been for good reason. She has to trust me completely and I'm not accepting partly. José, if I bend because she says something hurts, then it's on me. I won't give into her pain - I won't help feed her fear of this entity or man she is afraid of." Despite my obvious infatuation for Amanda influencing my every thought, and making me sound like a love-sick paranoid fool, I still sounded convincing enough for José to do as I asked.

Chapter 4

"We are drowning in information but starved for knowledge"
John Naisbitt

After delivering Amanda's train case José returned to our Pop's study, and sat next to me. His piercing glare and clenched jaw were obviously meant for me.

I pressed, "She said something, José. Get that look off your face and tell me"

"I don't know, Antonio. I hope you know what the hell you're doing. I hate to see you blow it over a stupid train case of herbal medicines." I wanted to say, I wished that was all I had found, but I couldn't bring myself to actually voice that suspicion.

Pop tried to weigh in, "I learned long ago, the answer isn't always what it seems. José now is not the time to withhold information from your brother."

José declared. "Antonio, I don't think OPERA is what you think." I wanted to laugh at that, hell; I wasn't even sure what I thought.

Pop asked, "José, what do you think it is?"

"I don't know. I told her it wasn't worth abandoning their relationship over this problem. She said the bond would suffer damage if she had to go to hell and return for 'it'. In fact, she claimed, she had already done that more than once. " José collected his thoughts.

"Antonio, it doesn't sound like an abusive man. I mean, it kind of does. What if it's only a part of it?" José finished.

I always assumed it was a husband, or a man. What else could it be?

Pop spoke, "I agree with José. I give her more credit than you do, Antonio. She's tough, no one man alone could do this to her. It may involve a man, but it's larger than one man could ever be. I agree with José in thinking you're wrong about the man, in the sense that the man represents someone close and personal-a relationship."

Pop confused me. He tried to help clarify, "Antonio, son - think, you surely have more clues. You need to look with different eyes."

I wasn't sure who I was convincing, but I participated in the game. "Amanda never lies, but there are these things she will not open up about." I replied. I replied, but was it true, hell I was no longer sure.

José added, "She used the word violated. That suggests something intimate." I thought about her alone in the bedroom with her case, she would surely discover that I had removed the listening device.

"Wait…" I remembered something. "When we drove to the Mountain, she told me all sorts of things she knew about. She called it 'The Institution' meaning 'Big Brother'.

I told them about our conversation that day, she mentioned

her computer was hacked, and then used the word violated to explain how private a computer is, even without discriminating pictures. She claimed it was like baring your soul.

"You know son, for a Midwestern girl, she possesses a remarkable insight into the races. You know, I got the distinct impression she hated it where she lives." Pop was right, only this point that was so obvious had just gone right over my head. I continued to process aloud. "I wanted to tell her where I secured the Scrolls, she didn't want to know.

She uses two Latin phrases often to strengthen her position. Avara k'davara, 'I create as I speak'. The most relevant, Veritas omnia vincit, 'truth conquers all'. She's clear the truth will eventually come out, and she will be vindicated."

José finished, "But not if the truth comes from her?"

The three of us stared at each other.

Pop elaborated; "Because, if it came from her, it would not be believed?"

I asked. "Pop, who or what is it?"

"Son, I can't say. But, I can tell you this, Amanda is far more than a pretty woman with boundary issues. From a distance, a person can see her more clearly than you can, as close as you are to her; you're blinded by the all consuming desire to protect her. That is normal, but at the same time you, Antonio, must see her for what she knows she is."

We sat in silence for a few moments. I asked, "How does it all tie together?"

Pop admitted, "That's not for us to say, but it does. Antonio, you need to get her to talk, Son. She knows more than we do. You need to try to get her to open up, but without revealing this conversation. You must be prepared to accept what you don't expect. Amanda has an uncanny ability to know things before they happen."

I felt as if my father had a placed a knife in my chest. "Pop, what in the hell are you suggesting?" In spite of my injuries, I stood, and began making my way to the door.
"I'm not suggesting anything in particular. Son, I only ask you to prepare yourself for anything. I saw her exchanging text messages earlier. My presence unreasonably startled her."

I felt sick. I didn't respond to my father's implication of subterfuge. Accepting the oblique idea that my Amanda was more than I wanted her to be, was a thought that would need more time to process-even though somehow I already knew he was right. I refused my brother's help, and hobbled out of the study to make my way to the library. I needed some time alone, some time to try and put the pieces together.

Chapter 5

'If a person studies too much ana exhausts his reflective powers, he wili be confused, ana wili not be able to apprehena even that which haa been within the power oj his apprehension. For the powers oj the body are ali alike in this respect."
— Maimonides

Sometimes, rationalization manifests out of irrational behavior. The information begins to flow like a river during a springtime rain. I guess that explains why interrogation is so effective. However, in my encounters with Amanda, I never seem to be afforded the luxury of preparation. What I discovered behind the bedroom door was a prime example of my disadvantage.

Time passed slowly from morning to afternoon, and when I finally made my way back to the bedroom and opened the door I observed Amanda hunched over a suitcase using her entire upper body to flatten the contents. I swallowed hard. "Amanda, are you planning on leaving, soon?"

Her strong short words stung like a slap in the face. "I have to get away from you."

My breath stopped. "I'm sorry you felt I violated you. I never want to disappoint you."

Her face tightened as she struggled to hold back tears. "No. Antonio you misunderstand. You have never disappointed me."

I couldn't help myself, in my one track mind, her answer was absurd, so I reacted with blatant irrelevance. "Amanda, let me set the record straight about one thing, I'm slow, I admit it. I underestimated you; I made assumptions based on my rationale. The enemy with a strangle hold on you is not a man in your past, but someone or something much greater. "

Her eyes pierced through me. She no longer fought tears. After a long moment she shrugged, and turned her attention towards the luggage.

"How long Amanda? How long has this ...whatever or whoever violated you?" Her flushed hot face glared at me. "What do they want from you?"

She shouted as she slammed the suitcase closed. "I do not know."

"Amanda...Who is it?" She began to check around the room, ignoring me. "Why didn't you let me die, Amanda?" I demanded. If nothing else I had learned that one sure way to garner a response when she was set on silence was to get her annoyed enough that she forgot she was ignoring me; I wanted her as hot as lava in a short time.

"You know why."

"No, maybe I don't. Right now, it seems you played a cruel joke on me." Her lips were so tight they disappeared from her face. "So, you proved you could. Why not? After all, you've got me wrapped around your tiny finger... Enough... Amanda...punches my buttons...I play...Turn me on...Turn me off." My anger had everyone in the house alerted.

She yelled back. "That is ridiculous Antonio!"

Good! Because...I'll go to this Hell of yours if that's what it takes. How bad is it, Amanda? This Evil - how bad does it get?"

A long period of silence preceded her soft response. "With me - you are in Hell."

"Oh, I get it. You think if you abandon me, you're giving me a get out of Hell free pass. Pardon me, Saint Amanda."

She shook her head. "Shut up, Antonio."

"That's it! You're a Saint, Saint Amanda... She'll release you from Hell, and then leave you like Mary Poppins."

Her voice was oddly calm, which further fueled my rage.

"Antonio, you know enough about the truth. Why are you doing this?"

"I know nothing, the bits and pieces I have are so disjointed they create a worse than nothing puzzle."

"You lied to me, you said, 'Antonio, truth conquers all'. Well, you really didn't give me a chance did you? Amanda they want you to leave. Do you always give them what they want?"

She didn't do what I anticipated at all. Her whisper was barely audible. "Yes, now I do, that is exactly what I do. You made me say it. Are you happy now?"

"No, I'm not one bit happy. Beaten, bruised, and hanging on to life by a thread, I felt happy yesterday. I'm certainly not happy today. Oh, and stop the presses if Amanda's ever wrong."

"I wanted to be wrong."

I limped to the door, tripping over one of her bags. "This time you are dead wrong, Amanda. I'll go to them, now. I've never been more serious in my life. I've got nothing left to lose."

"That would be suicide!"

"I'm glad to see you recognize it. You've been participating in it so long, I didn't know if you could. "I opened the bedroom door and moved out into the hallway, not surprised to see my family standing there listening to our shouted conversation, I turned and moved towards the front door.

Amanda looked towards my family, the audience. She moved in front of me, and whispered, again. "You're right. I should have let you die. Hell is worse than death." She paused. Her voice trembled. "Antonio, fine, do it! But, understand, I would rather kill you myself."

It was an epiphany I finally understood an important element. "Why? Why, Amanda? The enemy never kills? That's how you knew that they made an error when they attacked me so brutally. They never kill. That would be too kind." I dropped into the closest chair; the anger left me as quickly as it had come, making me weak.

She started pressing her fingertips into her temples. Her sentences became incoherent laced with aphasia. "Sometimes I think yes. Other times, no. I even start thinking..." she sighed, "...that I brought them to you, along with Solomon's Scrolls. It is the same."

Hell, it didn't sound as if she knew that I had found and removed the listening device.

She rubbed her temples, deeper. "It is complicated, I... I can't think." Her hands began to tremble. She sank into the chair across from me, dropped her head and whispered; "Antonio, let me go." She closed her eyes.

"Antonio, I would prefer you hate me..."

"I will never let you go Amanda, and for sure I will never hate you." I answered quietly. Her distress was eating away at my soul.

"There is nothing you can say or anything they can do to stop me from being beside you." I moved to kneel down in front of her and took her cold hands in mine.

"I know you have been feeling overwhelmed and your illness is affecting you more than you have let on. Together we will beat them, and we will make you well."

"Come with me now, and get some rest." I pulled her to her feet, and she wrapped her arms around me and whispered;

"Together we can do this." She repeated my words like a mantra. "

"Give me your strength and I can beat anything." She softly vowed.

I led her to the bed and helped her as she drew the covers over her body. "Let me rest now, and later we will...we will work it all out." She promised.

I watched over her until her eyes closed and she slept fully. I walked out of the room and out of the house to the garden. I stood there in the deepening twilight and watched the palms sway softly.

I approached our room quietly, and breathed a sigh of relief to find Amanda sleeping. There was time enough later to continue the discussion; she looked so exhausted, and as I eased down beside her, I finally gave in to my own weakness and slept through till morning.

Chapter 6

"Oh, the comfort, the inexpressible comfort of feeling safe with a person, having neither to weigh thoughts nor measure words, but pouring them all out, just as they are, chaff and grain together, certain that a faithful hand will take and sift them, keep what is worth keeping, and with a breath of kindness blow the rest away."
--George Eliot--

Safety, on the surface, is basic. If you have it, you generally take it for granted. If you don't, it rules you're life. Under the circumstances, I didn't want to push Amanda into revealing her personal experiences with OPERA. For once I was able to approach Amanda's hesitancy with a clear mind; acknowledging that perhaps her fear was not so unreasonable, I was beginning to see where that fear had led her into a secretive world she truly was afraid to let me enter. All I had to do now was convince her that the more information we shared, the better I would be able to help her, and just maybe save us and save the world as we know it.

Amanda looked peaceful sleeping. She slept more in the past two days than she'd slept since meeting me. Despite everything, maybe she felt safest here, with my family.

Unfortunately, her concern encompassed an outside force, with repercussions that severely influenced her confidence in our survival as a couple.

Over the years I have had to sleep in some pretty serious and awkward situations and areas. If that has taught me one thing it is this; sleep can allow the mind to process information and give you brand new and heightened perspectives.

As I lay here watching Amanda sleep, I make a vow to let her tell me in her own time anything she wishes to share. Slowly as her eyes open I see the truth of how she feels about me, before words or feelings get in the way, morning eyes tell the truth.

Kissing me softly, she brushed that glorious hair of hers over my face and chest. "Come on lets go have breakfast on the lanai." She rushes from bed full of energy and life. I can't help but laugh as I join her in our morning absolutions and rush downstairs for breakfast.

After we have eaten, I expect Amanda to offer another excuse as to why she cannot tell me all. When she finished her organic tea and carefully placed her cup on its saucer, I knew she was going to speak.

It was the words she spoke that left me with my mouth hanging open! With no intro or fanfare, she simply began to tell her story.

"Antonio, some of what I am going to tell you loosely relates to religious dogma."

"Okay." She was going to offer information; I would have been less shocked had she slapped me in the face.

She took deep breaths. "Did anyone ever tell you the danger in saying the name of a demon or the devil? I mean the real name."

"Yes, I've heard that." It wasn't the lucid beginning I was hoping for, but it was a start.

"I think that is why it is so hard to say. Not that I am going to give you the real name of the devil, or anything like that. It just feels like that. I know, it is childlike, but I feel as though I would disintegrate if I used the common Christian terminology."

"Would you like to write it?"

"No, that is the same thing. I will try to define… It is the ultimate evil, currently penetrating multiple levels, multiple places, and multiple people. It is not a single person, instead one enigma. The purpose is the same, no matter how it appears. It is power, just power – 'The Power of God status."

"I know what it is. It's the evil of Revelations, the warnings from John the Beloved."

She didn't exactly welcome my analogy. "Yes, but not literally, you see, it cannot kill some people. In John's version, we are led to believe it can easily kill. I believe it longs to kill. "

"Why can't it kill some people, Amanda?"

"I have surmised it is because they belong to God, the enigma wants to kill, but it can't kill His. However, you must not mistake this for weakness. The Evil can do other things."

"These things, they are worse than death?"

"Right, you see, they must take full control of America, and then install a dictator."

"Why?"

"America has only one King. A man, they despise above all others"

"I don't understand. What King?" America had not had a King since before the American Revolution.

Maybe I had been wrong, maybe the tumor was affecting her ability to rationalize reality and differentiate between it and a dream world of waking nightmares. Never letting my doubts show, I just listened and hoped I could bring her back to a real world soon.

"The only true King of a Christian Nation; the Jew they call Jesus." Maybe I am the one who needs a reality check. Of course Jesus was the King, the only one recognized by our forefathers and the people who believed in the Christian Dogma.

"You're right. Amanda…it's so obvious."

This resonated with me it was so damned obvious. She was right about America. The entire structure was based on Judeo-Christian values, and for the most part the Forefathers paralleled the foundation with the laws of Moses. These laws were palatable among both Jews and Christians. In other words, the issues behind the Constitution they agreed upon.

She continued. "They will stop at nothing. Even more frightening, they are showing signs of a new sense of urgency. Perhaps, they might be running out of time. I read their playbook, and it is advanced. The progress they have made recently is really eerie."

Astonished, I interrupted her. "You mean they really constructed a manual?"

"Yes, of course, I understand there are many manuals in use by the organization. They use overseas publishing facilities. They are extremely organized."

I thought organized was an understatement; I was processing all she was saying at a fast rate-endeavoring to keep up with OPERA's plans. Was it possible these maniacal groups actually had put in writing their diabolical plans?

"Tell me some of what you learned from their manual."

"Okay, let's begin with freedom. Antonio, define freedom." She loved having me define terms, sometimes I found it annoying. This time it seemed to fit the circumstance.

I thought for a moment before responding, I was sure she was asking me as an American, how I defined freedom. "Freedom has several connotations, an absence of restraint; in a constitutional sense, it is not feeling unduly hampered or frustrated by your countries laws and idioms; better yet, a lack of oppression."

"OPERA's playbook does not recognize freedom in nearly the same way. Instead, they have a freedom from mentality. On the surface it seems reasonable, at its depths, it is unadulterated control."

"Amanda, I don't understand; freedom from what?"

"Opera has a clearly defined propaganda, in order to control the populace; they must subvert the very protections that maximize the ideal of freedom. Here in this unique country people have freedom from harm, freedom from fear, freedom from want; those three ideals are perfect-but what if OPERA was the one who defined harm, fear and want? If they took control, infiltrated completely all tiers of government, controlled all means in which an individual obtains information and education; what would that do to those three basic ideals of freedom?"

"Amanda, that's Marxism."

"Exactly, at least it's Marxism with a perfected propaganda campaign. Antonio, keep in mind, I am not sure that this movement is in its preliminary stage any longer. At strategic times, it has penetrated both political parties. Now, in advanced stages, it stands on its own two feet. Are you thinking I am deranged, yet?"

I hated to admit that I doubted not her sanity, but the truth of her words based on an ability to think clearly due to her illness. Perhaps it was time to judge just how much she doubted her own ability to rationalize clearly.

"Amanda, do you doubt your own sanity?"

Her head moved slowly in an up and down motion. "Yes."

"Amanda, explain it to me. What triggers, or events, have made you question your own mental stability?"

"I know I am not crazy, but at times, I have wondered. Imagine this Antonio - you're on an enemies list. The list is not a murder list. It is a list about all things not tangible. The hits come in waves, or maybe you just never find out about them."

"I think I'm following you."

"You start to notice things that happen to you. Soon, you realize it has been too coincidental, and cannot be bad luck. Concerned, you tell someone, or a few people around you. Due to the time frame, they cannot seem to understand the relevance. Often, they forget the previous events, and lack enough reference to fully comprehend."

Hell, I wasn't sure I was able to comprehend the concept, but I wasn't about to interrupt the flow of information. I listened as Amanda's voice grew stronger as she saw my true interest in her words.

"While I cannot convince others these changes are real, and continuing, I know they are. I have experienced things that were so confusing and invasive.

The ability to admit you have no control in your life is frightening. The mind has absorbed certain truths about daily life, about history, about probabilities and statistics. Especially here in America where freedom is such a part of our life and we take it for granted. We trust those in power because we believe we empowered them.

Perhaps, within many Americans, there is a mechanism built into their brains, designed to send them into denial. For the most part, they simply are not capable of seeing that freedom is retreating. That is why I believe, if we are going to have a chance,- we must rely on the 'so-called immigrants', the Ethnics, and the Natives, to stop the take over and ensure our future. They are the only ones who have had their freedom removed in the past and can recognize the truth of the present situation. We have to take this issue to them and with my contacts I have already set in motion a meeting that just might bring new allies to our cause."

I could not possibly imagine this working the way she dreamed it could. "Amanda, many imbedded aspects are at work here, you're right. Do Immigrants and Ethnics feel they have the right?"

"You are observant, Antonio. I fear most of them believe they do not. OPERA is moving too fast. Yet, within every small Native group and Ethnic neighborhood, there are those who have an ability to hold onto the ways of the ancients, hold their history not in books as modern Americans do, but in their hearts and minds. This gives them the sight to see what Americans have chosen to ignore; history repeats itself and one must always be ready.

Once, in my early 20s, I had the opportunity to listen to an old Polish man. Unfortunately, some of the details escaped me and I am sure my youth robbed me of a lot of the meaning. Nevertheless, I will never forget that wise old man and how he warned me. He feared how naïve Americans would be when it came to the infiltration of Socialism and Communism.

He painted a picture of the Polish takeover. It all happened -

so…incredibly fast. I found myself going through history books to check the facts of his story; the real amazing part was his explanation of how the masses embraced each change.

Until finally, waking up one morning, they found they had nothing, starving and no jobs. Complete devastation took over. The story is the same as we have heard about Hitler's Germany, Russia and many others.

Speaking to someone who lived it and experienced the harsh reality is much more dynamic. I often talk about that old man and his story. It is so crazy, I remember him like yesterday, but I cannot remember the reason I met him. I cannot remember the people that were with me, or anything else.

He gave me a warning, long ago, of events in the future. His words offered an awareness of the greater scheme of things to come. Antonio, the awareness has stayed with me ever since."

"Amanda, it's your ability to empathize, that made the old man's story your own. I've seen your empathy in action, and you feel what others feel, often without any reference from your own past. On top of that, you have an otherworldly intuition. I question whether both rise to a level defined as psychic." I wanted her to see herself as I did.

"Antonio, you would believe in no such thing."

"I no longer think I have a choice. In my defense, I've never dismissed, or embraced it. Recent events I've personally experienced support psychic-type phenomenon. In my travels I have seen and heard things that were not explainable by Science or known facts. I chose to ignore them in the belief that what I could not explain in the present moment I could validate and rationalize later. We need to share this information with the others. There is safety in understanding, and it allows for awareness and preparation.

Amanda, I'm not asking you to address Harvard Hall. Please, explain the playbook and OPERA to José, Marc and Pop. Amanda, they need to know. We need for them to know. The truth is; there is no way I can convey the story with the detail and passion you can."

"Antonio I will, but understand for years I have dealt with this. Many times, I have tried to tell people. I even sought professionals. In all those years, I have met neither soul, nor professional bold enough to give it credence, even with proof.

Often times, the professionals found truth. Afraid, not one of them would touch it. I trust you and your family. Only once has anyone afforded this issue the attention it deserves. Eventually it was like all the rest. Every time my mouth opens about this, I start getting visions. I see you, your family, others from the past - all turning their back on me. It flashes before my eyes like an old movie."

"I know. That's why I want you to do it. This time it is different... Amanda, Pop understands, he lived through a similar situation in Cuba. I'm sure you struggled in your hometown. Amanda, you aren't there now, things are different other places. Will you try?"

"I will try, but I cannot guarantee anything."

"That's good enough"

"The sooner the better, Antonio, I hate waiting."

I laughed, "I know, you really aren't good at waiting."

"Antonio, I said I will try, and I will. Are you always going to do this to me?"

"What do you mean, Amanda?"

"Make me go public."

"You're worried about your research, aren't you?"

"Yes, are you always going to feel uncomfortable when I do not want to go public?"

"Amanda, that's a complicated question to answer..." She held a finger to my lips, stopping me.

"Let me clarify. I am not talking about presenting anything you do not understand or believe in. I am not suggesting you vicariously attach your name to something. I need to know your answer, Antonio."

"I understand. I know you wouldn't consider some vicarious situation, so let's remove that completely. Now, I can't understand why you don't want credit for your work. Amanda, many universities would give you a PhD for the work you've already done. Your fear of OPERA keeps you from wanting credit. Do you know how much I would love to take your work to my University? I talked to Kevin Collins about it. I want to take it for you, but I cannot take it from you; do you understand the difference? Don't you see that I want you to gain the credit you deserve?"

"I do not think it is OPERA. I just, do not like going public, I never did."

"This information needs to be shared among a select few; the general public would not understand and in most cases not even have an interest in the subject matter."

"I know. The thought stresses me out, I mean, it seriously stresses me."

"We attack, slay OPERA, and then we reassess. I promise, regardless, your research will reach Humanity. I'll make sure it happens. Understand, I want you to get credit and all the kudos, all of them Amanda. My getting credit doesn't compare to my witnessing you receiving the honors. Honestly, there is no comparison."

"I know you feel that way. At the same time, it concerns me to reveal the information, and its future."

"I understand your passions and fears. You have to trust I'll keep my word. I have a tremendous, new passion myself, and that is you. So much of you is captured within this research. The victory for you, Amanda, I'm obsessed with it."

"I do not understand you, Antonio. You think I am better than I am, that frightens me."

"Amanda, you're overwhelmed right now. You're brave. After all you have experienced, laughing in their faces."

"No, Antonio, you said it yesterday. It is true. I gave it what it wants. I fight, then things change, and I give in, that is the truth."

"Amanda, I shouldn't have said that. You stayed to expose OPERA. You're not weak. You're a survivor. Now is the final battle, and we will band together to destroy it for good, because of you."

"I would like to believe that, Antonio."

Thinking fast on my feet, I tried to come up with something to make her feel better, and take our mind off the present situation.

"How about I get a car, and we take a drive somewhere?" Not waiting for her response I shuffled off to find some wheels.

Chapter 7

"The great art of giving consists in this: the gift should cost very little and yet be greatly coveted, so that it may be the more highly appreciated."
Baltasar Gracian

Not wanting to ask Pop for his car keys, I limped around my parent's house trying to find a less opinionated donor. I was in a good mood, and had no intentions of a teen flashback starring Pop as the Judge giving a lecture about all the dangers I might encounter.

Just about the time I was prepared to give up, I bumped into my brother Marc. It was my lucky day. I couldn't have drafted a better candidate. Marc's laid back nonjudgmental attitude was a refreshing break from the rest of my intense family.

He nudged my shoulder. "Hey Antonio, you look much better today. Almost good enough for a little payback for that stunt you pulled at the sink."

I spoke with a chuckle. "Not quite, but I need to get out of this damn house. Can I borrow your car?"

He smirked. "You don't want to tell Pop? Great Antonio, I have to go over these documents with him, now. I assume you are going to have me tell him after your gone."

I nodded. "Come on Marc; ignore him when he starts to rant. Hell, I've done plenty of ignoring Pop."

He hesitated. "Yeah… Okay, but you owe me, Antonio."

I agreed, and with that my kid brother handed over the keys

to his BMW. Fearing Marc might change his mind, I developed a quick shuffle to the bedroom to get Amanda. Her giggle when she witnessed the comical sight was refreshingly worth my idiocracy.

Although Amanda is beautiful with mounds of the most stunning hair I've ever laid my eyes upon, there is a downside. The woman will not go unnoticed in a crowded room. I thought for a second, and turned to the closet. Inside I found an assortment of hats my mother had lovingly kept. My mother was a gentle sentimental woman. My childhood room was proof positive.

I fumbled through the hats and picked out a couple that had us both looking as if we were headed to Africa on safari. What can I say; I always wanted to be an explorer. Pop doubted, but I never did.

With the hats resting comfortably on our heads, I grabbed Amanda's hand and led her out of our confinement and into the welcomed sultry Miami air. We were a couple of kids longing to be alone, sneaking out from under our parent's watchful eye. The mere act invigorated me.

Once inside my brother's car Amanda's laughter became infectious. Yes, Amanda is a daredevil; I know it now; I knew it then. Even at our age, neither one of us can turn down an adventure.

From inside her joy, she spoke. "Antonio, where are we going?"

I shrugged, and mustered up my most arrogant tone. "We are going to a place where you can see things; things that are going to blow you away."

Her smile revealed her perfect white teeth. "And where sir, might that be?"

"The National Oceanic and Atmospheric Administration…"

I thought she was going to have a stroke, and then she grabbed my arm as I tried to keep the car from veering off the road. "You are taking me to NOAA?"

Continuing my arrogant game; "Yeah, I'm taking you to NOAA."

At the security check I pulled out my identification and gave them my colleague's name, geophysicist, Dr. Braden Aguilar. Braden and I were longtime friends attending the same grammar school, later we both found ourselves in graduate school at Duke University.

After security waved us on, I decided Amanda and I could safely remove our hideous hats. My tender leg muscles were infringing upon my ability to satisfy the burning urge I had inside of me to run over to Amanda and escort her into the building. Instead we had to slowly make our way up to the entrance.

When we finally made it to the atrium Braden was waiting for us.

"Geez Antonio, you said you were pretty bruised up, but I must say you look worse than I expected."

I accepted my friends hand and shook hard despite the sharp pain. Then I went about the task of introducing Amanda, a task I always had mixed emotions about performing. On one hand, she was incredible and I was proud; on the other, sometimes my friends looked at her in ways that I didn't particularly appreciate.

Earlier, I had exchanged messages with Braden and he was well prepared to grant my favor. He guided us through a maze of hallways and into a massive viewing room with gargantuan screens. Amanda was excited. She didn't speak a word, but I knew, because her grip was causing excruciating pain in my injured arm. I grimaced and switched sides. Hell, she didn't even notice.

Braden tapped a few buttons and the screens came to life surrounding us with current weather photos from around the globe. I didn't think it was possible, but Amanda's face lit up more. Braden and I exchanged glances; he seemed to be enjoying her reaction as much as I did.

After he allowed her to digest for a few moments, Braden shared a couple of facts. "We are in the middle of an enduring heat wave. The world is averaging the warmest temperatures since 1895, and it seems to be escalating, last month alone, we recorded 15,000 record breaking high temperatures." In response, Amanda's hand flew up and rested in the center of her chest.

Since, Braden could only reserve use of the room through

the lunch hour, he moved to change our view. In a millisecond the screens flashed and seven angles of the burning sun enveloped us.

Amanda let out a gasp as she absorbed the brilliance from within the violent fire. Braden began labeling the areas of ferocious activity, solar storms, solar tsunamis, and potential solar bursts threatening to be thrust out into space by the catapult action of the sun's indescribable energy.

Braden shared a frightening fact. "If a Gamma Ray penetrates Earth's atmosphere it would take 10 years for it to return to normal. In the meantime, the United States would only be able to sustain 10% of its current population."

No doubt, the concept supported King Solomon's warning. The idea of science and prophecy converging in such an obvious way sent chills up my spine. With that last piece of information, we had to clear the room for the returning employees.

On the way out, we stopped by Braden's office. In our previous conversation, I had asked him to compile a list of magnetic field weaknesses, a request that would not have been welcomed by the agency. Never-the-less, Braden was a good friend and scientist that shared our concerns; therefore he completed my request on paper and handed it to me in an envelope.

Amanda was still in a daze of happiness, and barely noticed saying goodbye, as she clutched the data to her chest in anticipation of new research.

Chapter 8

"A foolish faith in authority is the worst enemy of truth."
Albert Einstein

After taking a short stroll after lunch the following day, I went into the bedroom where Amanda was returning research to her precious cache. She glanced at me with a smile as I approached.

"You are walking much better today, Antonio."

"I am, still limping, but it's a huge improvement."

I took her into my arms. "Amanda, you really are brave."

"I wish I were more so."

"I'm with you."

"I do not recognize myself when all this comes up."

"I know." I kissed her with sweet lips. "They're ready."

"Take me to them."

"Antonio, I am not doing this for nothing. It will cost you dearly."

"I smiled. "What do I have to do?"

"You have to plant grapes in New Mexico."

"You want a vineyard there?"

She stopped, and turned to face me, tears threatened to roll down her cheek. "I want a vineyard there."

"Amanda, I will give you three vineyards there."

She grinned. "Why three?"

"You have three sons." The tears came.

"I do not want you to give me or my sons the vineyard."

"I know. I want it to be your vineyard from me."

She moved back beside me as we resumed our walk.

"Do you want it in the south pasture, as a backdrop to the swimming pool?"

She grinned. "You knew."

"Yeah, I knew."

We entered the study and took our seats on the smaller sofa.

The Judge spoke softly to her, "I know this is difficult Amanda, we admire your courage." She smiled softly.

José told her, "You do the best you can. If you need a break or anything at all, tell us. I think everyone would agree - to us, it's just family here."

She reached to José and squeezed his hand. "Thank you José. That means a lot."

She pulled out her notes as she prepared to begin. I asked, "Amanda, did you get up and make notes last night?"

"No."

"Where did the notes come from?"

"I made them when I thought I was leaving. I planned to leave them here for you." All three of us were flabbergasted.

"Why, Amanda, why would you leave us the notes?" I was astonished.

"You needed to know, you wanted to understand. You are more important than protecting myself from the pain."

I closed my eyes, my breathing felt labored. She glanced between us. "Should I begin?"

The Judge and José nodded their approval. I still tried to get a grip. That was when I truly looked closely at Amanda. She was not just stressed, she was terrified! I could not allow her to continue, I realize now just how hard this is for her.

"Amanda, stop. I will do this for you."

The look of sheer relief on her face was enough to let me know I had made the right decision. "Stay if you want, and chime in if you think I am missing something vital." I assured her with my words that we would think no less of her for this.

"Antonio, thank you, I will begin and when I can go on no longer, you can take over." Her bravery was so real. I nodded okay, and she began.

"I would like to start as I did with Antonio earlier. A little background will help make sense of it all. When it comes to religion, I do not subscribe to one in particular.

Truthfully, I do not like religion, but I am a staunch believer in God and the Divine Order. However, my beliefs are strongly supported within Judaism. Yet, I practice yoga and meditation in a more traditional sense.

I believe that one group of people cannot define spirituality. We can only define it from within our own mind and soul. Life is a journey, which demands a culmination of wisdom and truths on a personal level.

In addition, one must become proficient in these two areas

to advance to an ultimate understanding. In order to achieve this, an individual must discover and unite with their polar opposite, their Yin to their Yang, male – female. However you want to term the concept.

Through this unity, with proper care, intention, and love, mortal man can reach enlightenment. This is the window to the divine order, if you will. It is a place that gives us the freedom from doubt." She paused.

"I know this information may not seem necessary. However, it is important to me. I should reiterate, I believe in the Prince of Peace, Jesus, brought gifts. It amazes me to comprehend the impact he has had over the past 2,000 years.

I am an advocate for freedom. I do so, from the depths of my soul. God gave us free will. As a parent, I understand the magnitude. It must be continually difficult for God to keep from interfering with free will. As a parent, many times, I could rest at ease by taking away my children's free will. I cannot, nor will I do that to my kids. I condemn evil men and women to Hell that wish to infringe upon the freedom of other human beings. No man or woman should take the rights God has given to us.

It is also important to point out that America has had one King. Never, has a dictatorship or monarchy existed in America. Yet, one King always reigned in this Christian nation and that King is Jesus. It is not a fact based on one person's beliefs. It is a fact that this country is overwhelmingly Judeo-

Christian. Jesus is King."

José commented, "I have never thought about that."

"Exactly, but others have not only thought about it, but obsessed about it. To a more precise point, they have obsessed enough to form a coup d'état.

Now, as I have told Antonio, this is where it becomes difficult for me. I am completely aware of how silly and unreasonable it is, but I have yet to rise above the repercussions."

She took a deep breath. I held her hand. She looked at me, and I took over.

I explained as she had about the machinations of OPERA and their deep penetration into our lives.

It is the ultimate, penetrating evil. It operates in multiples; multiple places on multiple levels among multiple people. There are also many facilitators. Some do not even know they are codependents of the evil. It is not one person. It is one enigma. It is all about power, God-like power."

"I told Antonio I have seen the playbook, or at least one of them. I understand there are other books. In fact, I own one of them. First, he will outline some of its contents. This will help to clarify my actual experience. "Amanda interjected.

"OPERA's agenda continues with government-controlled agencies, designed to provide protection. These include; Army, police, fire departments, the environmental protection agency, consumer and worker protection, health care, Social Security, public health, food safety, disaster relief, disease control, and everywhere else you look."

I went on with all that Amanda had told me, and looking at her notes I read what she had discovered through intense research.

"The movement accused Conservatives of using symbols and images to provoke specific emotions, then adopted their methods and adapted them. Such things as repeated talking points are a part of their process. Using specific language to provoke their negative agenda, they succeed in deterring any new modes of thought.

This is important. They gave the Conservatives credit for the process. So much, that OPERA developed a model based on the Conservative's success, as if countering their strength.

OPERA has instituted the Conservative system, but with their own language of choice, images, symbols, and ideas. This designation strengthens the mode of thought in their direction, on their agenda.

The word OPERA believes most powerful is the one they call upon the most - empathy.

This propaganda campaign's indoctrination is based entirely on the Conservatives own system, and has birthed a veritable how-to set of instructions. It is a sprinkling of terms proven to provoke positive images with people.

However, they have attached new meanings to these terms. In their new definitions are underlying tones of Socialism and

Communism. They mean to replace the U.S. Constitution, which they claim to be outdated. This is about the destruction of the American Dream, and the hope of prosperity destroyed."

I continued, "They suggest Human Reason misleads political ideologies and hides the real conservative's agenda. Human Reason can hide the most important issues. It can keep OPERA's movement from presenting its vision of a moral-mission based government. Human Reason causes the movement to lose members. They have a high dropout rate because members surrender their ideals. Human Reason makes the movement ineffective.

Americans are divided within their brains and it creates their understanding of the world. This division cuts Americans into two groups, one is fundamentally democratic, and the other is anti-democratic.

If you believe in the Forefathers of the United States, you will look, and be weak according to OPERA. Those that vote and support the Forefathers, and their constitution, are ignorant. These ignorant people need to know the facts. They claim others with similar views are greedy, corrupt, or duped. The old enlightenment of our Forefathers is obsolete. It has run its course.

Ready or not, the movement's new enlightenment is here.

The government as a family is the new way. There are several notes and steps I can present.

The government institution is the family.

The governing individual, as the president, is the parent.

The governed, the government officials, are the family members.

I have to mention empathy is the power word. The movement promises to remove administration and profit from health care. The scope of that is nearly 20% of GDP. The first steps are already in motion.

OPERA outlines their methods for framing. Frame realities. Construct them to fit your agenda. Remove concepts, reframe it, and rename it. Learn to overcome your fear of framing. Be careful not to let conservatives intimidate your faith in framing. Confront stereotypes. Recognize them, and then confront them.

When it comes to accountability, find the targets. You must anticipate it, and insist upon it.

Recognize contested concepts, or terms in general, and be careful with these: freedom, equality, fairness, and opportunity. Make sure to use the movement's version of these concepts, and keep them uppermost in the public mind.

Say things that are powerful and evoke emotion. One example is Democracy is anything but private. Say these things repeatedly. Repeated activation of these ideas will change brains.

I hope that provides enough of an overview of their dogma to help understand the issues which threaten this agenda."

The Judge supported her method, "Amanda, you have done a fine job informing us of the enemy. You are right. We have to know, to understand the big picture."

"Amanda, we are stunned at the complexity and incredible organization OPERA has achieved." He applauded her efforts. She looked so pleased, and smiled at me as she gestured for me to continue.

We decided to break for a while to eat something and check phone messages. Amanda would proceed with her personal story after lunch.

I urged Amanda. "Please, come eat something."

"Antonio, go ahead, I have something I need to do." She had to get away for a few moments, and went back to the bedroom. Her head fell back into the chair as she rested her eyes.

She didn't hear me enter as I approached her chair. I struggled down to my knees and put my hands on her thighs, startling her for a moment.

"I didn't mean to spook you." I told her.

"It's okay, I was distracted."

"Amanda, you've done great, you've given us a huge amount of information."

She sighed, "I hope Antonio. I want to convey the seriousness. It's hard. The real threat is hard to understand, their definition comes through the repetition of events. Therefore, you lose something when you pass it on verbally."

"Amanda, you keep forgetting we've already witnessed some of their threats, we're not a brand-new, naive audience."

"True, Antonio. I failed to really consider that."

"What about the grapes? Tell me."

"Tell you what? Surely, you know what a Concord grape is."

"Amanda, of course I know Concord grapes. Why didn't you tell me the trouble you experienced where you live?"

"Do you mean how I've always wanted to leave?"

"Yes, why didn't you tell me?"

"Considering our situation, it sounded too convenient. I didn't want that perception. Besides, the ties that have always bound me there still exist."

"I see now. Honey, you despise it, and it has nothing to do with me, you've hated it for a long time."

"It seems like forever, and has been as long as I can remember."

"You will see. At times OPERA has trapped me to the point of a virtual imprisonment."

I shook my head, unable to imagine having to live like that or just how bad it must have been for Amanda, then rested my head on her lap. She played with the waves in my hair. I thought of the doctor coming that afternoon. I wouldn't tell her until she was finished with her story.

I raised my head. Our eyes met. "Amanda, what do you want?" I didn't know what compelled me to ask.

"What do you mean?" She was confused.

"What do you want now, and in the future?"

"Gosh, Antonio, that is a huge question. I do not know. Do you know what you want?"

"Why don't you know Amanda?" I avoided her question for now.

"A few weeks ago I had plans. I've always had plans, even when it seemed hopeless. I do not know if my plans have ever been about what I ultimately want. Want is different from making plans or goals within constraints.

I can't answer want. I don't think it's anything I ever truly considered."

That was the point I intended to make, I wanted to plant that in her head.

"Amanda, do me a favor, think about what you want. We are talking Amanda. It's only about you. I want to know you. I don't want you to think about what your sons want or what I want. Don't think about what anyone else wants, just you."

"Why? I just do not understand. I am not an unhappy person," she didn't see the point.

"It amazes me, but I know you aren't unhappy. Besides, Amanda, I didn't ask what makes you happy. I ask what you want." I tried to clarify.

"I see… I will consider the question."

I hoisted myself off the floor in front of her. Standing, I thought I had begun to understand her, even without fully divulging her private hell. My anxiousness was mounting, while she was surprisingly calm. I didn't really understand my own emotions.

She was amazing. Not angry or unhappy, she was in fact,

quite the opposite. Someone would have to know her long and well before she opened up. I didn't think anyone had gotten close enough to find her fear. There was no doubt I was the first.

I pulled her close and held her with raw emotion. Wanting to control it, I hadn't mastered it yet. I wanted to suck OPERA out of her, out of her life. I wanted her to know, at least once, the freedom she was so passionate about saving.

"Antonio, what is wrong with you?" Did I say something to upset you?"

"No, Honey." I held her tight.

"Something happened to you." I released my grip on her.

"Let's go, Amanda." She took my sweaty hand. I still limped and was unable to take my usual long strides, so we walked slowly. When we were close to the study entrance, José asked to speak with me. Understanding, Amanda left me with my brother, and headed into the study and sat down.

José asked, "What's wrong with you, Antonio?"

"Suddenly, I'm more afraid to hear what she has to say, than she is to say it."

José squeezed my shoulder. "I understand. I have scripts from her doctors in 90-day increments. We can have them filled here in Miami."

I thanked him, and we both entered the study.

Pop noticed my agitation as we walked in. "Antonio, did something happen?"

"No Pop, I'm fine."

I was short with my words. José gave Pop a look that said 'Let it go'.

Chapter 9

"That which can be destroyea by the truth, shoula be"
P.C. Hodgewell

After we returned to our room that evening, Amanda walked over to the box of files she had had delivered. She knelt down and pulled out a stack of printed papers at least a foot high. She carried them with her back to the chair placing them on the desk between us.

She spoke in a quiet voice. "This is a minute fraction of the studies the Government has done over the past couple of years on the effects of solar magnetism on humans. The trend started about ten years ago. They have known and manipulated the problem; some areas of the Government are already in danger. Many residents are already suffering from the disappearance of the magnetic field. There are anomalies within the earth in specific areas, which are already exacerbating the problem.

There is an interesting split within the political arena concerning this problem. I should point out this is deep within the Government where things happen. This is not your local congressman. Part of the Government views this as a problem needing minimization and the citizens need protecting as much as possible.

The other side of the Government prefers to view it as a form of population control. The odd thing is the sides are totally different with their stances. Their propaganda would suggest otherwise. OPERA is an advocate of population control.

Those that ascribe to OPERA historically will deliberately react slowly or not at all during a potentially dangerous situation; and therefore benefits in several ways. Slow response allows OPERA to let the disaster get more media coverage so, more panic takes hold and later a vote for a takeover is much easier. In some instances, it is conducive to contributing to population control.

During the past decade, the studies were much greater than this stack. These were most likely in reality funded during another administration. This has stopped.

During magnetic dips, some people are vulnerable to electrical charges distributed through their bodies. This triggers different neurological, hormonal, even cardiac emergencies. These manifest as serious seizures, migraines, psychiatric, and cardiac episodes, to mention a few.

Furthermore, pacemakers and nerve stimulators can malfunction. Antonio, dogs have died from their electronic collars malfunctioning." Her tone was solemn.

"Amanda, you have known about this a very long time haven't you?" I already knew the answer. Her silence and the look in her eyes was enough to confirm her knowledge. I watched as she carefully replaced the notes back in their box, closed the lid and gently smoothed her hand over the surface. For Amanda all knowledge, good or bad was precious; and even now her vast respect for the written word of another showed in her reverent care of its safe-keeping. I waited for her to say something more, but watched silently as she left the room and closed the door.

Left alone with only my thoughts, I knew the burden of the content of our conversation was weighing heavily on her mind.

Chapter 10

"Every man is afraid of something. That is how you know he's in love with you, when he's afraid of losing you."
— Unknown

That afternoon I returned to the bedroom after an attempt to strengthen my body with a short walk in the garden, to find Amanda huddled over the commode heaving terribly. I wet a cloth and helped her wipe her face and then assisted her back to the bed. Amanda plopped onto the bed and crawled under the covers. The minute I said her name, she yelled, cutting me off. "Okay, you're right I'm sick. Leave me alone."

"What would make you this sick?" I asked.

"I do not know, let me rest here, I do not want to talk." She was peevish and sharp, so I thought the best way to help her was to leave her alone-for now.

Everything we packed was dirty, so I volunteered to wash some clothes. Her eyes followed me out of the room. José spotted me in the hallway, and followed to the laundry room. "Are you out of clean shirts?" He teased.

"Pretty much, I'm also not used to living in Miami anymore. There's no one around where I live. It's so secluded. If Maria and Joe, my hired caretakers didn't come regularly, I wouldn't need clothes at all."

"Wow, Antonio. I can't imagine you living in a place like that."

"Be careful, José, it's contagious. Remember I warned you."

"No, I love Miami, little brother."

"We'll soon find out, José. More importantly, I just learned Amanda's been throwing up since Saturday. That's why she hasn't eaten, she's too nauseated."

"Pop said a Doctor's coming...

"Yes, I just wish he would get here and give us some answers."

Jose placed his hand on my shoulder and squeezed. "We are here for the both of you, and we will find out what is wrong, and fix it." With that he left me to finish the laundry.

Amanda's symptoms were escalating, but why?

My thoughts continued to race as I walked back to the bedroom. She couldn't hold food down, and she'd been losing weight faster than Wall Street lost money on Black Monday. Something was going on, but what?

Amanda was still in bed. At least she looked less Gothic. I could see she lay awake. Should I talk to her? Earlier, she didn't want to talk. Instead, I decided to put a shirt on. Maybe I would go out and wait for the doctor.

"Antonio, don't leave me." I rolled my eyes. I thought she wanted me to leave her alone. She didn't even want me to talk. Now she wanted me to stay?

"Amanda, I would never leave you." I brushed her massive waves of hair back from her damp face.

"Antonio, come hold me." I sat down with my back against

the head of the bed. I pulled her upper body against my chest and held her.

But, a tap on the door interrupted our peaceful moment.

"It's open."

José stepped in. "Antonio, you need to come out here." I moved her over and followed José out of the room.

"What's up, José?"

"Dr. Martinez is here, he wants to meet with you before he goes in to see Amanda."

Pop introduced me to Richard Martinez, MD, and then left the room so we could discuss Amanda's illness in private. I revealed a piece of paper with her current health information, and medications to give him. Then I explained recent episodes. Finally, I told him about the nausea, vomiting, and weight loss. The Doctor reviewed the sheet of information.

"Antonio, why don't you take me to Amanda? I will examine her, and discuss these issues with her, if she is in favor of you knowing I will come out to talk with you. Okay?" The Doctor spoke soft, but direct.

I wasn't sure that's how I wanted it to go down, but I didn't seem to have a choice. I led the Doctor into her room, introduced them, and then left.

In my father's study, I waited, and worried.

"Antonio." Dr. Martinez came in, shut the door, and sat down.

"Amanda signed the release. I am free to speak to you about

her health." He spoke slow, articulating his words.

"Good, thank you, Dr. Martinez."

"I'm sorry to say, I do not have much I can tell you at this time. I need results from her blood tests first. I took some samples and I will drop them by the lab. I should have something back as early as tomorrow afternoon. I can let you know when they are available.

I understand you are going back to New Mexico the day after tomorrow. Amanda says she does not have a doctor there. I think it is imperative she have a doctor nearby that understands her health issues. I have a colleague in New Mexico, and with your permission, I could telephone and share my findings with him. Perhaps, he could see her soon."

I nodded, "I would appreciate your help."

"She is very dehydrated." The doctor opened his bag and pulled out a huge bottle of liquid, and some pills. "I want you to mix this liquid with whatever she will drink. These pills should keep her from vomiting. If this does not work by morning, call me. We will have to put in an IV. There are simple directions listed on both of the items I am leaving with you."

"Thank you. What could make her this nauseated?"

"It could be some of her blood levels, however unlikely in my opinion. It sounds like she has taken her medications regularly, except for one day. I do not believe one day would create such an imbalance, not as substantial as this.

A hormonal imbalance is doubtful, but maybe. A virus, no,

it's been too many days now. I hope that the results of the blood tests will show us the answer. I believe they will."

"I really appreciate everything, Dr. Martinez. I will be anxious to hear from you tomorrow." I showed the Doctor out.

I rubbed my head, needing to go see her, but afraid to go see her.

José walked in. "What did the Doc say?"

"He doesn't know. He took blood. Some of the tests will be back tomorrow afternoon."

Chapter 11

"One is very crazy when in love."
— *Sigmund Freud*

Amanda was sitting up when I entered the room. "How did you get along with Dr. Martinez?

"Well enough, how about you?"

"Yeah, about the same..." I realized I wasn't at all prepared to face the possibility that the test would show Amanda was fading faster than we thought. I choked, so I gathered the drink mix and went to the kitchen to stir up the Doctor's concoction. I returned quickly with a pill and the drink. She took the pill.

"Antonio, what's wrong with you?"

"Nothing," it was the only answer I could give, given the circumstances.

She wanted to know. "What did the Doctor say to you?"

"He just said he would have to wait for the results from the blood test to give an official diagnosis."

"What else? Tell me now." She demanded.

"Nothing Amanda, aside from the fact that he also suggested we contact a colleague of his in New Mexico once we get there."

"Something else is going through your head." She knew.

I sat at the head of the bed and drew her close. Her hair smelled of sweet almonds. I smoothed the beautiful locks, her head rested on my upper chest. I needed the peace I only found in my beloved New Mexico. I was equating the mystic aura that surrounded my home with the hope that once there, Amanda would begin to heal.

"Amanda, I'm so ready to go. I want to take you back home with me."

"Just what is bothering you Antonio?"

I finally admitted my greatest fear. "I don't want to lose you. I can't fight this illness for you. I can't take it in my hands and make it go away."

"I am sure the doctor did not give you the impression that I am on my deathbed Antonio." She smiled when she teased me.

"Amanda there is nothing light about that topic!"

Amanda drew my face down close to hers. Looking into her eyes was like diving into a pool of colored crystals. With clarity and firmness she said; "Nothing in this world or the next will take me from your side. I do not know how I know, so do not ask, but we will be together long after this is over."

I tried to interrupt, but she silenced me with a finger on my lips. "Trust me Antonio, whatever is going on in my body right now, has nothing to do with the tumor. I can feel the wrongness, just not where it comes from."

"Like an allergic reaction, an allergy to something?"

"Possibly, but to what I cannot say."

In my worry, I had over-thought the possibility of her tumor causing these new symptoms, and here she tells me it feels like an allergic reaction, her Levite DNA in action! Those damn Canary in Gold-Mine genes! Now I was mad, not at her but at my lack of fruitful thinking that was feeding my insecurity of facing life without her.

"I swear Amanda; you are like a divining rod for anything that could possibly affect the human body!" I snapped.

It is amazing how fast fear turns to anger, and as soon as I said it, I was sorry.

"A divining rod; you think I draw trouble to myself?" Oops, I think I went too far. Amanda was coming off the bed, her hair seemed to crackle around her, her eyes were flashing, and I was looking for the door.

"Just how do you go from worry over losing me to being a complete ass in two minutes?"

"Now Amanda, I admit my choice of words was wrong, but all I was trying to say was…"

"I know exactly what you were trying to say. The mighty Judean is stuck with a sickly Levite!" Her ability to be sarcastic while angry was almost equal to mine.

"Amanda, I did not say that!" I had to get her to listen, and I had to do some serious apologizing. She was a whirling virago! I wasn't sure if she was looking for a weapon or her suitcase, but in either case I needed to calm her down. The only problem was she was not in the frame of mind to listen.

"Antonio, I have never been so insulted in my life. I thought you cared about me. That is what you said; you said we would fight together. Now here you are saying that since my new symptoms are possibly due to my biological inheritance, I must be faulty in some way."

I walked over to Amanda, as softly as possible I used my voice to reach out and touch her.

"I love you, and I am sorry. I lost it for a moment. I never meant that your Levite DNA was a fault. The idea of losing you is so painful; I was relieved when you said it might be something else. Unfortunately, that relief was a sucker punch that let my fear turn to anger, never at you, but at myself. For a moment I saw my fear as a weakness, but my love is not a weakness, it is a fount from which I draw strength."

For a moment I thought she was going to stay mad, but then I saw her eyes change.

"Oh Antonio, what is happening to us that we allow something so small to come between us?"

"Stress, it is just the stress, and worry over your health. These obscure symptoms are creating havoc on your body and making me crazy!"

"Antonio, did you know that when I get angry it makes me feel hot?" Amanda's voice had gone sultry and she was lifting her hair and fanning the back of her neck.

"Would you like for me to turn up the air-conditioning?" I deliberately answered as if I misunderstood.

"Do not play dumb Antonio. You may not be a complete ass but half an ass is just as bad."

I winced at her reminder. I reached out one hand and ran my fingers down from her chin, over her throat and allowed them to move and cup her breast. Leaning in I took her lips and feasted on their heat.

Amanda unbuttoned my shirt and pushed it off my shoulders, and played her hands across my chest.

I jumped when I heard a knock on the door.

"What?" I called out, in anger.

"Ruger's here to see you. He's in the study." José called back.

"Tell him I'll be there in a minute." I planted a couple more kisses. "Damn it, this hurts, but I have to go talk to him."

"Okay, Antonio."

"Like hell it's okay. Amanda, I want you so bad right now."

I put my shirt on and she buttoned it for me. Our lips played as her fingers worked. I clutched the back of her neck, placing my hand in its favorite spot.

"Honey, you're incredible. You make me crazy, don't go anywhere. I'll be back as soon as I can."

Chapter 12

"Never regret yesterday. Life is in you today, and you make your tomorrow."
— L. Ron Hubbard

Ruger and I talked for several hours in Pop's study. We had a great deal of information to share. I relayed, in as much detail, as I could about the facts I had gathered of Amanda's experience with the enemy.

Ruger, very familiar with OPERA, shared Amanda's malcontent. Worried about their power, he knew the movement gained terrifying strength amidst the recent economic crisis. Ruger revealed his enormous concern. The group's influx had infiltrated the government, and the military, and their reach spanned across the globe. His greatest concern was about the unlimited access OPERA now attained through what most of the population believed was the legitimate government.

Ruger described the country as 'on the brink of no return,' and this deeply worried me. Having served a lifetime as a Navy SEAL, he maintained contacts with high-ranking Military Officials, both active and retired. I understood, and now I had more knowledge than I ever wanted.

The former SEAL, whom I had employed, reported his security precautions back at my estate, and his preparations for our return arrival. He then revealed a plan for escorting me and my entourage back to New Mexico.

I informed him of the warning OPERA's hoodlums gave during their attack on me. "Once we're back in New Mexico, they promised to get Amanda." I had never told her. Pop and Jose` knew, but no one else.

I stressed my safety concerns regarding Amanda's sons, especially once the enemy realized our tenacity. Soon, they would know I wasn't suffering brain damage, and was no longer in a Miami hospital. I recommended Ruger spend his time prior to our departure, examining and securing pertinent safety precautions. Amanda shared earlier that they had just completed the harvest at the vineyard.

"Ruger, since the Harvest is complete, there is no reason to hesitate. If we have to take drastic action…if it is even remotely necessary, I want it done."

As a man of action, Ruger wasted little breath on assurances, we both knew time was of the essence and running out. He departed as quickly as possible, already formulating a plan, I knew he could handle.

I grinned when I entered the room. Amanda lay sideways across my bed asleep, with a book wide open. I picked up the book, marked her spot, and lifted her into a more appropriate position. I kissed her cheek, and then covered her with more kisses. My clothes removed, I crawled up next to her.

I turned on my side to face Amanda. Seeing her there next to me, felt great. It made the world seem less ugly. Her life, so difficult, yet somehow she inspired me.

"Antonio, how did it go with Ruger?" She whispered.

"It was productive, but I didn't intend to wake you." I drew her closer. She smoothed my face with her soft hands.

"Antonio, you seem depressed."

"I'm not depressed, but it does sadden me, Amanda. You are so right about the power OPERA has gained, and they continue to progress."

"I wish I was not right."

"Amanda, you have no idea how much I admire you. There are so many things about you that inspire me, without you…I'm not sure I would believe enough hope exists."

"Yes, you would, Honey. You need to go back to New Mexico. The Natives have maintained hope for more than 2,000 years. Your words are sweet, but there are lots of people who epitomize hope more than I. You know Antonio… I think I lied to you."

Stunned, I didn't know what to think. "Lied, about what?" She hesitated, and turned away. "I really do not think I am sorry I fell for you. Sometimes I feel as though I should be, but, I certainly do not think I am."

"You should never feel guilty about us. Amanda, we're good together, but evil is around, closer than ever, and maybe even trying to separate us, but it's not us. Honey, we're not bad."

"Antonio, I have another confession."

"I'm no priest, Amanda."

She smiled. "No, Antonio, this is really ugly. You may want

to take the hope thing back." I raised my brows at the implications.

"I would be extremely worried right now, if a baby came to one of my sons. If extremists gain much more power…I believe it will result in catastrophe. I cannot fathom giving life to a baby without affording that baby freedom within our society."

"Do you want a baby Amanda?" I felt a deep need to know her answer. While the thought of a child in our life was unpleasant to me; she might feel different. I did not want to share Amanda with anyone right now; I had waited all my life to feel what I felt for her.

"No Antonio. I have my sons, and I have you. I could not as I said knowingly bring new life to an uncertain world."
Her words resonated through me. I felt like scum, my reasons were selfish and ego-driven. Hers were genuine.

"Amanda, that's one of the most selfless things I've heard anyone say. You truly care. How can you apologize for that?"

She justified through her unique spirituality. "We are meant to support life, and have faith in God, and the Earth, to sustain it."

"I know it isn't enough to have your own baby live a life that is merely 'sustained', especially not in your mind. Amanda, that's caring and loving a child you'll never meet."

"I hope it isn't horrible, but it is what I feel."

Thinking back to the number of times we had made love without protection, I had to ask; "Amanda, how do you know you're not pregnant right now?"

"Antonio, I would feel it. I knew instantly with Sam. I felt the life. It was amazing, Honey. Babies are born every day. When it happened to me, I behaved like no one else had ever done it before.

I really wanted a baby conceived by love. In my situation, that could not happen, not in a relationship. The Doctor told me the chances of me getting pregnant, although not totally impossible, was highly improbable. Antonio, I'm a sperm killer."

"What in the hell is that?"

"My body kicks into an allergic immune-response, and takes the little guys out, one-by-one. Years ago, they told me 'yes,' it may be possible for one of the little guys to get past my artillery, and fertilize an egg, but not likely due to my body's reflexive response."

I interrupted.

"That's why you don't believe you are pregnant?"

"Right, but if one made it through, I know I would feel life. The quintessence of life is powerful to me. It surges through my body. Besides, I do not feel it is a part of our purpose or destiny right now.

Please do not confuse my words, I would love to share that experience with you, Antonio. A child conceived with you, would feel most incredible to me. I would love to have a part of you in that way, and experience such an amazing beauty. I pray that in another lifetime we have that opportunity. Right now, the conditions are not right. Maybe, I am wrong, that is certainly a possibility."

"I don't know what to say, Amanda. I don't feel like sharing you. I'm afraid I would be jealous of my own child, hanging on you, breast-feeding, I feel like such an idiot."

She laughed. "Gee, I'm kind of flattered, Antonio. However, you know the psychology behind Fears - Fears are different, in a deeper sense, than how you allow them to manifest."

"True, I still don't think I really want to share that much of you, with anybody. But I swear - I would, if I had to."

"I know that, Antonio. You are a sweet, noble man who does the right thing, even when it hurts."

"You think so?"

"I know so."

***

I curved, so that my face was near Amanda's, now buried in my chest. Then I spoke. "You see it wasn't the books. The incredible person that you are nurtured part of yourself into each of your sons. Despite your imprisonment of circumstance, you escaped.

You did a beautiful thing for each of those kids. You did it well. Those kids are astute enough to know you did. You merged like a transfusion your mind, body, and soul into them. You saw each child's individual strength, and you have made a piece of each child a part of you.

Their strongest traits became greater. This not only gave them strength, it gave them a unique sense of character because individually they share a unique part of you." I paused tightening my hold around her.

"Josh is the physical you. He is your body, fit, good-looking, strong, well-dressed, and well-mannered, when he is not protecting you. I suspect he can decidedly make people like him or hate him, like his mother. He is concerned with everyone's physical well-being. That is why he had to come to Santa Fe physically to check on you. He is the one that appreciates physical beauty, architecture, landscaping, even fashion. I suspect he will clean up a mess or straighten a picture on the wall. He is completely about the manifest world. He shares your love of the crafted arts.

Sam is your mind. He is all about what is in his head. He is the mental genius; the two of you share an intellectual bond. He is the one you are most likely to argue with to the point of distraction. You both like to argue. Like his mother, he is quick to be funny. He loves books, even writes. His imagination and creativity are monstrous. He often over-thinks a situation, like his Mom. He is a sponge soaking up, loving knowledge, the problem solver. The two of you have a great deal of fun, but sometimes only you two can understand it. Nevertheless he is fun."

"David is your soul. He is sacred to you. In your mind, he is King David, the soul of Israel. You share your soul with this boy. He is about how you feel. You are about what he feels. He is the one who protects feelings. The kid understands and reads people in a super human way. His personality defines love for you, the beautiful, and the ugly. He shares, sees, and understands things others can't see. His situation gives him the ability to see the spiritual world. However, he struggles with it. The love for music, you most share with him.

You have used the music with all of them, but for different reasons. Josh will sing and dance with the music. The music with Sam is mathematical. He plays the instruments making sounds from the equation. It is intellectual. David shares the part that communicates with your soul. You share all kinds of music because it is about what words cannot do. You and David haven't finished." I had to pause, my eyes filled with water.

"You are correct about the Divine Weave Amanda. I believe if you were able to think back precisely to the time of my concussion I bet you had an epiphany at that moment. A realization that your life was changing, Josh and Sam were ready. You are still their Mom and all that implies, but you taught them well. They were extraordinary students. Your mind and body were free. Those parts of you were again your own. Those are the parts easiest for you to share with me. Your mind and body fascinate me, I long to experience you through your children." I kissed her hair.

"Your soul is not finished, not ready. However, David is your best student. The two of you have journeyed and fought Goliath. I think you have caged Goliath at times. You have not succeeded in slaying Goliath. You are beginning to fear Goliath might win. Amanda, you wouldn't have ever come with me except for the Scrolls. They might hold the key to slaying Goliath, Honey that is where you started all of your wild research. I think there was a thread of hope when you saw the Scrolls. Otherwise, you wouldn't have agreed to stay, you would never stay away from him this long unless it was for him.

Amanda, I swear to God, I don't know what it is or how it correlates but it does. That is what pisses you off most about OPERA. The first violation was the information and research they took from you, research that you hoped could save your David's life. They were stupid, were they not? Feeling threatened by you for the wrong reasons. In fact, you weren't a threat to their cause; really, you were always on a journey to save him, the one who shares your soul. That is how you could so easily equate it with the ultimate evil. It is evil of an unspeakable kind. Only the ultimate evil could interfere with a mother trying to save her child's life. You have dared them to get you, have you not?

"You know, I feel like I've waited a long time for you. Now that you're with me, it's enough. I want to do so many things with you. You've missed some things too.

I hoped my sharing of this now would show Amanda that I saw her sons as a significant part of who she was; and I would never come between them, or ask her to step away from them. The idea of a kid of our own scared me just now-but who knows what the future will bring…She lay quietly beside me, and I started to get worried then I heard her soft voice.

"Well, you did promise to take me to Israel, Antonio. I believe it to be unhealthy to pack a tiny baby across the desert." While her voice held happiness, I could see the tracks of the tears on her face.

I laughed. "Correct! I promised, but it is contingent upon a contract."

"Yeah, well you better decide what you want in return for the trip, in case I find the price too high. I might have to secure a different, less costly escort," she grinned.

"Amanda, I've known all along what I want out of this contract. Like hell you'll secure another escort, only over my dead body."

"Antonio, please, do not use that pun. Considering our circumstances, I find it plain creepy."

"You're right. I'm sorry."

"Have you decided on your price for this middle-east expedition? Why have you not told me?"

"You haven't asked."

"What is it you want?"

"You," I smiled.

"Antonio, Lincoln abolished slavery."

"I see…that you are silly." She smiled, shaking her head.

"Not really."

I didn't push. I wanted the perfect atmosphere before presenting her with the details of our contract.

Chapter 13

"Expect the best, plan for the worst, and prepare to be surprised."
— *Dennis Waitley*

I kept busy with some paperwork. Pop and José weren't in the study by late morning this was unusual. I watched the clock in anticipation of Amanda's blood tests. Despite her tutelage, she failed to convince me that she wasn't pregnant.

The study door opened. José stepped in.

"José, you're just the guy I need right now."

"Hey, Antonio, I've been at the office, preparing for the trip."

"Not just any trip, the trip of your life, Josie!"

"Really, we'll find out soon. What do you need?"

"As usual, something in a hurry, I laughingly replied."

"Shoot."

"José, you compiled a blanket legal document to take care of my business, in the event I became ill, or died. Everything's changed. I want a more detailed set of documents before we board that plane to New Mexico.

Since the current papers didn't require it, I've never given you specific instructions, or a list of my assets. We need to change that, now. I prefer you do it, but I'm okay with Xavier doing it, so long as you and Pop check it."

José grabbed a pen and legal pad. "We'll get it done."

"I didn't want to get on my computer, so I could've missed something, but I wrote out all I could think of, which I'm sure covers the significant items of concern. In the event that something may happen to me, I want my caretakers, Maria and Joe to have enough to keep them comfortable. They are much more than just employees." I paused, handing the list to my brother. José could glance it over, and capably understand with which it dealt.

"Damn, Antonio, I had no idea… You've done incredibly well. You're a damn investment guru. Not only that, you pulled out before the crash. Apparently, your poker is no small potatoes. Sorry, I'm shocked, Antonio."

"Well, you're really the first to know, outside of the IRS."

"Amanda, doesn't know?"

"That's funny. I would tell her, but we never talk about money. I know she's done well, especially in the last few years. She has assets I'm aware of through conversation. Money isn't a part of our relationship. I mean, we could discuss it, but it hasn't been necessary."

José had a tone that expressed his admiration, "Wow, you two are in a league, entirely of your own."

"Anyway, Amanda has her own money. I know she's fine, but I would want her to be more than fine, before anyone else may be consulted. I don't know how you need to do this, José."

"Tell me what you want, I'll tell you if there's a problem."

"The estate goes to Amanda. She belongs in New Mexico.

There's a lot of land there. If it's too much for her, I really don't want any of it sold. I don't believe she'll have a problem, but if all, or part, of the land is too much for her, please, I want family to have it, our family, or her boys. I want the integrity of the entire property maintained. You have to find a way to put that in the document."

"I will, Antonio." He jotted his notes onto the legal pad.

"I want Amanda's security – always as first priority. Someone needs to watch out for her. As far as money, if for some reason you find Amanda needs it or anything at all, I want her to have it.

I don't think she needs the money, and I feel that if we weren't married when something happened to me, she could get deeply insulted. Therefore, I need to ask. How is the money situation of our family members?"

"Antonio, as far as I know...very well; Marissa and her husband are just getting started, but he has an excellent law practice. Plus, Pop and Mama have a very large estate that will leave significant funds for everyone."

"If anyone in the family was in need, I would want them to have it. Otherwise, I want a fund set for the Natives and a couple of scholarships, one especially for a Native from a New Mexico tribe. Anything else is at your discretion. Oh, Amanda's charity should also get something. I want Amanda to have all my work; all my books, papers, anything she wants. I have a lab that I use to authenticate and examine artifacts, if she doesn't want it, see that it goes to the small University in the Highlands of New Mexico.

"There are a few things in the house Maria should have, I have written those down. I would want you to have Raven. Everything else is at your discretion, but you ask Amanda first, and always.

She is very unpredictable. Hell, she might want something you think is trash. On the other hand, she may not want something that is incredibly valuable. She always has her reasons. Please, include Pop, I want him to feel like a part, and I don't want him to feel like I've cut him out of my life."

"We'll take care of it, Antonio, and you'll have it at the end of the day."

"Thanks Josie."

"You bet."

Chapter 14

"A fraudulent intent, however carefully concealed at the outset, will generally, in the end, betray itself."
Titus Livius

I opened the door to look in on Amanda, her appearance was ghostly. Beads of moisture were forming on her pasty skin. Concerned, I placed my palm against her warm wet forehead. In a tiny voice, she assured me, she took all of her medications. I simply could not understand the uncharacteristic nature of her bouts with illness.

Her moans sent me to retrieve some cool wet washcloths from the lavatory. I rushed back to her side and began using them to lower her body temperature. Again, she spoke, but her ability to sound coherent was fading.

Just as I picked up the phone to dial for help, José burst into the room with Dr. Martinez.   The slight man glared at me, as he threw open his bag and pulled out a syringe.

He got my attention when he shouted. "This woman is poisoned. Someone is trying to kill her."

José and I exchanged looks.

The Doctor continued his rant. "She's not getting some medications and said she took them." With angry intention, he removed instruments from his bag.

José shouted with his cell phone to his ear. "Antonio, get her medicine case." He walked into the hall, yelling. "I'm calling

Detective Johnson. We need him here."

The Doctor's stern looks in my direction were beginning to unnerve me. His rhetoric began to mimic a quasi-accusation. "Why would someone want to kill this woman?"
I offered a firm voice in response to the doctor. "That's what we'd like to know. We'll talk in my father's study, once you have Amanda stabilized. Can you stabilize her? She'll recover right, won't she?"

"Antonio, I think so, but her blood levels were very alarming." The Doctor worked to set her vein for an IV and medication.

I shouted around the corner to José. Get Pop on the phone, and tell him to come home." Oddly enough, we needed the side of my father I often despised, the judge. Pop and Dr. Martinez were friends. He would undoubtedly be beneficial.

"She felt great last night."

"Then she is probably getting it in the morning, or maybe in sporadic doses." The Doctor stayed busy, setting the correct dose to drip in her IV.

Within seconds I could see the medication dripping down the tube. I stared at Amanda. Shocked by her state, I began grilling the Doctor. "What's wrong? She's worse…Do something…Damn it you're giving her something she's allergic to." I grabbed her purse and pulled out the small red case with the allergy syringes.

"She has these for an allergic reaction. They're kept separate from her other medications. It wasn't tampered with."

The doctor took one, inspected it, and hesitated.

I yelled, "She's having a Damn reaction, Do it, or I will!"

The doctor failed to react. I wasn't about to wait any longer, so I snatched the syringe out of his hand. "Get out of the way." I held her thin arm out, and injected her. Without delay, I pulled the tube from the feed to stop the drip from entering her arm. José watched with intensity from across the room.

As soon as she was stabilized, I instructed my brother. "José, take him to Pop's study…get Xavier to watch him…then come back… Under no circumstance is he to leave this house…Where the hell is Pop?"

José bellowed from down the hall. "He's on his way."

By the time Jose returned, I had shoved the IV stand out of the way, and began snapping more orders. "José, get the Detective back on the phone. Tell him not to come. Explain, you made a huge mistake. Do it now, and then get someone to sit with Amanda."

Within minutes José brought Carmen in to sit with her. "Antonio, I took care of Detective Johnson."

"Good, Carmen you scream bloody murder if she shows any signs of negative change. Do not hesitate."

I knew Carmen had no idea what happened. Now wasn't the time to answer questions. "I will, Antonio."

I rushed into the bathroom, dumped out my shaving bag, picked up the .738, checked it, and put it in my belt behind my back, in plain sight.

"Come on, José." He followed as Pop met up with us in the hallway. We all three entered the office, shut the door, and stood in front of the Doctor, who sat on the edge of the small sofa, his hands lay on his lap in tight fists. I stabbed a disgusted look straight through the man's heart, and began my interrogation.

"Dr. Martinez, I'm going to talk - you're going to listen. Then, I'm going to ask questions, and you're going to answer. Do you understand?" The doctor nodded.

"Doctor – I suggest you use words. Do you understand?"

"Yes."

"Good, you have known my family for some time, correct?"

"Yes."

"You know all of the Judge's children, correct?"

"Yes."

"Except me; correct?"

"Yes."

"Do you know why?"

"No."

"You see, I couldn't come home for fifteen years and I'm guessing you didn't know the Judge had another son; right?"

"Right."

"Do you know why?"

"No."

"Because, I'm the maniacal son, I left fifteen years ago with a gun in my boot, a gun at my waist, and a pack on my back. I trekked all over the world to pick-up dead guys, primarily in the deserts."

My performance had José rolling his eyes. Pop's expression scolded him.

"Good, now that you understand who I am. I want to ask you some questions. Remember that woman who almost died in there, just a few minutes ago? She needs me. So, don't waste my valuable time.

Doctor, is there any part of what I just said that you don't understand?"

"No."

"Good, now we're making progress. You said when you came in, that her blood tests showed the presence of poison, then stated that she wasn't getting the medication, that she believed she took. Do you maintain that as the truth?"

"Yes."

"Now, you gave her a shot, and plugged her into an IV, which included several other medications, correct?"

"Yes."

"I'm not a medical doctor. So you tell me, is it unrealistic to assume that we should expect her to appear better or without change following your administered medical treatment?"

"Yes."

"If she became worse, or lost consciousness, would a professional find it abnormal, or reason for concern?"

"Yes."

"We have your medical bag, if we examine its contents, will we find medication to treat an allergic reaction?"

"Yes."

"Did you try to administer it when Amanda took a nose dive into oblivion?"

"No."

"Why?"

"I was stunned."

"Okay. Then when I took one of her syringes from her purse, and gave it to you for injecting into her arm, why wouldn't you do it?"

"Liability, I couldn't be certain of its contents."

"Okay, let me get this straight. You know the woman was poisoned. You know she has lacked the necessary nutrients, hormones, and God-only-knows what else. You even have tests to support this as evidence. I handed you a syringe that you could have kept as evidence after you injected her. It is my responsibly at that point for what was in it. The woman was dying from an allergic reaction. Not only did you fail to inject her, you didn't remove the drip from her veins. Are you stupid, Dr. Martinez?"

"No."

"I didn't think so either. Do you think José and I are stupid?"

"No."

"How about Judge Dominguez, is he stupid?"

"No."

"Good because, we are really skeptical about this liability theory of yours. We don't see that you were in a compromising situation that would suffice as a plausible excuse. It's not smart, Doctor. Now, is there something you would like to share with us?"

"No."

"You came in ready to accuse me of poisoning Amanda. Correct?"

"No."

"Doctor, you were - but when José phoned the Detective, you realized it wasn't going to fly, correct?"

The Doctor didn't answer.

The Judge stepped in, "Richard is that true?"

"Yes."

I resumed, "Now, you're in trouble Doc, so it would be a really good idea not to jerk us around. Surely, you, all by yourself, didn't try to frame or kill someone in the Judge's family. Is that correct?"

"Yes."

"I'm assuming you were approached after leaving here yesterday. Is that correct?"

The Doctor looked at us. His eyes wanted to lie. I ripped the.738 out, and lunged towards the Doctor, holding the gun to his temple, I warned him. "You son-of –a-bitch, I'll splatter your damn brains all over this room, don't think I won't.

The Judge interjected. "Richard, he'll do it."

I directed to my father, "Pop, let me, she almost died, damn it."

"Get a grip, Son. You don't want to go away again, do you?"

"Pop, I don't care."

The Doctor begged, "Maurice, make him put that gun away, and get his ass out of here. I will tell you everything."

José looked stunned by the turn of events in our game.

"Pop?!" I exclaimed.

"Antonio, I will call you back in if he doesn't cooperate. Go."

I left, slamming the door, and went immediately to Amanda.

"Carmen, any change?" I asked.

"Sorry, but there has been no change Antonio."

"I may need your help." I told her.

"Sure." She looked worried.

I got into the Doctor's satchel, removed a new IV bag, some tubing, and set them aside.

"Carmen, put these gloves on. I'm going to take this stuff apart. Make a place to set it. It's evidence. My prints are already on it, we'll deal with that later." I took everything apart and handed it to Carmen. I left the needle in, and connected the new bag of fluid.

"Carmen, go to the study, knock, and get José. Tell him to have the Doctor call, and get, let's say, four bags of IV liquids delivered ASAP. We're going to run these through her like crazy. Carmen, on second thought; ask him to force the doctor to have an unopened case delivered, fast."

"Okay Antonio." Carmen ran down the hall to the study. I pulled the bedside chair right next to the bed where Amanda rested, sat and situated myself over her, so that my face lay next to hers.

"Amanda, can you talk to me?"

Her voice was barely audible. "Yeah…"

"When you have an allergic reaction, what do you need besides the shot from your purse?"

"Steroid shot."

"Is the steroid in your purse?"

"Yes, I keep it close by at all times."

"Good girl, Amanda."

I picked up her purse, dumped the contents at the end of the bed, and found the bottle. "Amanda, I have pills is that it, try to look?"

"Yes, but…"

"Is there something else?"

"Yes, a small bottle of liquid, in the pocket with the money." Okay, good, the pills didn't seem right. I opened the zipper and found an enormous wad of bills; inside where she kept the money at the bottom, padded by the bills, a glass bottle. More, sublingual drops.

"Honey, I've got the drops to go under your tongue. Is that

correct?"

"Yes."

I read the instructions and measured using the dropper.

"Okay, open up. Let me get this under your tongue. Good we've got it. Now, do you take a round of the pills?"

"Yes."

I located her drink, removed a pill, lifted her limp body up and slid the pill between her lips.

"Does it work pretty quickly, Amanda?"

"Yes."

Her voice already sounded better. I laid my head on the bed beside hers. I felt relieved. With closed eyes, I tried to calm myself. Glad, my plan seemed to work with the Doctor. I really wanted the information more than I wanted to come unglued.

My goal was to get Amanda strong enough before our flight back to New Mexico. Miami had played serious hell on us. I knew the Doctor had blown our deception anyway. Now, OPERA knew I wasn't healing in the hospital.

The sweetest words interrupted my thoughts. "Antonio, are you my Doctor now?"

I chuckled. "It looks that way. I'm gonna try, for now."

Her tiny voice barely climbed above the sound of the ceiling fan.

"I think I prefer you."

I kissed her. "Amanda, I'll always take care of you if you will just let me."

"I know."

I noticed Carmen across the room. "God Carmen, I'm sorry, I didn't realize you were here."

"It's okay Antonio, you were busy. I'm glad she's coming back to us."

"Oh, Carmen, come here." I gave my sister-in-law a giant hug.

"Carmen thanks so much. I think she's pulling out of it."

"She looks better, too." Carmen pointed out.

"Not so much like a Gothic Princess now, huh?" I teased. Carmen laughed. José came in.

"Antonio, how's she doing?"

"Better, we found a couple more things to help. I'm running IV fluids through her now, as I guess you probably figured out."

"Yeah… You did a great job with the Doc, Antonio. Are you sure you didn't go to law school?"

"I'm sure. Maybe there's a little in my blood. You didn't leave Pop alone with the bastard, did you?"

"Hell no; he could murder the Doctor right now. Marc showed up. He's keeping Pop from killing him."

"Marc, bad choice, he's as bad as me. Marc's a daredevil at heart; him and Pop together might murder the guy anyway. By the way, how much did they pay him, José?"

"A bunch, I'll let Pop explain the pay-off."

"Damn…"

"They really wanted you arrested so they could get to the Scrolls. It seems they've infiltrated Miami PD pretty deep."

"Now what do we do?" I sighed.

"I figured Pop would know… I don't know." José said.

Amanda asked. "Antonio, what did you do?"

I smiled at her. "I did some acting, Honey."

She pleaded. "José, come tell me please."

Delighted to tell the story, José went to her side and sat down in the chair. "Amanda, he put on an awesome act, won an Oscar, and made the family law firm look like a debate team. Did you know Antonio is the maniac son who left fifteen years ago, packing guns and picking up dead bodies all over the world?"

She giggled. "Antonio, did you say that?"

"Honey, it's true. I never said when the guys died. Besides, I always pack a gun out there in my boot."

We all laughed, and Amanda made José tell her the rest.

Marc ran down the hall insisting he needed to talk to me. When José finished his story, he went out with them. José told Carmen to find a video camera. Pop wanted a taped confession from Dr. Martinez, before he telephoned the authorities. I came back in and sat down by Amanda.

"Antonio…"

"What?"

"I'm ready to leave Miami, and I do not know when I will want to come back."

"I agree, they may have to come to us. We won't be returning for quite a while, if ever."

"Antonio, should I call you Indiana now? That was an awfully exciting story your brother told me."

"Please don't. I just needed to make a point."

"You're much sexier than Indiana anyway."
I laughed. "We're going to get your eyes checked."

"What about my hands?"

"Amanda, stop it. You're gonna be I-V'd till you wet the bed."

"Good thing we're leaving in the morning."

***

The next morning I sat at Pop's desk determined to complete my research criteria for the Chosen. Amanda sat beside me, quietly watching as I gathered my thoughts. She looked so much better this morning, and I was glad she felt well enough to join in. I was beginning to worry that I was failing our partnership by falling behind in my work due to obsessing over Amanda's health.

I organized the items on my desk while Amanda slipped her glasses on. Prepared to examine my progress, we began.

"Amanda, I want to go over the criteria that I'm convinced is important for the Chosen."

"Great, I am anxious for you to share your new information with me. You know, Antonio, as a rule you have been eager to provide me with details about everything. Your work on the Chosen is a contrast shrouded in mystery… I am truly perplexed."

The two of us shared sarcastic grins.

"It's important for me to do the right thing in regards to the '13'. Focusing on the religious practices only, seems counterproductive.

However paramount, the Chosen should be deeply spiritual, and dedicated to a humanitarian purpose. These individuals must be seekers of truth, movers, and shakers, with deep ties to the original platform of the United States and to Israel.

These individuals are most likely not living as Holy Leaders. They need to be humble and loving, free of exploitation.

The Chosen are seekers of light, truth, and love, people of passion willing to journey, sometimes even to Hell. These individual journeys may never reach their end, similar to Moses.

Amanda, after all, we don't want to end.

Humanity will face a turning point over the next few years. Possibilities, like God, are infinite. Right now, we're in 'Sodom and Gomorrah,' just like Lot and his family. We can't look back and dwell on the past, to do so is to die.

As individuals, we must move forward in seeking a new era. It's imperative we do so through freewill. The process, procedure, and ultimate journey are everything. Constriction by government, and institutions, will only smother the process."

Amanda's words escaped in a mere whisper. "Like you,

Antonio… The Chosen must be as you are - unassuming and humble…beautiful inside."

Astounded, I didn't expect such an emotional reaction from her. I decided to move on to trusted methods for changing the mood. "Don't get all gooey, Amanda. Prepare for victory!" Smiling, she refrained from addressing my declaration.

"On previous occasions we discussed using DNA tests for verification. I used the labs as part of the process. Prior to finding the Scrolls, I found the study fascinating enough to pursue further research. You said so yourself, the tests were how you learned you were a genetic Levite.

The professionals responsible for a similar experiment did a stupendous job, especially one Professor from the University of Arizona, who is solely responsible for the basis of the operation. In fact, I believe he deserves the Nobel Peace Prize for his work.

Having reiterated, it's not enough to select the Chosen based only on their Jewish genes from the blood work. This will require a Divine connection, and perhaps, these individuals are predestined.

Amanda, I've purposely kept this to myself. Not because I don't want you to know, but because of the conflict it manifests, and there it causes me problems. It required validation. I'm not a Psychic, and I'm not divine…

I resorted to search within your mystical madness and honestly found credence, and validity." I paused.

"The names of the Chosen are in the Codes of the Torah. I've found them there. However, I'm still using the other tests, and criteria to validate my findings."

"That is fabulous, Antonio, and I am pleased it is working for you."

Chapter 15

"Here in America we are descended in blood and in spirit from revolutionists and rebels - men and women who dare to dissent from accepted doctrine. As their heirs, may we never confuse honest dissent with disloyal subversion."
Dwight D. Eisenhower

I awoke with anxious anticipation. The arrangements were in place. Pop had commissioned a pilot and private jet to fly Amanda and I back to my home in New Mexico. My brothers Marc and Jose, along with Pop were joining us to offer their expertise to the completion of our plans for the Chosen.

I didn't bother to open my eyes, but instead, reached out to touch her, next to me. I smiled when my hand met the cool sheets, and for a few moments I lost myself in warm thoughts of Amanda preparing for our return to my estate in Santa Fe. I wanted her to love life there. Her affections could only assist my attempts to convince her to stay.

Soon, I abandoned my dream, and surfaced assuming my morning routine. Once showered, and shaved, I again, privately, reacted to Amanda's apparent urgency. She had already packed, and removed her luggage from our room at my parent's house. It was clear; she was more than ready to get the hell out of Miami. I couldn't blame her as I had grown weary of the chaos we had endured during our brief stay.

I sauntered out of the bedroom expecting to find Amanda in

my mother's kitchen having her morning dose of Greek yogurt. Instead, I was met by the long faces of my Pop and Jose. I recognized their look of pity. My Pop began with "son" a dead giveaway that revealed, he hated whatever it he was about to say.

"Son, Amanda has left." Pop paused.

I didn't wait, my voice thundered. "What in the hell do you mean, Amanda has left? You make it sound as if she got up and walked out of here by her own freewill waving goodbye."

Pop's eyes closed, his lips pursed as his head nodded. In contradiction, my gut wrenched as my Pop's fist pounded into it and resided into a grind, repeatedly.

My hands, on auto-pilot, began massaging my temples. I lowered my voice, and enunciated each syllable. "How do you know she left willingly, and more importantly, why in the hell would you let her?"

Pop snatched a deep breath. He articulated the words in a tone barely above a whisper. "Antonio, Amanda left with her luggage in tow by water."

An insane chuckle escaped me, my voice wreaked with sarcasm. "You're telling me, Amanda, so desperate to leave me, hopped onto your yacht, and embarked across the Atlantic Ocean, and to top it all off, you watched her."

Pop shook his head, and Jose jumped in to respond.

"Antonio, a man in a scarab, cruised in, Amanda boarded and they raced off across the water. By the time we caught sight of her it was too late."

Suddenly I knew just where she had gone. Her first mistake was leaving; her second was thinking I would not follow. I abruptly turned and left the room, letting my long strides eat up the anger burning inside. I needed a plane and I needed it now.

Chapter 16

"When you are courting a nice girl an hour seems like a second. When you sit on a red-hot cinder, a second seems like an hour. That's relativity."
— *Albert Einstein*

Just before sundown, the pilot landed the plane at the obsolete airport in Amanda's hometown. The small facility used for private aircraft was absent runway lights. Subsequently, we slid in just before the facility closed for the night.

Moments before landing, I telephoned a couple of services hoping to secure a car and driver. Unable to complete the task, an eerie truth was beginning to manifest. Forced to improvise, I took a cab to a car rental facility. I couldn't help but notice the peculiar looks I received as I went about my tasks.

Amanda had provided a chilling description of Glendale. She told of a mob-style organization with outgrowths that controlled the area's business, and legal institutions. Cognitive dissonance and indoctrination kept the citizens functioning beneath, like fine-tuned machines. I was beginning to fear, she had not exaggerated.

I felt genuine relief once inside the rented black Cadillac. The GPS programmed, I set out to locate Amanda's house. The city owned the appearance of a quiet wholesome existence. A church occupied space on nearly every block. Glendale, surely, held a world record for the most churches per capita. The population was anything, but diverse, and the residents were obviously unaccustomed to anyone that did not fit their limited idea of an ordinary profile.

After about twenty minutes, I realized, I was entering the neighborhood Amanda called home. A sign with a familiar name grabbed my attention, Zin, fine food and drinks. Amanda claimed this was the place where things happened. I decided to take some time to relax, and pulled in for a beer. It had been a long day, and I wasn't sure where the hell the night would lead.

It was Thursday evening and the parking lot was packed. The establishment shared a strip with several other businesses, but they were all closed leaving me to assume the cars belonged to the Zin's clientele. I made a full circle around the property before I spotted an empty space to park.

The aroma hit me when I opened the door, nice. I personally loved a place that felt like it had been there for years, and the scents that hit my nose one step inside were of micro beers on tap, old wines, grilled onions and beef tenderloin!

The décor was relaxed yet upscale, a rather out of place Zen environment. The area dividers were lined with identical three foot tall clear glass vases filled with a variety of rocks and stones. The pattern was broken periodically by the same vases filled with wine corks. It was odd, but it did work; I liked it. The main dining area held tables for two and large family gathering options. I located the curved stainless bar on my left, lined with men in suits and construction guys, separated on each end; normal male behavior; separating the haves from the have-nots.

I made my way to the empty bar stool in the center.

I have been in enough bars around the world to know that the locals usually take a minute to look you over. I returned the favor by nodding to the men nearest me. I could not help but notice that the reflection of our gathering in the large mirror behind the bar was a stark reminder of just how different in appearance I was from the local crowd.

Now, I'm a Cuban-Jew with strong Spanish traits. My ancestors originally escaped Spain during the Spanish Inquisitions, and settled in my father's beloved pre-Castro Cuba. At 6'2", I'm rather tall, but I still run, and my years in the field have contributed to my muscle mass. I have deep brown curly hair, Amanda compares to deep rich dark chocolate. Hey she said it, not me. My skin is a deep olive tone. In fact Amanda thought I was an Argentine when we first met.

I have not suddenly decided to become obsessed with my appearance, you see that is the issue here, my appearance has served me well, and so have my instincts. I have travelled the world, and in the places that it mattered most I blended in. In Israel, I look like an Israeli, in Egypt an Egyptian, in New Mexico; I'm thought to be a Native. It has worked beautifully. Never had I attracted the attention I received in Glendale.

The bar nearly went silent as the patrons turned to take in my presence. Finally, after an inordinate delay, the bartender came over to ask for my order. At first, his line of vision had me thinking I had spilled something on my shirt. I looked down and realized the medallion Amanda gave me was in plain sight. I was an idiot; this was a problem Amanda mildly warned me about, but I assure you I had not comprehended until I landed in her hometown. It seemed the Hebrew words comprising Aaron's prayer on the symbolic scroll with the Star of David were compounding the problem they had with my ethnic appearance.

I took a deep breath and ordered a bottle of Corona, I thought it was best to stick with the theme, but I couldn't think of any Jewish beers so, I went with a well-known Mexican brew. The barkeep set the bottle down hard on the surface. "That will be $8.95." Hell, I didn't think a Corona was that expensive in Miami?

I grinned. "I'll run a tab."

His reply was surly; "Can't run a tab without a credit card."

I chuckled, and pulled out a credit card with my full title and insignia, then slapped it down on the bar top, and smiled. I stared at his face as he fumbled to pick it up off the slick surface. He looked at my name and title, and then up at me, before returning to the register.

The tension around me was rising; slowly but rising. I could hear murmurs from down the bar; just loud enough to be sure they were heard, but not enough to see who said it. I could hear them discussing my appearance, and for a moment I thought they meant my clothes. Nope, they were discussing my darkness, my curly hair, and my overt strangeness in this part of the world.

Suddenly my idea of a relaxing moment held a myriad of danger. I waited until he turned around and then I called out to him in a loud voice. "Go ahead and run my card, I think one beer is enough for me here, tonight."

In a disgusting motion, Amanda would not have approved of; I chugged down the beer, and slammed the bottle back down. I stood slowly, and with a glance at each of the patron's faces, and the last to the bartender, I gave a brief nod and bid them a good day; "Shalom." With my back held straight and my head held high I walked out of there vowing to myself that I would in fact return soon to rock their world. I feel like I need a shower. Getting into the car I see that a couple of suits have followed me outside, and I barely refrained from a juvenile instinct to shoot them the bird; I don't though. I just held my impulse and my dignity and drove away.

I rounded the corner into Amanda's neighborhood. The homes were an eclectic mix of middleclass, and upscale residences. The architecture suggested the area was developed during the '70's with newer homes sprinkled throughout. The gentle hills added character to the unique design of each property. The lawns were large, and well-manicured with mature trees. The air smelled of freshly cut grass. The car rolled past three small lakes, home to an impressive flock of ducks and geese.

My thoughts had never ventured to imagine Amanda living

in a neighborhood, but expected her out in an open and yet, secluded suburbia area.

The car crept through the winding neighborhood streets. A hammer inside my head knocked harder as I realized I was approaching her address. Confusion stampeded through my mind. I wondered if anything I believed was factual. Hell, my trip to Glendale was a shot in the dark. I didn't know where she was or where I would find her, but I had to start somewhere.

Numbers against chestnut brick divulged the truth. Amanda's house sat in front of me. The rather expansive structure nestled behind a couple of majestic oaks and a circle drive was natural in a nondescript fashion. In contrast, two massive stone lions were perched on pedestals guarding the entry. The heavy wrought iron covered entryway was constructed of an elaborate open design, one that was gaudy and almost made you wince, until you spotted what it was protecting. The wooden doors behind the iron entry featured an exquisite stained glass much too beautiful to be camouflaged. The unusual design appeared to have been altered. Two rows of shuttered windows rose above the height of any man.

A scattered array of light from inside was visible. I pondered, without a proper plan, and maneuvered the Cadillac onto an adjacent street. At the very least, I needed to cool off; my trip at the bar had me boiling. My location provided a full view of the three garages as well as the front of the house. I simply sat and watched.

A couple of hours passed without incident, and just as my eyes began to feel heavy a dark sedan pulled into Amanda's circle drive. A man stepped out and went to the door. Nausea flowed upward into my throat as I watched Amanda open the door and invite in her guest.

Our intimate snapshots flashed behind my eyes, and I prayed out loud to God hoping he was not a lover. I pleaded for him to quickly leave. I couldn't endure visions of Amanda with another man.

After only a few moments, my breath hastened, my chest tightened, my body pleaded for air. A tap on the window startled me into a gasp. I released the car lock; Amanda pounced inside the passenger side.

"Antonio, you have sat here for more than two hours. Why?"

Perplexed by her knowledge of my whereabouts, it was the most ignorant question I had ever felt the need to address.

"Amanda, did you honestly believe you could just leave and I would do nothing?"

Fidgeting, she looked around. "You cannot sit out here, any longer."

I ignored her warning. "Amanda, what in the hell is going on? Better yet, who in the hell is that man in your house?"

She avoided the questions, but instead, ordered. "Start the car; pull into the center garage stall."

Without hesitation, I did as she instructed.

We got out of the car, and Amanda grabbed my hand, and steered me inside. The savory aroma of rosemary calmed me as we entered the kitchen. The surroundings distracted me. The cool stone counters were the perfect contrast for the warm wood cabinets. The six burner Viking and hanging pots created a space fit for a chef. I was most intrigued by the double ovens and dishwashers. It suggested Amanda did a lot of entertaining or her kitchen was kosher. I smiled at the well utilized space.

However, Amanda misunderstood my amusement. Her words exploded out of a loud whisper. "Antonio, this is not funny. We are in the midst of a very serious situation."
I began responding in a normal tone, but by the end my voice thundered. "Amanda, I'm not unaware. I realize the seriousness, but since you have failed to believe I am worthy of knowing what in the hell is going on with you. Yeah, I'm operating in the dark of night, oh and, by the way, who in the hell is that man?"

Her stunning eyes struck me down before she turned and walked over to a pot on the stove. Without answering me, she filled a bowl and set it down on the table.

Her eyes met mine, and for a moment, it was familiar. She motioned for me to sit at the table and eat. A man under the spell of a woman, I did. I gasped when I felt her hands steady my head. She whispered in my ear. "Antonio, you must listen, do not ask any questions. Please understand, if you cannot respect this, you must leave."

Before releasing me her soft lips grazed my right cheekbone.

I vigorously shifted my face, secured hers, and covered her lips with mine. She responded to my passion.

"Amanda." Her feminine finger touched my lips.

"Antonio eat some chowder, you must be ravenous."

I grinned, and looked down at the bowl. The contents looked organically anemic. The aroma and taste of the corn and chicken was an interesting mixture of a sweet milky cheese with hints of mild herbs. My stomach growled with anxious anticipation of finishing every bite.

Amanda brought over some huge chunks of crusty bread. She filled my glass with wine without ever taking her brilliant eyes off of me. She watched me chew every bite. I watched her watch me. My senses were so heightened; I thought it was the best meal I had ever eaten.

After I finished the last morsel, I reached for her hand, but the moment was interrupted by the elusive houseguest. He spoke softly from a Hebrew accent, judging by his appearance, he was likely an Israeli National.

"Amanda dear, are you going to introduce me to your guest?"

Amanda looked down, and rubbed her hands together. "Yes, of course, Ari, this is Dr. Antonio Dominguez, he is a professor of anthropology from the University of New Mexico. She paused and stared at me, before continuing. "Antonio, meet my cousin, Dr. Ari Sternen, professor of religious studies. He is staying here in my home while he studies unique religious practices in this area."

We shook hands. I inspected Amanda's so-called cousin. He was our age, average height with dark peppered hair. His physique was lean and fit clearly he worked to maintain such a build.

I intended to strike up a conversation with Dr. Sternen, but Amanda was too sharp. "Antonio, take your things into the bedroom past the stairwell. I will check on you, shortly.

I couldn't control the smirk plastered across my face. Hell, I didn't even know where to find the stairs. Amanda read my mind, and pointed me in the right direction.

I could not establish a good reason to rush to the bedroom. My pace was slow, and I pretended to lack true direction as I wandered through Amanda's finely decorated eclectic rooms. At the center of the main living area, a stunning grand piano caught my eye. I wondered if I would ever hear her play.

My images were broken by a teenage boy with a backpack and a load of luggage. His dark hair was unruly, and in bad need of a trim. The moment I saw his sparkling eyes, I knew this was Amanda's youngest son.

He paused when he noticed me, then grinned, and removed an ear bud. He held up his hand and said.

"Yo."

I chuckled. "Hi, let me guess, you must be Sam."

He nodded with a questioning look on his face.

I held out my hand. "I'm Antonio Dominguez, a friend of

your Mom's."

"Just friends, or real close friends?" My eyebrows raised, I shrugged. His boldness startled me. He was definitely his mother's son.

"Are you going away?"

"Yeah, I've got to catch a plane back to MIT?"

"Great, how does it feel to be such a young student on campus?"

"I don't really feel like I'm that young."

His confidence amused me.

"Well, I won't keep you, have a safe trip."

"See ya." He waved, replaced his ear bud, and was off.

I spotted double doors at the end of a short hallway. Passed the open staircase, I approached the entrance. Slowly, I turned the doorknob, hoping it was Amanda's personal bedroom. Immediately, I knew, my wish was granted.

Just as I was entering, Amanda's raised voice startled me. She was confronting Ari. "Where have you all been? The entire charge of the D'affaires abandoned me the minute I was diagnosed, and now, you waltz in as if nothing happened."

Her words stopped. I wanted to go to her, but I didn't dare. I slipped inside the room, and quickly, sent a message to Jose. I simply let him know I was in Glendale with Amanda. I wanted to mention Ari and the D'affaires, but I refrained I didn't possess enough information to coherently inform him of the circumstances.

My eyes darted around my surroundings. The massive bed demanded my attention. The carved wood posters mimicked giant columns. The covers were soft cotton clouds, layered in white. I sat on the side, removed my boots, and hid the Glock under a pile of pillows.

From the side of the bed, I noticed a doorway. I rose and walked over and pushed it open. It was Amanda's study. Bookcases lined the walls. The shelves were filled with books, and icons primarily Jewish, and Israeli art.

From the doorway I looked around in awe, the contents surprised me, since Amanda claimed; she had never traveled to the Holy Land. I shook my head. Every time, I thought I understood, something would emerge, and contradict.

She was Jewish, but did not strictly practice Judaism. Israel's wellbeing was of utmost importance to her, yet, she was not a Zionist. In fact, extreme Zionists annoyed her. At that moment, I realized, I had fallen for a woman that I knew nothing about.

A small spiral staircase within the study led to another level. I wasn't about to pass up the opportunity to explore. My ascent was awkward as the design was not intended to accommodate a man of my height. At the top I wandered through a jungle of bookcases, each filled with books. No expense spared, the room was climate controlled with a clever ventilation system.

Beyond the rows of books, the room opened into an awesome solarium. This was where Amanda became the artist. Her paintings intrigued me, but it was the work in progress that took my breath. It featured the naked trunk of a woman with ivy wrapped around her body. Two male hands appeared to be freeing her from the tendrils. On one of the hands was a small scar, above the knuckle of the pinky finger.

I glanced down at my hands. The hands in the painting were mine. How could this be possible? Amanda would have to have painted it before we met. A strange sensation sent a tingle up my spine.

The books in Amanda's library unveiled a portrait of the woman. The words she once said ran through my mind. 'Antonio, the books saved me. Everything I am, everything I know, it came from the books.'

The place felt sacred. I wished I could stay there, and read her books. I knew, then, I could understand. But, my exploration was about to end. Her voice startled me.

"Antonio"

She jumped into my arms. We stood in a desperate embrace, surrounded by her books. I began to caress her back. My wandering hands produced yet another surprise.

I took the liberty, and removed the loaded Beretta tucked in the waist of her jeans.

"Amanda, why are you packing a Beretta in your own home?"

"Antonio…hush, we must not discuss this, now."

Lowering my voice, I asked; "Then when Amanda?"

"Tomorrow, I promise, but not here."

She didn't allow me to respond. Her lips pressed hard against mine. She began devouring me. Amanda had never loved me in such a way.

Somehow, she guided me to her bed while unbuttoning my shirt. At the edge of the bed, I lifted the pillows, and placed her Beretta next to my Glock. She nodded, and began unbuckling my belt. Her kisses covered my body. She stopped, only long enough to remove her own clothing.

I didn't question, why we could make love, but couldn't talk. I assumed the situation was so volatile that she didn't care if someone eavesdropped on our lovemaking.

I sat on the bed with my back against the headboard. Amanda hovered above me loving me, wildly. I moaned as she tasted my earlobe just as my passion ignited to meet hers, she whispered in my ear.

"Leave in the morning, go to the campus coffee house…I will meet you there."

Without pausing she assumed her loving torment. We didn't talk that night. From a place within us, a power possessed. We made love for hours in silence.

I waited until I was sure Amanda was sleeping, soundly. Gently, I rolled out of bed, and crept to the door, opening it soundlessly, I moved out into the darkened hallway and made my way to the stairs and quietly climbed to the second floor. There were several doors, but only two were closed. I walked over to the first; I reached out my hand to open the door….

And an arm locked around my neck from behind.

With just enough pressure to prove a possible threat, I was immobilized immediately. I didn't try to get away.

"Listen, Dr. Dominguez, you go back down the stairs, keep your mouth shut, and I won't tell Amanda you were sneaking around. By the way, I'm a friend, not the enemy." The whispered words were from Ari, and I knew he meant what he said. Whether I chose to believe him or not, the idea of having to face Amanda like a reluctant bad child was enough to stop me in my tracks.

I nodded and he let go, and I promptly responded by turning quickly and jamming two fingers into his left kidney. As he doubled over and went to his knees, I leaned over and whispered in his ear; "Never sneak up on me again Ari, I may be a scholarly man with an extremely deep respect for the human condition, but I am not weak, meek or mild." With that I patted him on the head and calmly returned back to the bedroom like the good scholarly professor I am.

Chapter 17

"Never be bullied into silence. Never allow yourself to be a victim. Accept no one's definition of your life, but define yourself."
— Harvey Feinstein

The campus coffee house was the epitome of a techno college hangout. The mid-morning patrons were scattered, busy cramming for their next class. I scanned the area, and located a rather secluded booth on the far side.

Amanda entered just as I ordered a couple of lattes. She smiled when she saw me, and rushed over. A quick kiss on my lips, and she sat down across from me.

The barista brought out lattes and Amanda asked for some yogurt. At least her yogurt consumption had not changed.

Once the waiter left Amanda spoke. "Antonio you have to trust me. Circumstances require my attention, our relationship is important to me, but there is a cause I am devoted to that is greater, even, than us.

I left Miami hoping you would stay away, and remain safe. You followed me here. Now, you have a choice to make. You can leave or stay. If you stay, you must simply listen and trust me." She paused briefly. "Inside the pocket of your jacket you will find instructions for a plan to leave here tomorrow. Read them, and then, destroy the paper. Tonight, we must not speak of these things at my house. Ari believes it is not secure."

"I'm not leaving, Amanda." I thought to ask why she claimed

Ari was her cousin, but I didn't. The situation had me perplexed enough to play along. Besides, I had some place I wanted to take Amanda.

She squeezed my hand, and grinned. Damn, she knew exactly what I would do. She knew I would come to Glendale to find her after she left Miami.

I was not surprised her semi covert exit from my parents' house in Miami had little to do with me, and everything to do with her association with the D'affaires, whatever that meant.

It was a test, after all, trust is greater than love, and to truly trust another human being is rare. Love can exist without trust, but trust cannot exist without some semblance of love.

Did I trust Amanda or was I just curious? I had a lot of reasons not to trust her, but I did, anyway.

Claiming she would meet me back at her house in a couple of hours, she stood and leaned over to kiss me goodbye. I gripped her arm, and spoke softly. "I want to take you out tonight for dinner and drinks."

She smiled big with squinted eyes. "Are you asking me out on a date?"

I guessed I was. "Absolutely, go out with me in your hometown."

Still smiling she bit her bottom lip; "Okay, yes."

I could tell the idea thrilled her. We kissed and she rushed out of the coffee house.

I stayed for a short while longer and processed the ever

changing situation. In the relatively short amount of time Amanda and I had spent together, most perplexing was her ability, to not only know things, but to interject the information at precisely the right time.

I had fantasized about a long term relationship with Amanda. I believed, we could share a life together. I could continue my work as an anthropologist, with Amanda at my side. She could write as we traveled the world, broken only by extended hiatuses at my estate in Santa Fe.

Now, I had to reassess. Amanda wasn't exactly the type to act as anyone's sidekick. The only thing I knew, for sure, was that I had to see this escapade to completion.

I had possession of King Solomon's scrolls and OPERA still wanted them. How it all intertwined, well, I didn't know.

The one thing I did know was I was going to have dinner out that night with an incredible mysterious woman. Beyond that fact well, it was anyone's guess.

*****

When evening came, I waited for Amanda from within the formal seating area of her home. I began to wonder if my obsession with winning Amanda was out of control. I wanted to go out to dinner with her, yet, I worried that part of it was to seal my own deal.

Before I could finish my thought, the stunning woman emerged. I had not seen her look this gorgeous since my niece's celebration in Miami. No the dress she wore was not nearly as formal, but none the less, she was exquisite wearing it. I indulged my desires with a deep breath as I stood to acknowledge my approval.

The tight dress she wore was literally the color of fine champagne with tiny silver studded circles scattered across the waves of fabric. She smiled and handed me the Cognac Diamond necklace I had John Bear make for her. I stepped behind her and placed the pendant around her neck. Once the clasp closed, I leaned in to enjoy her scent. It wasn't the normal smell of sweet almonds that surrounded her. It was a subtle hint of India; a mild undertone of the incense present among the temples. For me it was downright erotic. I lingered with a soft wet kiss against the side of her neck. Her shiver made me smile.

"Antonio, do you even know where we should go eat? I am so sorry, since you do not know the area I should have taken care of the plans."

"Shhh Honey, no problem, I planned on taking you to the place where everything happens." I couldn't quite decipher the look on her face, either she was very excited or very disappointed, either way it was extreme.

Regardless, this time when I pulled into the parking lot at the Zin I was prepared. Earlier, I had made a reservation making damn sure they knew I was returning to torment them with my presence. With my arm around the small of Amanda's back, once again I entered their establishment.

With large eyes the hostess approached us. I spoke without giving her a chance. "Dr. Antonio Dominguez, I have a reservation for two, but we would like to have a couple of drinks in the bar area first." The expression on the young girls face didn't change as she nodded and directed us with a wave.

Taking a seat at a table near the bar, Amanda seemed a little uneasy. There was no doubt the piercing eyes of the patrons were familiar with Amanda.

"Antonio, I know you were here last evening, what happened?"

Damn her, how the hell did she know? I stopped at the bar before I ever entered the neighborhood. She spoke before I came up with a response. "Antonio, word travels fast, and you made a rather large impression on the group."

Frustrated, I rolled my eyes and took a deep breath. In need of a distraction, I glanced down at my watch, we had seated ourselves 15 minutes prior and still, no one had ask for our drink order.

The snobbish group of want-a-be tough guys and superior racists had resumed their prospective conversations, but still I feared later they would all be diagnosed with serious whip lash from the constant snapping of their necks in our direction.

30 minutes had passed, still no drinks, the table next to us had received a couple of trips from the waiter. It was clear; they had no intention of serving us. I gazed around the room at the superficial crowd of bigots. The sight sickened me.

I watched as a man approached Amanda. Without as much as an acknowledgement of my existence, he bent over to whisper in her ear. My teeth were clenched together so hard in my mouth, I'm surprised I didn't break a tooth. The mere audacity of the jerk had me fantasizing about his death. Amanda shook her head at the dumbass. I could not believe I was setting in an upscale business in this day and time in America, and experiencing such blatant racism.

I stood, and Amanda immediately started to react. "Honey it is okay, I'm going to walk over to the bar and get our drinks myself."

Her eyes locked with mine. "Antonio, please be careful." I nodded at her and made fierce strides on my way to the bar.

The same bartender from the night before stood behind the bar. I glared at him and belted out my order. "My lady and I would like a couple of Courvoisier's, please." He turned and grabbed the bottle off the back shelf and began pouring the drinks. I glanced back at Amanda and saw a couple of women talking to her. I could only imagine what they were saying. I took a wad of bills from wallet and threw them across the bar when he returned with the glasses.

A patron sitting at the bar spoke with a smartass tone. "Hey, why did you do that?"

I shrugged. "Sorry, they just slipped out of my hand."

Of course the fool of a man didn't stop there. "It's Friday evening, shouldn't you be at home with your kind."

At that moment much of the anger escaped my body. "If

you are talking about Shabbat, well you see that beautiful lady over there, we decided to celebrate the evening here with you fine folks." Empowered by the harsh reality of the man's utter ignorance, I returned to our table with the drinks. I placed Amanda's in front of her and kissed her cheek, she smiled, and I whispered in her ear. "You look magnificent." I heard a slight breathy giggle escape her as I set down.

Watching Amanda's throat move as she sipped her drink was mesmerizing, and for a few moments I forgot about our surroundings. Apparently, Amanda had not. "Antonio, I think we have proved our point. I do not wish to have dinner in this environment."

I stared across the table at her and nodded in agreement. After a few more sips, we rose from the table to make our way to the door. Our exit had us both sighing in relief. The tension inside was unbearable. I had no idea what triggered such incredible hate in Middle America, but I could now say, I had in fact experienced it.

Chapter 18

"Out beyond ideas of wrong-doing and right-doing there is a field.
I'll meet you there.
—Rumi

The next day Amanda's instruction sent me to a farming area, ten miles south of Glendale. I passed the synagogue hidden on the secluded farm road. Amanda once told me, there wasn't a synagogue in her hometown.

Driving down the country road I needed a distraction; I tuned the radio to a news station. My fears of dramatic changes to the planet were beginning to come to fruition. Temperatures were registering twenty to thirty degrees above average, and solar storm warnings were being issued every two to three days. I was hoping for more time, but that seemed unlikely. The ancients warned us. Were we prepared?

It was too risky to use the GPS; therefore, I had to rely on my memory of Amanda's sketchy map. I spotted the dirt drive ahead of me. I scanned the road behind to make sure I wasn't being tailed.

I followed the rough dirt path for more than a half a mile before catching sight of any inhabitation. Finally, an old four square, run down farmhouse appeared resting in the midst of several utility buildings, and an oversized dilapidated barn. The air smelled of horses, but I didn't see any animals.

A stocky older man stepped out of the house

before the car came to a stop.

"Are you Dr. Dominquez?" His dialect caught me off guard.

"Yes sir. Please, call me Antonio."

"Prove it."

I paused, cleared my throat, and reached for my driver's license.

After a cursory glance, he introduced himself; "My names Larry."

"Yes, Amanda gave me your name."

"Well, I got everything Miss Messenger told me to get. You'll need to get changed inside. Your ride is out in the barn, packed and ready to go. Miss Messenger said to wait, and then return your rental car tomorrow."

I nodded pretending to know what Larry was talking about. He walked me inside to a bedroom, then left, and shut the door. I glanced at the clothing arranged a top the worn quilted bed. I chuckled. A sleek black leather jacket, pants to match, and boots that would make any biker enthusiast proud.

Decked out in my new biker gear, I followed Larry to the barn. The ground in the barnyard was pitted and dry. In less than five minutes my new boots didn't look so new. Larry threw open the massive barn door. The screech caused me to wince.

"Here's your ride, Doc. She's a beauty."

I started laughing at the massive piece of awesome machinery standing upon the scattered old and smelly hay; "A Harley Fat Boy! This is what Amanda wants me to drive?"

Larry spoke while I admired the bike.

"That's right. She wants you to drive this girl down to Muskogee to meet with the Yuchee Indian Chief. Miss Messenger says, he will tell you what you need to do. After you finish with the Chief pick Miss Messenger up at Tinker Air force base."

"Anything else I need to know, Larry?"

"Nope, that's all I got."

"When did Amanda purchase the bike?" I could not imagine Amanda driving such a huge cycle, alone.

"Oh, about a year ago; after that incident when the rest of the Militia moved into these parts, but she never did use it. It's been sitting here ever since."

"I see, what about the clothes, when did she bring them?"

"Yesterday, and gave me the message to give you. Maybe, it's not my place to say, but I sure hope Miss Messenger keeps safe. She's too nice a lady to be in all this danger."

I wanted to continue questioning Larry, but I had a time constraint. I nodded to Larry and hopped on the bike. With a push of a button the engine thumped through my veins. I added the gas and she let out a ferocious roar. The barnyard dirt went flying in clumps as I sped away.

Amanda's plan was brilliant. The Yuchee chief was the only surviving member familiar with the native tongue. The ancient language of the Yuchee was consistent with ancient Hebrew. Many of the tribe's rituals mimicked those of early Jews. It only stood to reason that the chief could shed a great deal of insight into the mystery behind King Solomon's Scrolls.

Apparently, it was too risky to meet on the reservation. I was to visit with the Chief after sunset at a Best Western outside of Muskogee, Oklahoma. Three hours of road ahead of me, I raced down the interstate, excitement pulsated through my body. The power of the Harley, the sensation of the ride cutting through the wind, taking me to meet the iconic chief all followed by my rendezvous with Amanda at Tinker Air force Base. I felt damn good.

After a quick bite to eat in Tulsa, I opened the saddle bag. Riding clothes for Amanda, she evidently intended to join me on the road. I anticipated seeing her in the leather. My beautiful biker babe, her arms wrapped around me, flying down the highway, it seemed likely only in a dream for a professor like me.

A short time later, I rolled into the parking lot of the Best Western Motor Lodge. I scoped out the numbers, Room 17 was in a corner on the lower level near a dark stairwell. I parked the bike, and walked over to the door. I tapped on the worn metal.

***In my travels I have had the honor of meeting several different Chiefs of indigenous tribes around the world; the Lacandon who are direct descendants of the Maya, the Guarani and Yanomami, the Akuntsu and Kanoê of Brazil, and most of the Native American Indians. No matter how many Chiefs I am introduced to, I can never seem to completely hide my awe at their absolute sense of natural power. This time was no different.

The true stature of the man who stood before me was not bowed by age or minimized by his modern clothing. Like the proud members of other Native American tribes, he held himself erect, and his piercing eyes belied the grey in his hair.

His voice while gravelly was filled with the connotations of his Oklahoma heritage. He spoke to me as if welcoming an equal, and one who would automatically accept his words as truth. My height usually intimidates people, but his only sign of acknowledging the fact that I towered over him, was a slight widening of the eyes.

"Doctor, it is a pleasure to meet you; Amanda has spoken of you often." As he moved back from the doorway, he gestured me inside to a small table where he had placed several documents, a glass of water, a wooden bowl of dirt, a feather, a box of large matches, and a small cedar box.

"Thank you." I accepted his invitation and waited for him to be seated before sitting down myself; I hung the bike helmet on the back of the chair, loosened my jacket and prepared for obligatory inspection. We sat there in silence for five minutes. He simply stared at me, and I did my best not to flinch or fidget. It was a lot like being in a room with a panther. I just knew if I made the wrong move, it was all over! Not physically afraid, but mentally. I had undergone several of these silent inspections from others and the protocol was to act as if you were being examined by a doctor; just remain quiet and he would tell you what you need to know at the end.

Finally, he nodded his head as if satisfied with his inspection; I passed the test, and now the conversation would begin. I watched him visibly relax, and take on the once more friendly persona he had exhibited at the door. With a somber voice he began;

"The young ones believe we should not share our culture with the white man. They say we have had too much taken already, our tribe has almost disappeared into many others, and we should hold our sacred knowledge of the "lost Ones" and the old ways tightly in our hands, wrapped in a closed fist."

"Do you know what happens when you squeeze water in a closed fist Doctor?"

"You're left with wet palms and no water." I answered.

His deep laugh surprised me. "Absolutely right Doctor and wet hands cannot quench the thirst of a people. Nor can it put out the fire of hatred."

I watched as he took a deep breath and the air around him seemed to vibrate, and a glow of pure light seemed to suddenly imamate from his face.

"If you will listen, I will tell you of the things revealed to us from the "Others", those who speak to us from the Cracks in the World.

I was speechless already! Just sitting here with him, was an experience beyond time.

He touched the objects on the table with reverence, and one by one told me of their meaning.

He picked up the dirt in his fingers and allowed it to sift back into the bowl; "Earth, the foundation of all things. It supports us; it is fruitful, moist, and nurturing. The Earth holds power over a compass, and always leads it north where lays the darkest and coldest parts of our world."

Next he dipped his fingers in the water; "Water, it purifies us, it is always moving, and our sub-conscious minds are like the sea, dreaming of the places and things hidden in her depths."

With a brisk move he lit one of the large matches; "Fire, man's greatest fear, and comfort in the darkness. In the Sun we can see the divine light of the Power that rules all, and in a candle flame we can see the spark that represents the life in all things."

Waving the feather about, he allowed it too waft slowly back down to the table top; "Air, breath of life, breath of knowledge, it moves us toward realizations of the known, manifestations of the unknown."

"These then are the four elements that make up the culture of the Yuchee as you call us, but within we are known as the 'Tsoyaha'; Tso (Sun or sacred) ya (fire) ha (people) you would interpret it as "Children of the Sun,". As such, we have traveled from the Maya lands to the New World. Our tribe split many years ago due to political differences and one became lost over time. The lost tribe is the one who held the ancient writings of our people.

It is said that we were always lost, from the beginning. Tales told of a great voyage across the sea from the hot, dry deserts to the lushness of rain-forest we came. We knew nothing of where we were and how to survive. But, we had a secret, we could talk to the animals and they could talk to us. It is from them we learned of the Cracks in the World, and the knowledge to be found there.

Our world Doctor is not just this ball upon which we spin daily. This is the Middle World; home of man and beast, above us is the

Upper world, home to those who would rule us with peace and goodness, below us is the Lower World; it is from those who live there, and share their knowledge we gain in progress and from which comes the terrible price of that knowledge.

From the Earth we have gained knowledge that advanced civilizations. With every advancement came the mechanical wonders and technology we have today. With each advance, we stepped away from the earth and her nurturing. We cut our ties with the tree magic, the healing power of plants and flowers, the acute ability to feel one with the earth through the stone and rocks that once sang to us, and the price has been high and now will be higher. Turning our back on the earth has resulted in the greatest time of strife and turmoil for every individual and on a global basis, the world has ever seen."

"What do we do Doctor, to heal the earth? What do we do now to stop the spread of evil across our lands and our world?" With that question he looked at me with blazing eyes, and for once in my life, I had no ready answer.

"Do not look so lost Doctor. I have the answers and so do you. We just have to bring them together and introduce the one element that binds them; Amanda." He slowly opened the cedar box and removed a small bead covered bag. He carefully untied the frayed knots of an ancient binding. Then he tipped out onto his palm one of the most beautiful Mayan Kan Cross Symbols I had ever seen.

Reaching out my trembling hands, I silently asked for the pleasure of holding it. It was only when he allowed me to grasp it in my hands that its true weight and beauty felt real. On closer examination under the light of a nearby lamp I could see the Paleo-Hebrew writing, "Only for the Judeans!" The same inscription found on the Bat Creek Stone in Tennessee!

"Where did this come from?" I whispered hoarsely.

"It has been in my family since the before time. Only two people know of its existence, besides you that is; me and my Grandson. We have kept it and others hidden from view, along with several other artifacts. Would you like to see them Doctor?"

"More than anything on this earth at the present moment; I would be honored if you would allow me to see them!"

Smiling, the Chief motioned at the papers before him. "These were put together by my Grandson, and hold as much value as that which you hold in your hand. Take them, share them with Amanda. Come with me now and see the treasures of the "lost Ones". He put the Kan Cross back in its pouch, after I reluctantly gave it up. Once more it was placed in the reliquary of cedar.

I gathered the papers without even looking at them; I took his word on their value. Together we walked to the door, and before opening it, he turned to me and said.

"Doctor, Amanda is precious to all the worlds, and as her protector you must use the knowledge you hold in your hands to heal her; for all our sakes. The laxPé nõKá - tah weh, "13", that you gather must be close to the earth in all ways, remember that." With those final words, he opened the door and motioned for me to precede him.

Just as I stepped out, I remembered the bike helmet hanging on the chair. I turned to go around the Chief, and the sudden sound of a high-powered rifle rang out and a bullet screamed out of the dark hitting the chief in the side of his neck.

I never caught sight of the assailant. I tried hopelessly to stop the fountain of blood gushing from the old man's wound. The chief was dead within seconds. The bullet had been meant for me, I was sure of it. If I had not stepped from in front of him, this wondrous soul would still be alive. My grief was powered by my guilt, as I gazed at the blood on my hands. How many more lives would the seekers of Solomon's Scrolls demand?

For a period of time, after the Chief's murder, my memory became clouded. I spoke to Amanda, but I don't remember initiating the call. Shortly, after our conversation, three men showed up at the crime scene. Two of them identified themselves as federal agents and the third, introduced himself as Ben. I point this oddity out, because Ben was in charge of evacuating me from the premises. I was never interrogated.

Ben handed me the cedar box and the papers the Chief had intended for me. He tossed me a towel, and escorted me into the front seat of a black, box style utility truck. He demanded my keys to the Harley. Without question, I handed them over to him. He loaded the bike into the back, and returned to the driver's seat.

Before starting the engine, Ben spoke. "Amanda Messenger is waiting for you. I will take you to her."

I turned and stared out the dark window of the truck. During our drive the night sky turned black, and an annoying mist covered the windshield. My heart rate increased with each swipe of the blades. Anger began to build inside of me. Like it or not, Amanda was going to explain everything, I would stand for nothing less. In the meantime Ben would have to suffice.

"Ben, exactly who do you work for?"

He glanced over at me. His deep set black eyes were wide open. I noticed he swallowed hard.

"You don't know?"

His response infuriated me.

"Hell no, I don't know. Do you work for OPERA?"

Ben laughed, softly.

"No"

"You're Israeli. I've spent a lot of time in the Middle East."

"Yes, I am an Israeli contractor. I broker manufacturing agreements with American companies."

"Is that right?"

My pointed sarcasm clearly annoyed him. We drove in silence until Ben answered a call.

"Yes, but I do not feel Dr. Dominquez trusts me so much... Okay, goodbye."

Awaiting his explanation, I glared at him.

"The plan has changed. You will meet Amanda in Oklahoma City."

"How long have you known Amanda?"

"I have not met her in person, I only learned of her a couple of days ago.

Chapter 19

"Grief should be the instructor of the wise. Sorrow is knowledge: they who know the most must mourn the deepest."
Lord Byron

Walking down the corridor of the hotel, I felt genuine relief. My ride with Ben was less than enjoyable. Covered with the Chiefs' blood, I wanted a shower, and hoped Amanda had brought the luggage I left at her house.

I slid the key card in, and swung open the door. Amanda stood staring in my direction She remained frozen as I moved towards her. When I reached her, I noticed a tear race down her cheek. I took a deep breath, and tried to deliver my firm message,

"Amanda, as much as I would like to put you on that bike with me and drive back to Santa Fe, well, it will have to wait until another time. I'm in charge now; a plane will pick us up here in Oklahoma City, tomorrow. We are going back to Santa Fe."

She nodded in agreement, and whispered. "Antonio"

"I'm not finished Amanda, I need answers. Tell me, what in the hell is going on."

"We needed help, Antonio."

"D'affaires, what does that mean?"

She closed her eyes before answering. "It is a French word"

"Damn it Amanda, I know that…In translation it means

agency. In context, I want to know what agency."

"It could mean any agency."

"Amanda, tell me the name of the agency, you refer to as D'affaires."

"I cannot"

"You can't? The hell you can't. Okay, tell those cronies, I don't want their help, and furthermore, you can stand for whatever you want Amanda, but you can't die doing it. That's counterproductive."

She remained silent, so I continued my rant.

"A good man died tonight, I felt him leave as his blood dripped through my fingers. I do not want to feel your blood on my hands Amanda, but by all that is Holy, they will pay for this."

"He said we have all the answers we need, all we have to do is bring them together-his knowledge, yours and mine." I dropped to the bed and put my head in my hands.

Looking up at Amanda, I tried to explain how much was lost tonight. "He was taking me to see the treasures of the "Lost Ones", he was going to share with me…so much.." My voice broke and I could not go on. Then my anger returned, and I bounded to my feet and went off again.

"You see, I'm confused, you want me, you don't want me, then, you don't want me involved, and you do want me involved." I paused not expecting her to respond, but she did.

"Exactly"

"Why Amanda, tell me why?"

"You make me tingle."

That stopped me in my tracks. Then I looked at her face and saw the compassion there, and I realized what she was doing. She had turned my own trick of distraction against me. For my minds sake, and my hearts sake, I let her distract me with the most beautiful passion that only a realization of just how close death can be, can bring to a man.

***

The next afternoon I was sitting in the Hotel Suite making plans for our return to New Mexico, while trying to comprehend exactly just how devastating the day before had been, and I was still unsure of how the Chiefs death was going to impact our journey. The knowledge he held could also have helped me find a cure for Amanda. As I brooded, I stared at the documents with the dried blood of the Chief dotting their surface, and the cedar box gave off a scent of freshness that was in contrast to the moment. I heard the far off sound of a doorbell, and soon heard soft footsteps coming towards the quiet corner of the large bedroom Amanda and I were sharing.

When I looked up, it was to see a younger version of the old chief standing before me. He was maybe 30, and held himself with confidence, and the marks of his recent grief were etched in the lines around his eyes. I immediately stood and waited for the condemnation I was sure he was going to reap upon my head.

Like his Grandfather he stood silently, and then came forwards and put out his hand.

"My name is 'Ge wan o ya ti yuba, but my family and friends call me George. My grandfather believed in keeping the old names, and I have tried to maintain that tradition. But in a modern world a name that means 'Spirit of Fire Mountain' can be perceived as presumptuous."

His soft smile was all that was needed to complete the vision of his grandfather in my mind. I took his hand gladly, and asked him to join me. For a moment I had forgotten the items on the low table, and his brief glance and twinge of pain reminded me that the blood there before us ran his veins as well.

"I am so sorry; please let me move these from sight." I moved to gather the items, but his hand on my arm stopped me.

"Moving them will not make them cleaner or make them not real." He sat down, and I joined him.

"I know grandfather gave you the papers, but the cedar box belongs to the tribe and I must return it. Despite my families inability to accept their existence, and therefore their knowledge…does not mean my sacred guardianship has ended with Grandfathers death."

"Of course, I was going to ask Amanda about returning them as soon as possible, I had simply forgotten up until this moment." I replied rather contritely. I was embarrassed to admit I had failed to contact him sooner. As an anthropologist I understood the value of the ancient reliquary and its contents, and would sooner have cut off my arm than allowed it to become lost from its rightful place.

"Doctor, death is a natural thing, only its delivery is often times unnatural. It was his time and his place, and he was happy about the meeting with you. He believed you are Khutane, a portal. Through you others will find the Yufala, the way to save all. Do not be sad Doctor, to us the blood is sacred, and the blood you held in your hands was the blood of Shawaeno Choyaha, the Priest of the Sun People. Through you, his blood has now found a new path, and will guide you when you need it most."

To say I was blown away would be an understatement. Once again I was speechless in the presence of a wondrous soul.

He stood up and I joined him, he reached for the cedar box, and then looked closely at its clasp. "You have not opened this since his death have you?"

"No, it was not mine to open." I answered.

"Doctor, what is inside is now more yours than mine, and has always been. I only meant to retrieve the cedar box and for now, the Kan Cross, not the other item it holds." He opened the cedar box, removed the decorative bag holding the Kan Cross, laid it on the table and then reached inside and removed one of the largest pieces of polished Lilac Sugilite I had ever seen.

"This is for Amanda, make a necklace, with a natural cloth

pouch, and have her wear it from now on."

"What will it do?" I asked as I took it from him.

"It will do what it does, Doctor. Just as you will do what you must do. Remember Doctor, the Kan Cross will return when you need it most, and never forget, when you are ready I will find you and together we will seek out the treasure of the 'Lost Ones' and the way to the Cracks in the World."

Before I could speak, he was gone. I glanced down at the beauty of the crystal I held in my hand, and I swear to you it was warming and vibrating. Stranger and stranger, this journey I am on.

Chapter 20

"If I had a flower for every time I thought of you...I could walk through my garden forever."
— Alfred Lord Tennyson

The view of the New Mexico landscape from the chopper was breathtaking. The mountain peaks captivated me from an entirely new perspective. It felt like floating amidst a master painter's endless mural that spanned across the Earth's expanse. The color appeared more vivid, the texture more defined. It mesmerized me with a surreal power. The Master's own hands carved these planes.

I glanced over at Amanda. She appeared equally enthralled. Her eyes glistened as she stared out at the art. She was a passionate woman. Despite the yellow flags that come with this type of personality, I enjoyed this side of her. Still, I needed to understand her true passion, and for a woman with many, this was not an easy task.

I awoke from my trance to exchange smiles with her. As we got closer, I reached over and hugged her. I lifted her headset, and spoke directly into her ear.

"The lavender," I said, as I pointed below.

Amanda loved the massive mounds of purple bathing the valley adjacent to the house. The field was now in full view. I pointed as we passed over the pond with the platform. She leaned in holding my arm.

"Antonio, it is so beautiful."

The chopper dropped down to the yard. Joe the caretaker stood by the pick-up truck ready to take our luggage. The place looked incredible. I was glad to be home.

The chopper touched down. As soon as the door opened Amanda jumped out. She greeted stoic Joe with a hug. The large native man gave her a quick pat on the shoulder, before moving to unload the bags.

Clutching Amanda's elbow, the wind blowing her hair across her face, I escorted her through the meadow to the residence. Pop, Jose, and Marc met us just outside the entrance. Accompanied by Ruger, the three had flown into Santa Fe the day before.

I could feel Amanda's body stiffen. She apparently wasn't prepared to meet them so soon after her escape from Miami.

Jose broke the ice, "Antonio your estate is incredible- it's huge."

I decided to remain true to the subject, and give my guests a little background on my once, not so grand, home. "Thanks Jose, it's great now, but when I bought it I had to restore two rooms in the guest house to make them livable. The house was in such poor condition, animals used it as a lodge. I lived out there almost three years while the main residence was restored."

My father patted my back. "Amazing son, this place is amazing."

We strolled inside where Maria waited. Maria, Joe's wife,

took care of the house. The two were and still are an invaluable part of my life. Without them, the estate would be in shambles. I travel too much to care for it all, myself.

"Maria, come give me a hug." The short plump Hispanic woman came running towards me crying out in Spanish. Her hands pressed against my cheeks as if I were a little boy. Maria had no children, so she often treated me more as a son than an employer. She was a nice surrogate in the absence of my mother.

Maria glanced at Amanda then back at me. She scolded. "Miami has no food."

"Maria, Amanda fell ill in Miami, I thought you could help get her back to normal.

She giggled. "You bet Antonio, I'll get cooking."

"Maria, you are the best, I missed you."

I was pleased to see Maria cheerful. I was unsure how she would react to Pop's visit. In Maria's mind, I was the perfect son. My new relationship with my formally estranged father wouldn't gain her approval any time soon.

Everyone gathered around the kitchen bar eating the finger foods Maria had prepared. Amanda wandered away. I watched her walk out, and set down by the pool. I waited a few moments before following her.

The outside felt crisp, and clean. The slightest hint of lavender filled the late afternoon air. It was truly a perfect place on earth.

My hands fell on Amanda's shoulders, her head tilted back. Fondling her extended neck, I leaned over and kissed her.

"I thought I would find you here."

She smiled. "I tried to sneak away. Please, go tend to your family. I am fine."

I laughed. "It's me Amanda. I'm not used to this constant string of people. I'm glad they're here. I just want them to go nap, or something - right now."

We laughed at my predicament.

"Give me an hour with them, and then meet me upstairs."

Chapter 21

"Ye shall know the truth, and the truth shall make you mad.
~Aldous Huxley

I breathed a sigh of relief at the bottom of the staircase. My Pop and brothers were excellent interrogators, but I wasn't ready to answer any questions about the recent events. An outsider might consider my thought process absurd. The truth is, I was protecting Amanda. My family's forte was discovering hidden issues about people. I wasn't going to smoke Amanda out through them. I also know, some might consider it a flaw in my character, but I didn't want her to know that I had not informed them. Besides, my friends, I am nobody's fool, at this point, I was fairly sure of my darling Amanda's situation and exactly with whom she was involved.

Anxious to spend a little unmonitored time with her, I ascended the stairs, two at a time. Amanda was seated in a chair by the bedroom fireplace reading something on a tablet computer. This was new. She had only used a notebook computer prior to her trip home.

My entrance caused her to look up. Her expression was blank, but her eyes were fixed on me, with obvious signs of anticipatory dread. She had shared a lot with us in Miami, but her active involvement was a mystery she had failed to explain.

"Amanda, no one is listening to us here. I had Ruger check.

Do you understand?"

She nodded.

"This time, I'm going to ask you to tell me what you understand about OPERA, and the role The Scrolls play in all this chaos. I'm not going to ask how or why you know. I'm going to trust you. Is that fair?"

Her lips tight, she placed her index finger over them as her eyes danced around, and then she said.

"Okay."

I had to contain myself. My biggest lesson on dealing with Amanda was in approach. All too often, she challenged my cleverness.

"Amanda, I'm listening, begin where you will, but I do deserve to know."

She cleared her throat and began. "I hate to disappoint you, but for everything I know, there is much more that I do not know. Antonio some things might seem irrational to you. Believe me, I should know. Perhaps, you will say, I have developed a coping mechanism that has caused my Psyche to block key information. I will tell you OPERA, and their right wing extremist counterparts have gained the vast majority of my attention over recent years."

She paused and looked hard at me. I felt like she was looking into me. Her hands trembled. How could the woman be so tough, yet find it so hard to explain this situation? I realized, she still believed, maybe even feared, I would not believe.

"Amanda, please continue without censorship."

"Very well, America is struggling for balance in the midst of extremism. There is OPERA on the left infiltrating the federal government with its Marxist style agenda. On the other hand, there exists an equally dangerous segment of rogue groups on the right that is controlling a great deal of our financial, and jurist prudence systems. Their slates are different, but for the masses the outcome is the same. 'The many will be ruled by the few.'"

She had my full attention with that bit of information, and I could now draw a few conclusions of my own. With that single bit of information, I was now able to connect all of the disjointed happenings of the recent past into one cohesive outline of destruction that had a single purpose. "Truthfully, we are in the middle of a civil war. We do not recognize it, because the weapons of choice are not military munitions. OPERA on the far left wants government control to allow them political power. On the right is the quasi-mob controlling money, lawyers, and judges for financial dominance.

The left wants to eliminate spiritual and religious freedom. The right wants to exploit religion as a means of justification."

She stopped, and looked down at her hands. I could see her squeezing her eyelids together. Without raising her head, she resumed.

"Remember, the left, meaning OPERA, doesn't kill. I falsely believed, we were only dealing with them. It is much different with their direct opponents. The Chief's death suggests the right extremists are now aware of the fact that you are the keeper of The Scrolls."

She rubbed her temples, and took my hand in hers. Our eyes locked. I knew whatever she was going to say next was most significant to her.

"OPERA wishes to destroy Israel or allow others to do the blasphemous deed. The militia mobs of the right are anti-Semitic racists. Both positions leave Israel standing without America."

The wind escaping my lungs was audible. Amanda moved into my space, and pressed herself against my chest. I wrapped my arms around her and enveloped her entire body.

Once more an ancient enemy has chosen the destruction of Israel, and this time they were using her most faithful ally, America to accomplish what so many others had tried before. I knew I had to join forces with Amanda and do whatever was needed to stop OPERA and their more deadly opponents from destroying the holiest of places and all Israel stood for.

Chapter 22

"You can discover what your enemy fears most by observing the means he uses to frighten you."
— *Eric Hoffer*

Amanda and I descended the stairs to meet the others for dinner. We agreed to continue our conversation about the enemies afterward. Amanda was nervous about dinner with my family. She expressed a great deal of concern over a possible confrontation. It was not the way my family operated, but I couldn't seem to convince her.

Maria had set dinner in the rarely used dining area. It was nice to see guests sitting around the massive table. Everyone stood until Amanda was seated. She gave a nervous smile with gratitude.

The conversation over salad stayed confined to talk about the estate. Maria entered and began removing the empty plates. Suddenly, music was serenading us from Amanda's phone. She looked down.

"I am very sorry, but I must take this call."

She stood, answered the phone, and quickly made her way out to the pool area. I excused myself, and strolled over to the double French doors. I glanced out the window. Outside, Amanda was pacing with the phone to her ear. Her free hand flailed as she spoke. I threw open the door, and marched out.

The second she realized I had come, her knees began to

buckle. I reached out to break her shaking body from the fall. Her voice cracked. "Sam is missing. Antonio, he never checked in for his flight back to Boston."

My chest tightened at the news. I thought about my exchange with Sam a couple of days before. I tried to comfort her, but the life was sucked out of her. She felt limp, and lifeless.

I demanded a response; "Amanda, who called with the information; who was on the phone?"

"Ari, it was Ari."

"We need to get you inside."

I scooped her up and carried her up the stairs. Marc ran over to us.

"What's wrong?"

"Sam has disappeared. I will give you all more information when I get it."

Amanda was now, positioned on the bed with a sweatshirt on. I had never seen her wear it, before. I sat beside her on the edge. She began speaking before I began questioning.

The only information Ari could share was that Sam's car was intact at the airport parking facility.

I squeezed her hand. "Amanda, I will get Sam back."

I stood, and started walking back and forth next to the bed. I began to speculate.

"Amanda, they took him at the airport, chances are they transported him to another location. Give me his cell number, it's a long shot, but we will try to fixate on his location."

I called down to Marc with the number, and instructions. Ruger joined Marc, and the two of them had every phone, and computer in the house set to trace incoming communications.

After a short time, Marc asked me to come down to the makeshift control room, now set up in one of the guest rooms.

My brother was sweating profusely.

"Marc, did you get a hit?"

"No Antonio, but I think you should know, Amanda's IPad is registered to an Israeli agency, and I swear, if I didn't know better, I'd say it's a direct link to the Mossad."

Damn, my suspicions were right on. Still, the news struck me like a fist in the chest.

Not sure who could be trusted, I shared my thoughts with him; "Marc for the time being let's keep this between us."

"Sure, but Antonio, this is huge. We all knew she had a secret, but the Mossad. Damn, we could be in the middle of some sort of International Espionage."

"I know Marc. However, we must focus on finding and rescuing Sam."

Chapter 23

"After all, everybody has secrets and there are some things that nobody knows about you but only you, right?"
— *Halle Berry*

A chopper and a plane were on standby. Marc and I were monitoring the electronics. Without a call or demand from Sam's kidnappers, we were paralyzed. Marc had pinged Sam's phone at the airport where a security guard located it in the parking lot. The trail was ice cold.

After several hours of staring at blank screens, I felt restless, so I slipped away from the monitors, and escaped to my upstairs office. Once seated, I removed my eye glasses, and rested my face in my hands. My inability to act… was drowning me in frustration, when I felt her palm against the back of my neck.

"Amanda, how long have you worked with the Mossad?"

She removed her hand. Her long silence annoyed me. Finally in a quiet voice, she began.

"I worked with them for three years."

"Worked? What does that mean?"

A short time ago, I was released by the Mossad. They concluded I was no longer fit to assist. I did not pass the medical assessment. I had no contact with the agency until after your attack in Miami, when they began sending me messages on my secure phone.

Antonio, how did you find out, and who else knows?"

"Process of elimination, it was the only reasonable assumption. I've spent nearly half of the last two decades in the Middle East, much of it in Israel. The moment I pulled in front of your house, I knew. Marc provided the confirmation from your tablet. For now, he is the only one that knows. Prepare yourself Amanda, because, Pop and Jose, even Ruger will figure it out, soon."

"I believe Ruger already knows or suspects, and as far as the others knowing, well it is time for no more secrets."

"What does Ruger know?"

"We had a talk, remember, in your home. At that time I asked him for assistance in keeping you safe. He made a few remarks that led me to believe he knew more than he was saying. He is your friend and loyal companion; he was trying to be sure I was no threat. None of that matters Antonio, Ruger and I are friends now."

"Is the Mossad trying to locate Sam?"

"Yes, of course."

"Good, I need a direct contact with the agency. Amanda, it is imperative. Can you arrange this?"

"I will."

"Amanda, there is something, I must understand. You told me, you had never visited Israel. How could an agent of the Mossad avoid a trip to Israel?"

"I am not an agent of the Mossad, nor have I ever been. I

was a katsca, and offered my home as a safe house."

I chuckled, slightly sadistically; "Of course, a well-studied informant."

Amanda answered my sarcasm with rational aplomb; "A woman stalked by OPERA living in a hot bed of anti-Semitism, and militia, and one who understands fully the consequences. Do not underestimate my abilities; I am trained. A katsca is not exactly an informant."

I raised my head, and turned to look at her. There were no words. I held her head in my hands, and stared into her eyes for a long moment. She blinked trying to fight the moisture's escape. I kissed her hair, and pulled her next to me.

Chapter 24

"Life is a shipwreck but we must not forget to sing in the lifeboats."
— Voltaire

The bellow of Marc's voice vibrated throughout the main floor. I raced to the monitoring room. Pop, and Jose, not far behind, joined us.

Marc was wearing a headset and jotting something down on paper. He lifted one side when he spoke.

"Antonio, does Sam have an IPod?"

"Yes, he was listening to it when I talked with him at Amanda's."

"WOW, this kid must be amazing. The message is silly, but I think he is sending Morse code through the music device to Amanda's cell phone."

I laughed. Sam could certainly pull off such a genius stunt. "Give me the letters Marc."

"Best I can tell his only error is leaving out the spaces."

Marc handed me the sheet of paper with the letters: T-H-E-Z-E-B-R-A-I-S-B-L-I-S-S-F-U-L-I-N-T-H-E-S-A-N-D

I interrupted aloud. "He left the spaces out on purpose, Marc. No error, he did exactly what he intended. The zebra is blissful in the sand."

Amanda rooted her way in from behind.

"It is Sam. He loves Zebras." She laughed and cried in

unison.

Mark asked. "What does it mean?"

I translated. "Sam is here in the New Mexico desert, at Fort Bliss.

A contagious excitement spread through our small group. The room filled with the sound of hands slapping. Amanda jumped into my arms. I think she was relieved it wasn't the militia that had Sam. OPERA was difficult, and ruthless, but far less deadly.

After our brief celebration, I gave Marc instructions.

"Just send the words- got it, without spaces."

Marc sent the message, and quickly jotted down Sam's response, L-A-T-E-R.

During our wait for another message from Sam, Ruger and I retreated to the guesthouse to prepare in case we needed to act fast. Ruger had turned the space into a weapons arsenal with all the gear ready for a quick deployment. In my mind, marching onto the military base demanding the kid didn't seem a likely scenario for us.

Walking back to the main house, I learned, talking to Ruger for him it wasn't out of the question. The former Navy SEAL saw it as a challenge.

"Antonio, if we can zero in on Sam's location, it's not impossible." WOW, I rubbed my hand across my head. I was not a stranger to danger, but rescuing a kid among military professionals was an insane stretch. Amanda would, certainly, have to reach out to the Mossad for assistance. At the time that did not set well with me. I was not quite ready to let go of the idea that she and I were an independent team.

Ruger and I joined the others anxiously awaiting communication from Sam. The moments seemed like hours, and Amanda was showing harsh signs of stress. Still wearing the sweatshirt, she could not sit. Instead, she would stand for a while shifting her weight from side to side, then she would walk around in circles going nowhere. It was during this time that I began to understand the deeper implications of Amanda's role as a mother, and how even OPERA understood. While hers sons were strong individuals; powerful personalities in their own right, each mirrored the essence of Amanda's core personality in some small way.

My mind drifted back to the moment during my beating when OPERA's thugs threatened to 'get' Amanda if I did not turn over The Scrolls. The clever faction understood her, even better than I. The most effective way to 'get' Amanda was to 'get' one of her sons.

I clutched Amanda's hand, and led her to a nearby guestroom. Behind the closed door holding her in front of me, I spoke.

"Amanda, I want to contact OPERA. We can offer OPERA The Scrolls for Sam's return."

Her head shook. "No Antonio that would be a mistake. We must be patient, and wait for their demand. We cannot give them such power. A power they can only use to further manipulate us, and harm Sam."

"Amanda, they're holding him at a U.S. military base, let's bring in the authorities.

Her eyebrows rose. "Antonio, I wish we could, but OPERA is deep within our government, we do not know who to trust."

Only a few days before, I would have considered this ludicrous, even paranoid. She was animate and sure. It was an area she knew about. This time, I was the subordinate. I would bow to her certain knowledge, after all, as her partner I had to learn to trust her instincts and her unusual ability to know things.

Chapter 25

"Create a definite plan for carrying out your desire and begin at once, whether you are ready or not, to put this plan into action."
Napoleon Hill

In the course of the night, Ruger assumed Marc's position in the monitoring room. Hours had passed without communication with Sam. The silence grew deafening, and we were weary. However, no one could completely pull themselves away.

The great room became a bunkhouse with bodies napping on the furniture. I roamed around the dim area hoping for an epiphany. My affections for Amanda left me with an unfamiliar sense of responsibility. OPERA was ruthlessly patient. Without a demand, we were left as pawns in a maddening stalemate.

My thoughts turned to a different issue, one that was constantly in front of us thanks to media coverage on all electronic devices. Natural disasters were occurring at such an alarming rate, they no longer were breaking news. Half of the country was experiencing multiple super cell tornados on a weekly basis. Major earthquakes were rocking every continent. No individual could escape the effects of the dramatic climate changes. The heat wave ravishing the country was becoming catastrophic. The science, and prophesy were converging. Change was not coming. Change was here. Seven billion people were experiencing it, but no one seemed to be dealing with it.

Amanda's soft touch interrupted my silent hell. I wanted to dissolve into her comforting caress, but I couldn't. I had to become a pillar of strength for her and Sam. In an attempt to defeat my dwindling courage, I turned, took Amanda into my arms, and held her tight.

***

By midmorning the sun came barreling through the windows. The landscape outside was bright and cheerful. Inside, the mood grew darker with each passing hour. We were approaching forty-eight hours since Sam's last communication. The psychological effects were devastating us all.

Collapsing under the pressure of time, we started to contemplate a reconnaissance mission of Fort Bliss. Ruger and I spent several hours studying blueprints of the facility Amanda acquired from the Mossad.

Fatigue had started dictating our thought processes. Amanda was exhibiting signs that suggested she was caving in on OPERA's stand-off. Oddly enough, it wasn't an incident with OPERA that had her doing an about face. No, it was the sun.

A solar burst had entered the atmosphere in the Midwest destroying all internet connections in the region. This incident destroyed her safe communication with Ari, the Mossad agent she depended on in the Midwest. Frankly, it was a blow to all of us. Ari's relationship with Amanda and Sam had become a helpful element in our dilemma.

I took over the communication helm, so Marc could take a call from his wife, Elisabeth. In a matter of minutes beeps became music to my ears. I pounded on the table to get the others attention as I scribed Sam's letters.

I-N-T-H-E-W-I-T-C-H-S-H-O-U-R-T-H-E-S-U-L-T-A-N-G-O-E-S-T-O-H-E-L-L-A-N-D-S-W-I-M-S-T-O-T-H-E-S-T-A-R-S

Amanda began deciphering over my shoulder.

"The power of a witch is said to be strongest at 2:00AM. They are going to transport Sam, somewhere. We need a map to break the code."

I quickly sent Sam a response. Marc put the headset on to resume his position. The rest of us raced to the dining room table with the coded message and a map. Time was imperative for success.

I translated the letters into words. 'In the witch's hour the sultan goes to hell and swims to the stars'.

Sam's reference to the sultan had us baffled. Was it a reference to his captors or a place? We spent an inordinate amount of time debating this issue. Finally, I broke up the argument with a shout of reason.

"For now, we must assume it is a place. I do not think Sam would confuse us with a statement about his captor's religious beliefs."

Amanda nodded in agreement. "Antonio, you are absolutely right, such a statement would defy Sam's character."

I smiled; "Exactly."

Out loud, I tried to direct the thought process.

"The sultan may not be literal terminology...think of similar words."

In a chorus we all shouted; "Salt."

Immediately, I knew, they were taking Sam on a route that would take them through Texas, and around the Salt Basin. Now, hell, Sam had to be referring to Carlsbad. The star reference was a cinch, Roswell, New Mexico. I blurted out the route.

"They will leave Fort Bliss at 2:00AM, taking highway 180 around the Salt Basin to Carlsbad. Once there, they will get on highway 295, which runs perpendicular to a river, this will take them to their final destination in Roswell, New Mexico.

Okay everyone, our mission is clear. We must greet OPERA at a point along this itinerary, and get Sam back."

Chapter 26

"A good plan violently executed now is better than a perfect plan executed next week."
— General George S. Patton

Pressure to succeed had never weighed so heavily on my consciousness. Our mission to rescue Sam left no room for errors. We were forced to put together a plan to pull off an event of international magnitude with a group of mostly rookies. Our target was OPERA, a well-trained fascist militant enemy. The victim was a kid, Amanda's son.

Our shortage of trained guns had Amanda and me in spotlight positions. Marc would continue to maintain his post in the control room. Ruger, the former SEAL, and most experienced was set to act as the distraction and if needed provide covering fire. Amanda and I would actually free Sam.

Bernie, the pilot flying the chopper was a Mossad agent none of us actually knew. I was concerned about this arrangement, but we had no choice. Ruger couldn't fly the chopper and be on the ground. Pop and Jose had few skills to offer. Pop was too old, and well, Jose was a clumsy Miami attorney. He wasn't even good moral support. He was like a nervous mother.

Earlier, Ruger and Joe returned after leaving Ruger's SUV on location in the desert area we had mapped out.

The night sky was black except for the occasional flashes of heat lightening. It was a strange sensation from inside the chopper. Looking around, I noticed our heavy breathing had developed synchronization.

Stoic, I strapped on the vest. A quiet robotic rhythm dominated throughout our small group. We became the dark shadows in the charcoal night. We wore black combat gear with bullet proof vests, and were fitted with earpieces connecting us to one another as well as Marc in the room, we now called control. Ruger outfitted Amanda with an extra device to amplify sound. Her inability to hear well was cause for great concern. On a mission sound was as important as sight.

Amanda possessed the skills for the mission, but the tumor in her head was creating a multitude of obstacles she would have to overcome. At times, she experienced problems with balance and vertigo. Her vision in her left eye was blurry. I was beginning to understand the Mossad's concerns. To top it all off, none of us were exactly young. Luckily, we were all fit.

After an hour in the air, we landed in a field near the Salt Basin. In the diurnal dark the dry desert felt cold. Ruger jumped out and got into his black SUV. Amanda and I stayed in the chopper awaiting the signal. During those few moments, we stared hard at one another. I'm relatively sure neither of us blinked once.

"Zebra!"

Ruger had the van in his sight. The pilot lifted the chopper. We watched Ruger slam the SUV into a sideways spin. At the door, Amanda and I stood with the cables attached.

Marc's voice came roaring into our earpieces.

"Abandon...Abandon...The Zebra is on 25 to Albuquerque!"

Ruger shouted. "Leave me...Get the Zebra!"

Amanda's eyes grew huge. I yelled to our pilot. "Go, now!"

In flight, we had to coordinate a new plan. Marc was working to maintain positioning on the van carrying Sam. It was at this point I knew, after years of packing a weapon, and target shooting, I was going to have to shoot at a human being.

In Ruger's absence I felt I was the obvious choice to become the distraction. Amanda would have to retrieve Sam, alone. Only Amanda took exception to the idea. It was a hell of a time for an argument, but we did it anyway.

"Antonio, I will act as the decoy. I have more experience in confrontational situations."

The shouting match was in full swing. "No way in hell, will I let you stand in the line of fire, Amanda."

"Antonio, I have shot someone before, you have not."

Her flat admission stunned me, but I didn't back down. "Amanda, just get your son."

She didn't say another word.

Marc gave Bernie the coordinates. Within moments we dropped down in the middle of the abandoned interstate. Much to our surprise, Bernie pulled out a Tavor TAR-21; the rifle preferred by the IDF, small, compact and deadly; and belted out the orders. "You two get the boy as soon as I wave."

Amanda and I exchanged looks, and the blasts began. The

continuous firing was deafening. Bernie fired, bodies dropped, and then there was silence. Bernie gave a little wave and we were in motion.

Amanda and I darted out, made our way into the back of the hostage van, and rescued Sam without firing a single shot. By the time we got back in the chopper, Bernie was belted into the pilot's seat. My leg was still hanging out the door when he lifted off. We had completed the mission in less than three minutes.

As soon as I got the door closed, Sam teased at least I think it was a tease.

"I can't believe you guys actually saved me. I thought I was going to have to break out myself." Sam was talking so fast we could hardly keep up. I enjoyed his innocent arrogance.

It was a great success. Sam was safe and sound. The sweatshirt Amanda wore the entire time Sam was missing disappeared as she was no longer cold.

The Mossad was assuming responsibility for the entire incident. Later, I discovered, Sam in his own right had gained the attention of the Mossad, and was under their watchful eye. Of course, back at the estate, Sam was the real hero, and needless to say, he loved the attention.

Chapter 27

"The treasures hidden in the heavens are so rich that the human mind shall never be lacking in fresh nourishment."
— *Johannes Kepler (1571-1630)*

Once Sam was safe, Amanda was so happy and her spirit lifted. In a moment of complete abandon we both jumped into the large Vaselli tub in the bath, and shared a bottle of Prestige cuvee that we did not treat with proper respect; drinking straight from the bottle. When we were both wrinkly, tipsy and weak from warm water acrobatics, we rose and I helped Amanda out of the curving tub. I didn't want Amanda to get dressed. A better idea came to mind. I grabbed two bath-sheets, wrapped one around her naked body, and the other around mine.

"It's a beautiful, clear night. I have a special surprise for you."

Amanda gazed up into my eyes, a rush of warmth flowed through me.

I picked up our bottle of wine, and held Amanda's hand in mine, "Come with me." I directed her down another hallway to a door. It resembled a smaller closet door. Instead, a steep, narrow stairwell hid behind the door. With my hands on either side of her waist, she held the bottle of wine.

"I'm right behind you. When you reach the top of the stairs, stop, and close your eyes. No cheating." Amanda did as instructed. At the top of the stairs, I took her hand in mine.

"Okay, come with me. Don't open your eyes."

We turned a corner and walked several steps. With her eyes still closed, my hands steered her into a specific position lining her up. Done maneuvering her, I pressed my chest against her back, and wrapped my arms around her. I lowered my head and placed a wet kiss on the side of her neck. She shivered.

"Amanda... Open your eyes."

"Antonio - this is incredible."

The solarium, constructed entirely of glass panels, sat atop the rest of the house. A magnificent telescope stood at center-stage making it an observatory. It felt like floating in the Cosmos. The room's design placed the two of us directly in the middle of the beautiful night sky. The massive telescope's view took us even further, until we soared around the Moon.

"Antonio, we are in a dream." She marveled. "You have taken me to the Moon."

I pulled a tall stool over, and sat behind her as she gazed at the Heavens. A small tug allowed the sheet to fall from her shoulders, and onto the smooth floor. My hands ran along her curves while moments drifted by. I lifted her up, sitting her on the stool between my legs and wrapped my sheet around us. The gorgeous woman made me happy.

Amanda hardly spoke. She let her head fall back on my shoulder, and closed her eyes for a moment.

She seemed to be absorbing the experience into her soul.

Her face turned towards mine as she placed her hand against my cheek, and gently turned my face to hers. "You have an understated genius within you, one you have no idea exists." In response, I spoke the words of Solomon against her lips and never wavered from her gaze.

"'And the roof of thy mouth like the best wine that glideth down smoothly for my beloved moving gently the lips of those that are asleep.'"

She answered with the next line, "'I am my beloveds, and his desire is toward me...'"

I responded with my own words. "Your beloved's desire for you is matched only by the consuming fire of the Sun." My desire devoured her breath and left her acting a little tipsy.

I wanted to share the Galaxy with her on that perfect night, but my earthly cravings were swallowing me. I summoned the Professor within, best equipped to rescue the silly lovesick man, and restrict his consuming desire.

"Amanda many ancient myths claim when we stare at the stars we are looking into the face of God'."

"Antonio, tell me, what do you think is out there? Is God out there?"

Her question amused me. "When I first started studying ancient civilizations, it was easy to study them and arrive at those conclusions. We have attributed myths, religious beliefs, and practices as the result of some naïve search for answers. As we learn more, it's hard for me to draw that same conclusion.

The one truth I do know is - Every civilization that has existed on the Earth has possessed a common obsession: The birth of his own kind and the creation of Earth, and ultimately, the end of Earth and extinction of Humanity. Man has always looked for mercy within the Cosmos."

My arms tightened around her as my lips continued to answer her query. I spoke softly into her ear. "Our bodies are stars. You and I are made of stardust. Every element of our body exists out there. Look out and see the stars. They talk, just like you and I. They communicate across radio waves. But what do they communicate? With whom else can they speak? Do they communicate with God?

Many, probably even most of my colleagues, believe it's all just an awesome chemical reaction, debris playing out in something called time."

"Antonio Tell me your soul's answer. The one you would not share with your colleagues. Share with me a secret answer, you have never shared."

Flattered, I kissed her neck and revealed her request. "Everything we ever wanted to know, or will ever need to know, is out there. Jesus said the same, 'In my Father's house are many mansions'."

"You know, I keep reading, hearing the Cosmos show signs of change, maybe even destruction. Is it true?"

"Jupiter has a new Red Spot and a never-ending electromagnetic storm. Auroras between Jupiter and its Moon

Io exist. As Io has lately experienced a great deal of volcanic activity, Jupiter's magnetic field has also increased. In addition, Uranus and Neptune have experienced shifts in their magnetic poles while the atmosphere on Mars has become denser. We can see light from the radiation on Saturn. Enceladus, Saturn's Moon, has produced Yellowstone like volcanic eruptions.

The Mayans claim the North Star will switch from Polaris to Vega for the duration of five Suns. Our beloved Venus is changing her atmosphere. As her levels of sulfuric gases decrease, it becomes apparent that her Luminesce is thicker than ever before. She's forming a tail around her Moon, with dark and light spots appearing on her surface.

Venus is the element that connects Earth with the Heavens. I fear changes to her would mean changes to everything as we know it.

Venus was important to the Ancient Cultures, and it is equally important that we quit discounting their beliefs. Venus is Earth's sister planet, known as 'The Morning and Evening Star'. The Ancient Mayans and Egyptians understood all of this. Even the Hopis placed great significance on her planetary cycles."

Amanda interjected, "King Solomon placed tremendous importance on Venus. He called it Shekinah, the essence of God, or the female essence of God."

I smiled, and added to her conjecture. "The Israelites identified profound changes on Earth within the cycles of Venus."

"Antonio, I would like to tell you an old Jewish Myth about Shekinah. Would you like that?"

Against her neck, I smiled. "I would like it very much."

"It is called: 'The Creation of the Sacred Dream.'

"In the beginning, God created a vast space for a dwelling place. God loved this makom, this sacred space, where divinity could spread out in all its glory. It was good.

Eternities past, and the magnitude of all this serenity and open space created a yearning, a desire to share this with another. The yearning that God did not know how to fill began to grow stronger and stronger, and it became painful. There was divine sadness because God did not know how to remedy this state of being. God began to withdraw into a void. This was tzimtzum.

One eternity, God fell into a very deep sleep and dreamed of four angelic beings that came and led God to a mirror. God gazed into the mirror and saw an image, which introduced itself as Shekinah. As God watched, Shekinah raised her hands and began to weave a most extraordinary vision. The makom began to fill with light and color that wove a new consciousness into God's reality. Shekinah wove for him the dream of future worlds, of creation, formation, and action, and of wisdom, beauty, goodness, and mercy. She wove the dream of the stars and planets, and the divine order of the constellations. In the weave appeared man, woman, child, the Jewish people, a land, Torah, on and on through the frame of space -- time until the weave was complete.

God was filled; the vision awake and such love and gratitude that God kneeled in front of Shekinah. As the remnants of the weave dripped from her hands, God reached out and kissed them, then led her to join him for all eternities on the throne of glory. Shekinah consented to unite with God beyond the worlds, so that together they could leave the great dream into manifestation.

As they stepped out of the dream into the morning, their light created a great explosion. Billions of light fragments scattered above and spread over them like a wedding canopy as God and Shekinah became the one. The Heavens sparkled with joy at this grand union.

The great dream was born."

"Shekinah, in Judaism, is the essence of God in the female form. Many believe Venus is Shekinah. Her cycles represent profound changes on Earth, especially among the Israelites."

Chapter 28

"I count myself in nothing else so happy, as in a soul remembering my good friends"
— William Shakespeare

Thanks to late evening we enjoyed last night, I was preparing an early lunch, and even if I'm the only one saying it, the aroma in the kitchen smelled rich, and pungent. The superb spices filled the air. Amanda peeked into the kitchen, undoubtedly, she was curious to know who was cooking. Maria seemed a little overworked, so I had given her and Joe some time to relax.

Amanda giggled when she saw me laboring over the stove. The laugh in her voice brought out an ornery side of me.

"Antonio, what are you cooking?"

I walked over and planted a kiss on her cheek. "An authentic Cuban meal, in fact, just for you, I'm making it from completely organic ingredients."

"It smells wonderful."

Caught off guard, she watched as I cut an orange in half like a ninja warrior. She jumped back when the blade hit the board. I laughed, picked up the half, and squeezed it into the simmering pot.

"Are you putting the juice in the rice?"

"Absolutely Honey, Cubans love oranges. We'll eat them in almost anything."

Taking the other half of the orange in my hand, I cornered

her, trapping her against the counter. I brushed the wet orange against her sweet lips. Squeezing ever so slightly, the juice dribbled down her neck, I helped myself.

"Open your mouth."

She tilted her head back, gazed into my eyes, and opened wide as I squeezed a stream of juice into her delicious mouth.

"Antonio, could we talk?"

Clearly, talking was not what I had in mind. My lips were close, so close. "Why?"

Right there in the kitchen, my hands ascended beneath her blouse. My fingers slipped under her bra. I whispered. "Talk to me or play with me, you decide."

She acted delirious. "What?"

My mouth teased her. "Decide."

"I need you alone, Antonio."

"Honey, we are alone."

A gasp escaped her. "Antonio, you are doing these things to me, and I cannot think. Besides, someone might catch us."

"Okay, talk to me, sweetheart."

Her exhale tickled my neck. She obviously dreaded saying what she had to say. "Antonio, I am sorry to say, we have to return to Hidden Mountain. I lost something very important to me in the cavern."

Her eyes were brilliant. I wondered if she knew the power they had on me. "Okay."

My acceptance seemed to upset her as she struggled to hold

back tears.

"Perhaps, you could tell me what we will be looking for within the depths of the old volcano.

"I need to find an ankle bracelet; one that was a gift from someone who meant a great deal to me."

Great, I wasn't overly excited about going out to find a piece of jewelry, likely, given to her by a man in her past. But, as usual, Amanda's story wasn't at all that ordinary.

"The bracelet was once a necklace given to a young girl by her friend. The girls eventually became women, one died. Separated by dimensions, her friend had the small necklace made into an ankle bracelet. Then she could always feel the tug of her childhood friend."

I swallowed the emotion in my throat, and asked. "What was the friend's name?"

She smiled behind the tears. "Kimberly."

"We'll leave early tomorrow morning."

She straightened herself, and walked away from the kitchen. On the way out, she noticed Jose.

"Jose, I did not know you were here.

I detected a nervous undertone in my brother's voice.

"Oh, I just got here. I need to speak to Antonio."

She left, and I began scolding my brother. His guilt was written all over his face.

"Damn you Jose, you were listening to us. Get yourself together, and start cooking as you can see, I have some business to take care of."

"Uh, Antonio, I don't cook."

"You do now, you damn eavesdropping voyeur."

He yelled after me as I exited the room. "Antonio, I'm warning you, I don't cook."

I ignored him, and retreated to the bedroom. Opening the door, I saw Amanda. Her gaze followed me. I sat on the side of the bed, removed my boots, and stretched out. The room remained silent for the longest time.

After a while, I broke our silence. "Amanda, what's the first thing you want to do when we are freed from the constant threat of danger?"

Her smile was sexy, and playful. "Date you."

I chuckled at the thought, hell, I would marry her. I was amused, and simply had to explore this idea further. "Tell me, what you imagine Amanda."

Her face did an animated dance prior to her answer. "I would put on a stunning dress, and you would show me the art while I hugged your arm. Later, we would dine in the finest restaurant in town. Then, we would dance until the night gave into the wee hours of morning. Truthfully, it really would not matter what we did, because, always, I would feel proud on the arm of the Mysterious Professor."

Flattered, and surprised, I reiterated. "You want to date me, Amanda?"

Her flushed face turned down. "It is all too silly, isn't it?"

"No, I would enjoy dating you, but know it is I that would be the lucky one."

She smiled as she came over to join me on the bed. I lured her onto her back. Hovered over her, I positioned my face next to hers, and spoke my truth. "Oh yes, my darling Amanda, with you on my arm, I would spark the envy of every man in town. Touting around with a beauty whose eyes alone can bring the strongest of men to their knees. The enchantress with locks so gorgeous, no man can look upon them without longing to touch. Yes, tis my lovely Amanda, a woman as natural as God ever created, with the heart of an angel, and the body of a goddess. It is I that is blessed for on my arm she will be."

Chapter 29

"The moments of happiness we enjoy take us by surprise. It is not that we seize them, but that they seize us.
— Ashley Montagu

True to my word, Amanda, and I threw caution into the wind. We headed to Hidden Mountain, alone. The cold and windy November day required cumbersome coats. The only positive was the pockets they provided for our extra gear.

I brought several powerful lights to help find Amanda's ankle bracelet. Her description of the tiny-style silver chain would create a haystack challenge in the cavern.

Parked in my normal spot near the railroad tracks, I changed my glasses, and got out of the car. Amanda and I met at Raven's trunk to gear up. Together, we checked and repositioned our weapons. Amanda with her Barak/SP-21, and I with the Glock in my boot, and the Desert Eagle Mark XIX-.50 AE in my belt, we weren't taking any unnecessary risks. In a matter of minutes, I had repelling equipment attached to both of us.

The wind cut like a knife as we traveled up to the summit. The ancient mountain felt cold and surreal on that gloomy day. With haste, we made it to the dugout we had previously camouflaged. Amanda insisted upon helping me uncover it.

"Antonio, I hate this coat. I need to hide it up here."

I laughed at her expression of annoyance. "We can roll them up and hide them under these stones.

My line secured, I positioned myself for my descent.

"Amanda, do you remember what to do?"

"Of course I do!" She paused. "Antonio do not catch me this time, let me do it myself, I want to learn."

She rolled her eyes at my laughter. After I began to repel, I heard her speak beneath her breath. "You are so hot."

Stopping myself midway down the hole, I looked up at her. "Amanda, did you say, I'm hot?"

"You are. I could devour you after watching you do this."

"Damn Honey, hold on to that feeling for me. I would love for you to devour me."

I finished my descent, and began coaxing Amanda down. "Come to me. ONE…TWO…THREE…GO!"

Once Amanda was safely at the bottom, I turned the flashlights on to illuminate the area.

"Perfect, Amanda."

"Antonio, did you bring earplugs?"

"Yes, but I see no benefit in returning to the maze, today. We'll go back when the weather improves. It's rained a lot, and I don't think it's a good idea."

After my last experience in the bowels of the volcano, I was in no mood to return. The strange high-pitched screams of the unknown nearly, shut down my nervous system. With the level of her hearing loss, it didn't bother Amanda much at all.

"Antonio, where does the strange sound come from at the end of the tunnel?"

"I don't know, but it sounds exactly like the stars in the cosmos. I listened to the recordings, once at the National Radio Astronomy Observatory, and they sounded like that—like an old science fiction movie… Come on let's canvas the ground and find your ankle bracelet."

We got down close to the cool volcano floor. I brought out a small UV light, and switched off the others to take full advantage of its unique properties. I flashed the light against the cavern walls. The unusual illumination made visible a sunken carving. I stooped to examine it closer. My fingers traced the grooves. The star of David, Solomon's seal, it was carved into the volcano walls.

Unaware of my discovery, Amanda shouted; "Stop!" She pointed to an area near where I stood. "There it is Antonio."

I got down on all fours in the direction she instructed. I too, saw the ankle bracelet, but it was laying on something spectacular. I flattened my body on the floor to gain a closer view.

"Amanda, do you see what's underneath your bracelet." Her high pitched tone was crackling. "Yes, and it isn't a ring at all, it too is a bracelet."

"Yeah, a ring would be too small to use as a key in stone."

Amanda sounded confused. "What?"

I moved the light upward, onto the wall, and pointed.

"Amazing…! Antonio, I believe we are standing extremely close to the edge of a supernatural event. This all seems too unbelievable to be real."

"Maybe, it is, but whatever is behind that wall is likely very real."

Amanda was visibly shaking. The tremble in her hands was debilitating her.

"Antonio, you're not saying this is the mine, are you?"

"Amanda, I had to have misinterpreted the Scrolls. "I took a deep breath of the musty air, and coughed.

"Honey, we have to take samples, and photographs. We must record everything.

Taking baggies from my pack, we scooped up samples of the sandy stilt around the area. After everything was tagged and photographed we stood staring at each other. Hesitant to expose Amanda to possible toxins, I paused to contemplate. She apparently read my mind.

"Do not even think of protecting me. You have the syringes. Damn it Antonio, we go in, now."

I shook my head, handed her the light and positioned the bracelet. Just as I was about to fit the two together Amanda grabbed my wrist. "No...Stop!"

I looked around, but I could see nothing that would prompt such an outburst. "What's wrong with you, Amanda?"

"Antonio, if we open this, we cannot deny it."

I pulled back, turned, and faced her. "You're right, plausible deniability. We need it."

Without further conversation, we packed up and prepared

ourselves for the climb out of the pit.

Chapter 30

"Nobody says you must laugh, but a sense of humor can help you overlook the unattractive, tolerate the unpleasant, cope with the unexpected, and smile through the day"
— *Ann Landers*

Still in the bed, I turned over, towards Amanda. When I noticed she was gone, I thought, hell, she's probably already out in the pool, she loved early morning swims. For a moment, I contemplated going back to sleep. The night before, I wanted to get some work done, so I got up after Amanda fell asleep.

Feeling mildly annoyed, I wished she'd stayed in bed with me. At least, she could humor me every now and then. Nevertheless, it was stupid to lay there thinking about her so, I decided to get up.

On my way out to the pool, I stopped by the kitchen for some coffee. With all the guests in the house, Maria and Joe were working diligently, so I had told them to come in late. I filled two cups. I always got a warm greeting from Amanda when I brought her coffee. Caffeine carried me through the French doors, and into the pool area where I sat the coffees down. Taking a huge drink from one of the cups, I scanned the area, and noticed Amanda wasn't in the pool.

I bolted to the balcony, rushed up the steps, and surveyed the bedroom. I called out her name. There were no signs of her. Behind my office door, I spotted a 'Dear Antonio' note placed on my desk.

> Dear Antonio,
>
> You are angry with me right now. I know. Settle down. I needed an overhaul. Do not worry. I did not take Raven and I have the Desert Eagle in my purse.
>
> Do not try to come after me. I will be fine. If you are thinking about coming after me or sending someone after me...DON'T... or you will find yourself extremely sorry. Remember those expeditions?
>
> Lets just say you will wave goodbye to Santa and blow Cupid a kiss, before you experience another expedition. If by noon you have behaved yourself and not reported the Escalade stolen, I will call you.
>
> Use your head wisely,
>
> Amanda
> 88

Furious, I didn't have a clue what to do about her. She was psycho. Why didn't someone see her get away? Insulted, I glanced at the note. Did she really think I would worry about the car?

I had no idea where the daft woman would go to get her so-called overhaul. I would have taken her. All she had to do was tell me. Waiting until noon for a call wasn't an option. At that moment, I thought, she was the craziest person I'd ever encountered.

How long would this damn overhaul take?

I rubbed my head and paced. Damn her. OPERA just got a free lunch. In haste, I put my clothes and boots on. Hoping I got to her first, I stomped my way to the other side of the house where Pop and José were staying.

"José," I yelled! "José, those sons-a-bitches we hired let Amanda get away this morning – Alone! Go kill them!"

José's look was that of an astonished man. "Not again, where did she go?"

Filled with fury, I handed José the note; "Without anyone noticing, she tip-toed out of here for a female overhaul."

"José, where the hell is Pop?"

Jose responded as he read. "Out in the guest house, he's going over some security issues. What is 'getting overhauled', Antonio? Did the Escalade have engine problems?"

I grabbed the note from my brother. "Damn it, José. You need to get the hell out of Miami Legal more often! She went to a salon, a spa. You know - hair, and whatever else they do there."

José had an "I got it now" expression; the one a younger man wore when women's mysteries are a topic of conversation; the one that really meant he had no idea what I was talking about.

"I get it. You better leave her alone, or she won't go on the expedition to Israel with you."

"José, she's not talking about a trip to Israel. Seriously, tell me you'll get out more. Read it. She won't make love to me until after Valentine's Day, if I so much as bother her. José we haven't made it to Thanksgiving yet." He shook his head.

"Tell Pop to kill the security and get your butt in Raven, you need a damn life. I need to find Amanda, or I'll have no life. I'll be like you." José ran to tell Pop, I yelled;

"I'll pick you up back there, José." Snatching Raven's keys, I got in and started her engine. Raven ripped out of the garage, pulled around the drive, and stopped to pick up José.

I sat, stroking my head and rolling my eyes. Pop was coming towards the car... no... not Pop, I could tell... it was the damn Judge that approached me.

"Antonio, son, think before you run off with your brother and get everyone killed." The Judge tried to reason.

"Pop, damn it, when those thugs attacked me they promised if I didn't take the deal, they would take her; they've already taken Sam. We just got him back."

"Am I the only one who remembers? Pop, José doesn't have

to go. I do have to go find her." I tried to make it clear.

"Son, when did Amanda last drive or get her hair done, alone? I know you are afraid, but she is a very capable woman."

"Pop, I don't want to hear you. I won't care what her hair looks like in a casket! José are you staying, or going?" José jumped in the car. I stomped Raven, leaving Pop in her dust. We tore out of the gate, and onto the state highway.

José asked. "Antonio, how far is it to the Spa?"

"Well, José, damn it, she didn't write down the name and address, or leave me a map. Amanda is a little too smart for that." I bled sarcasm. Hauling ass towards Santa Fe, I intended to find Amanda.

"Antonio, you don't have a clue where she is, do you?" José always wanted to get the facts straight, and point out the obvious.

"José, whatever she thinks I would think - she would do the exact opposite. I promise you, she flipped it around many times with the purpose of outsmarting my dumbass." I grew more irritable.

"Your Raven is a kick-ass bitch, are the tires even touching the road?"

"José, that wasn't natural coming from you. Quit while you're ahead." I would have laughed my ass off, if I weren't so infuriated. I pushed Raven harder. She flew.

I took my eyes off the road long enough to glance at my brother; despite his holding onto the dash, his face was filled with glee! Then his attire caught my eye, and made me wince.

"José, I need to take you shopping. The Miami look isn't working. With no socks, and Italian leather shoes, someone will kill you out here. You need some boots." Suddenly, I realized José needed some serious deviation from his norm.

A flashing red light in my rearview mirror had me swearing. "Son-of-a-bitch, José, I'm going to jail. I'm driving like a maniac going 90 miles an hour. I've a Glock .45 in my boot without my weapons permit. To top it all off, my damn attorneys are from Miami. Not to mention, Amanda may well be kidnapped and my wallet is in yesterday's clothes, all because I was feeling` love, last night.

You need to call Pop, now. Get me an attorney. Take my damn phone. If Amanda calls, you lie to her as if your life depends on it. Shit José, he is going to arrest me. This is a first for me. José, do you have your license with you? I hope he lets you take Raven."

I found a wide spot on the road and pulled over. Jose was yammering on the phone, and I watched in the rear-view mirror as the Trooper approached the car, with one hand on his weapon.

He stood looking at us for a moment, ran his eyes over me and Jose, then across the back seat. "Going a little fast there, and neither one of you look like you are in labor or bleeding."

"My girlfriend is in danger."

"Sure she is. Got papers on this ride?"

"Yes, the glove box… My wallet…I left it at home."

"Let's see the registration." He glanced down at the paperwork after I handed it over.

"Antonio Domínguez?"

"Dr. Antonio Domínguez, Anthropologist." I elaborated.

"Is that so? Well Dr. Antonio Dominquez, Anthropologist; your registration is expired, so are your tags. You are by your own admission driving without a license while exceeding the speed limit, and therefore I am going to have to ask you to get out of the car, and come with me."

As I opened the door and got out, I remembered the Glock.

"Sir, my boot, my permit is in my wallet." I tried to explain.

"I thought you said your wallet was at home, now you remember it's in your boot? The Trooper asked sarcastically.

I realized suddenly that this situation could get ugly real quick; I was standing on the side of the road, worried about Amanda, armed, without identification or proper permits; and I had to get a Trooper with a smart mouth.

Slowly, as if speaking to a child, I explained about the Glock.

"Yes sir, my wallet is at home, but in my boot is a Glock…" This was as far as I got, before the Trooper spun me around and tossed me face down bent over the hood of Raven. I knew that was going to happen! He pressed the button on his mike and called for back-up.

"Just be still. No sudden moves. I am going to cuff you, and then sit you down over here on the ground."

"You, in the car, hands where I can see them!" Stern, but fair, his voice implied; I could see Jose through the windshield, and his mouth was gaping open, and he had the phone resting between his ear and his shoulder; like a good boy he threw both hands in the air.

"Now get out of the car and walk slowly around to the front." I watched José, slowly lower one hand and open the door; he walked around to the front. The Trooper pulled me upright and walked me around the front of Raven, then sat me down in the dirt.

"Which boot is the weapon in?" I held up my left foot, and he jerked off my boot with a hard tug. The Glock was strapped to my ankle, so he released the strap, took the weapon and dropped my foot.

"Now, as a learned man, and an official of the law, I feel I must warn you I have judged the situation and come to the conclusion that the shit just hit the fan." He was looking at the Glock, and expertly released the clip, took note of the fullness, and then looked back down at me. Motioning, he gestured for me to raise the other leg. I held up the other foot and he used one hand to remove that boot as well. Satisfied I was not carrying an unannounced arsenal strapped to my other leg, he took a step back.

"This is not a weapon that needs to be carried by a man who is concerned about his girl-friend. No, this is a weapon a man carries when he feels threatened or wants to threaten somebody. So which is it Doc, you going to save your girl-friend or put a bullet in her head?" His voice had gone from friendly Trooper just doing my job, to cold and hard. In the distance I could hear the sound of sirens and knew more Troopers were on the way.

I tried to explain about Amanda being in danger, and how I needed to get too her as fast as possible.

"Sir, my girlfriend is in danger, I need to get to her, and bring her back home as fast as possible."

"Where is your girlfriend?"

I answered honestly. "She's in Santa Fe at a spa somewhere having an overhaul, not sure exactly which one."

I knew as soon as the words left my mouth the effect they were going to have. As if to prove it, I heard José hiss in frustration behind me.

"At a spa having an overhaul? You thought that was dangerous? What were you going to save her from…being tortured by the masseuse? Or, maybe there is a mummy running loose in Santa Fe I should know about. That is what you do isn't it; chase mummies?"

"Actually no, what I do is study the origins of human-kind, with emic and etic views of their culture relative to their location as well as ethnography." I automatically corrected. José was groaning now, and I knew I wasn't helping the situation.

"Does this study of human-kind include the habits of men who chase women with guns in their boots?" Apparently he did not like being corrected.

Before I could answer, two more Troopers arrive with sirens blaring, rushed from their cars with guns drawn. One went to stand behind Jose, and the other joined the Trooper who was interrogating me.

"What we got Bob?" The Trooper, who had now joined 'Bob', was looking us over with true diligence.

"Drop the phone hombre." Ordered the other Trooper giving José a shove to his knees and I knew this was getting out of hand real fast! Was it any wonder he thought we were dangerous? Jose was dressed like a South American Drug Lord, and we were both as dark as sin itself with our Cuban heritage.

I tried to gain control of the conversation. After all I was looking like a fool, and I did not care for it.

"Sir, if you would let me explain, I am sure I can straighten this entire mess out."

"Right now Doc, your explanations have not been a lot of help, if I were you I would be quiet."

He added; "Chasing after a woman with a loaded gun is never a good thing in my book."

He elaborated for the other officers; "What we have here is a fast as hell car driven by one Antonio Dominquez, or as he likes to be called; Dr. Antonio Dominquez, Anthropologist."

"Unfortunately for said Anthropologist, he is also driving without a license, and had a concealed weapon hidden in his boot. Haven't had time to ascertain who the other one is yet, but from his clothes I'd say he was a wanna be member of Miami Vice or just some poor druggy who is way North of his home border."

From behind me I heard José chime in. "Actually I am neither; I am a lawyer with a healthy practice in Miami, and his brother." He sounded insulted over the aspersions the Trooper had cast on not only his lifestyle but his clothes. Couldn't blame him in my opinion, but I couldn't blame the Trooper either.

"A Miami lawyer, well that explains the clothes."

"The Doc here says he has a great need to save his girlfriend from the dangers of a spa, although he is not sure which one; but apparently it required a fast car, a hasty trip to Santa Fe and a concealed, loaded Glock .45."

The silence that met that asinine sounding statement left no doubt as to the agreement among the other Troopers that I was in deep trouble and most likely a demented stalker.

José had called Pop before the Officer made him drop the phone. With any hope, he'd get my ID here before they hauled my carcass to jail.

I prayed Amanda was still alive, because I wanted to take care of her myself. Damn her, and her damn spa day. I was butt down in the dirt in handcuffs, with my boots off, and my brother the Lawyer beside me. Never in my life had I been this humiliated.

Thank God, I heard the sound of Joseph's car, and then he was there, walking slowly forward talking to one of the

Troopers; my Pop—the Judge.

While Pop couldn't stop them from taking me to jail he did stop them from taking José, and gave them my identification. How does he do that? How does the man manage to walk up on wary, suspicious Troopers, and within minutes have them believing that he is the most trustworthy soul in the world; he does it with everybody!

Then again being the Judge apparently is enough. Even here in New Mexico his judicial reputation was known; after a call to dispatch, the officers were able to verify his name and relationship to us, and by the same contact save José from being arrested.

Chapter 31

"A quick temper will make a fool of you soon enough."
— *Bruce Lee*

José and Pop waited for my hearing to begin. They had met and hired local attorney Michael Starr. I'm told that they attempted to explain disjointed parts of the story. By a stroke of luck, Michael knew me by reputation, and told them he was confident that barring an unforeseen crisis, the Judge would throw the charges out immediately. The story and circumstances of the situation apparently amused Michael.

They watched as I entered the courtroom and stood before the Judge in my socked feet. It was just a further reminder of the careless stupidity I often exhibited in issues concerning Amanda. Nevertheless, I hoped they would be able to retrieve my boots. I could not imagine ending the horrific day, and losing my favorite boots, too.

The charges were dropped against me, and the gate opened. My public record remained clean. However, I couldn't be sure about the gossip grapevine. It was sure to spin out of my control, and take on a life of its own. I could see it in my mind, highlighted this week, Dr. Dominguez's Run-In with the Law.

The awkward drive back to the estate had Jose at the wheel. I couldn't believe I was setting in the backseat of my beautiful car with my brother in the driver's seat. A short stretch before we reached the drive, José broke the dead silence with an insane burst of belly busting laughter.

When we got out of the car, I couldn't get away quick enough. Once out of their sight, I heard, José and Pop roaring in laughter. Sure they had a laugh, but I couldn't share in their hilarity; where is Amanda? My worry for her echoed with every step I took, it rang out like thunder on every riser! I had a feeling I could not shake, something was terribly wrong – somewhere the darkness was gathering and I was afraid Amanda was in the middle of it. I had just about made it up the stairs to get another pair of boots to complete my search when my phone rang.

Chapter 32

*"The meeting of two personalities is like the contact of two chemical substances:
if there is any reaction, both are transformed."*
Carl Jung

Damn the man! Why is he not answering the phone? First he hovers like a mother hen, and then locks me down in his home-made fortress, and now he refuses to talk to me; just because I chose to take an early morning excursion without telling him.

Once I crept out of the bedroom this morning, and made it downstairs, I had carefully eyed the assortment of keys in the kitchen drawer, it was hard but I managed to ignore the coffee pot, as much as I loved early morning coffee, the aroma would have drawn attention. I admit it; I snatched the keys to Antonio's Escalade for one simple reason; the extreme pleasure of driving that beautiful piece of machinery!

I made my escape out through the garage, avoiding all the security and family that now inhabited Antonio's home. Antonio would have been furious as the coast was clear, and I made it down the drive and through the gate without a soul approaching me! It was great fun eluding all the dramatic steps Antonio had taken.

Truthfully, after clearing the gate, I feel free as a bird. The surge thrust upwards from within me. I cranked up the radio and sang at the time of my lungs, it felt good. I did not really know my way around so I had to pay close attention to the GPS.

Believe me, the last thing I want to do is scare Antonio. I

honestly considered the long-term results of his once again waking to find me missing. I realize it might seem cruel to an onlooker, but there were still many things Antonio did not know, and did not need to know. In fact, he just was not ready or maybe it was me, I was not ready.

At least I left the obtuse man a note; one I was sure would get his attention. I know Antonio does not want to return to a life that leaves him sleeping alone, so, I knew any threat to our intimate relationship would certainly gain his attention, and he would think twice about compromising it even once. In planning I supplied him with although a hideous circumstance for my leaving the estate alone, it was reasonably believable. I decided this would fuel his anger and within his rage, he would fail to recognize the whole idea defied my character.

Daily, I had to remind myself to be cautiously careful about my feelings for Antonio. He is the most enticing man I have ever met, but I had a purpose and was long committed to obligations he is unaware of. Deep within me I felt a constant gnawing that sometimes overwhelmed me.

Before meeting Antonio, although nothing that happened was planned, I had come to terms with my destiny. I had learned to balance. As a mother of three sons this was not an easy task, but I was doing a relatively good job. That is until Antonio appeared out of nowhere, broad siding me into an emotional tsunami. With or without him, my life could never return to the normal I was accustomed to living.

Normal, I cannot believe I used that word. I hate it. What is normal? Who defines normal? Nothing in my life had ever manifested into the definition of normal. My normal certainly was not anyone else's normal. Well, I digress as Antonio so often reminds me.

I have left Antonio for a few hours to tend to some urgent business. Since, I have unofficially at this point returned to my duties with the Mossad, the organization has insisted that I see a Doctor about the nasty tumor in my head. The agency set the appointment for me, and appeasing the Mossad is important to me. After all, no one else had offered any support for my predicament with our enemies. Besides, Israel was and always will be of utmost importance to me, an issue that Antonio appears to understand, but he is not yet capable of rationalizing the extent of my involvement.

Despite the distress it will cause Antonio and me, I had to see the Doctor. My symptoms are worsening, yet I cannot fathom the sense of seeing another Doctor. I have lost track of the number of Doctors that have assessed my medical issue. The fact is I need a surgeon with the skills to go in my head, do a reconnaissance and then fix the damage. All the surgeons and Doctors I have seen want to start clipping muscles and nerves before they ever got started! I was not willing to be chopped up and potentially left unable to live my life the way I needed to for my cause and more importantly my sons. Antonio's entrance into my life added even more impetuous for finding a way to extend not only my life, but the quality of my life.

Luckily, I found my way to the clinic without taking any wrong turns. I considered this a success, since on a few recent occasions I had gotten lost despite the GPS. The early morning had me arriving to a rather deserted parking lot. Once the SUV was parked, my pleasant mood turned to an eerie nervousness as I crossed the parking area and entered the building. Since I was a special case, I was rushed in by the receptionist for my MRI.

They were ready for me. A nice looking dark haired, young man, not much older than my eldest son led me back to the room housing the huge machine that would soon swallow me down to my shoulders. An older blonde woman entered the room, and introduced herself as Diane the technician that would perform the MRI.

My body tensed as she aligned my head and neck into the restraints. I wanted to say something obnoxious when she told me not to move. The idea that a person could move was ludicrous. Only moments after she disappeared, the annoying sound of the equipment began grinding in circles around my head. The sound and vibration alone made me terribly dizzy. Even after it stopped, I could feel it continue tormenting me over and over.

From my state of nausea, I tried to focus as she was giving me directions to the Doctors private office where he would review the findings with me. I rolled my eyes as I made my way down the smelly alcohol infested environment. I was in no rush to talk with another doctor.

I looked up at the door Nigel Cooper MD, with a turn of the knob I went in and sat. Since, Dr. Cooper was apparently a friend of the Mossad I was afforded this little professional courtesy. I glanced around at the sparse southwest décor. I love the way the theme flowed through the entire state. Every business, home, and establishment seemed to adopt the look.

The door opened and the pleasant looking Dr. Cooper entered. I allowed myself a deep inhale as he was introducing himself. We agreed to use first names. He wasted no time.

"Amanda your situation is worsening at a very fast rate." He paused. I felt like someone else was sitting in the chair, and I was observing. I swallowed hard.

He reached across his desk and patted my hand. I felt my eyes grow huge. "The tumor has spawned five outgrowths; one is seriously threatening to interfere with your brain function, if it hasn't already. I agreed to share my findings with a couple of excellent surgeons the Mossad has suggested. Amanda a resolution is now imperative. "

I understood, but his words now seemed to come from a great distance. He talked a while longer; I do not know what else he said. We shook hands, feeling empty and lonely; I left the building and got inside Antonio's Escalade.

I sat in the parking lot for a few moments trying to process the news. Without a doubt the tumor was terrible, and I understood it was life threatening, but what about the visions. Did the tumors allow me to understand the other dimension or had it developed independently? It seemed silly to even consider yet, it was an important part of who I had become.

Right now, I had to put it out of mind. There was other business that needed my attention. John Bear needed to see me. I set the GPS to his jewelry store. Antonio had taken me there, but I did not trust my sense of direction. Thank Heavens for technology.

John Bear was a fabulous jewelry artisan. He had designed and crafted the stunning Cognac Diamond necklace Antonio gave me. He also took my drawings and created a fabulous pendent for Antonio's beautiful niece Rosie. Most importantly, John Bear was a wise Hopi sage. A man Antonio respected with utter reverence. Antonio claimed John had become his teacher and liaison to the tribes upon his arrival in New Mexico and had remained so ever since.

I too felt a strong connection to the man. I was anxious to find out why John wanted to see me alone. John respected Antonio, and believed him to be the man that would make a difference. The same one his ancestors spoke of when John was just a child. The truth is there were many in New Mexico, and across the country that shared John's hopes about Antonio.

I slid the SUV into one of the marked spaces in front of John's store, dropped in a couple of coins, and entered. At first, I did not see him. In a second he rose from his work behind the counter and greeted me.

"Ah, Amanda, thank you for coming;" He smiled and gently held onto my hand. We stood for a couple of moments in silence.

"I am more than happy to be here John."

The sage nodded his head. "Please, come and join me in the back." He locked the door and flipped the closed sign, and gently took my arm and led me behind the curtained doorway at the rear of his shop.

The aroma of Willow bark tea and Pinion incense teased my senses, and I saw where John had set a table for two. He motioned for me to sit, and prepared our tea.

"John, I am not sure why you wanted to see me without Antonio…"

He held up his hand for me to stop speaking.

"First, drink your tea, and relax. You are tense and the shadows in your eyes tell me you are in pain. The tea will help." With that he settled back in his chair and seemed to become a statue; what else could I do, I drank my tea.

Under his breath John began to sing. I loved John's voice, it was like a melody that drawled across his consonants, and sang a song my heart could hear. As I sipped my tea, John kept refilling the cup; I did not mind, the tea and his singing were having a wonderful effect on my mind, and soothing my soul.

"Amanda, you are close to Mother Earth, and you seek knowledge about the Sky God, our father. Let me share a bit of knowledge that will help you understand why I have asked you here, alone.

Our ancestors taught us that humans come from the earth; they entered this world through the sipapu, a crack that has widened greatly since we first came forth. What we call the sipapu, you call the Grand Canyon. All those who have gone before have left behind a bit of themselves, and it is in our Kachina that they rest.

Our lives are guided by adherence to the six cardinal points of the earth. Ours has not been the only people so guided; the ancients of Egypt also used the cardinal points to guide them. North, South, East, West, all these words are used for directions you will recognize; but you must also remember the zenith and the nadir."

"The days of darkness approach us."

I tried not to appear overly blank, but I did not know what the Native man was speaking about. Where was Antonio when I needed him?

"The day is approaching; our World will grow dark for three suns before the Great Mother is revealed from above. The dark demons will be unleashed, many will die."

Now I knew exactly what he was talking about! During the galactic alignment light of the sun would be hidden from earth. The magnetism from the anomaly would activate the inhabitants' pineal gland. Those unprepared would face their private hell as if they had received a hallucinogen. Basically, insanity triggered by a devilish inner demon would develop into an epidemic of suicides and fear related deaths.

I touched the top of John's hand, and spoke in a solemn tone. "I am familiar with the prophecy and the viable science that supports the theory, John. It is a ghastly thought."

"Amanda, there isn't much time, and I thought you should be the one to tell Antonio."

I gave the old man a soft sympathetic smile. "I am honored to gain your trust and confidence. Please trust; I will honor your request. I will share the warning with Antonio."

He stared into my eyes for the longest time. "Our Antonio is a good student. He feels stronger with you."

I grinned. "I am most flattered, but Antonio is worthy of completing his task independent of me."

The Sage's expression was kind as he raised his eyebrow of doubt.

Thanking him once more I turned to walk back into the shop, John called out to wait.

I watched him hurry across the room to his work counter, and retrieve a blue bag.

"Antonio asked me to make this for you, and I think now is a good time to give it to you." He handed me the soft bag, and I untied the delicate knots that held it closed.

As I tipped it out over my palm, a delicate silver chain spilled out with an intricately painted tiny bag attached to its end. The symbol of a bird in flight in a night sky against the backdrop of a mountain was perfectly completed on a surface no larger than a half dollar. I looked up at John in question.

"The other side holds a representation of 'Hon', the White Bear Kachina; a powerful healer. Inside you will find a stone crystal, one that was given to Antonio by the Chief Priest of the Yuchee. I only touched the stone long enough to insert the chain and place it in the bag, and that was enough for me to know its power. "

As I turned the bag over in my hand, the room seemed to spin for a moment as the crystal inside tumbled. "Why not just set the crystal in a setting and make it into a necklace?"

"Some things are not meant to be flaunted. Some things are not meant to touch the skin of a seeker or a seer. You are both, and even I am not powerful enough to capture that stones essence in a simple setting."

"It is a medicine bag Amanda, a powerful one that captures the symbols of two mighty tribes; I do not know its reason for coming to you, only that you need it now. Wear it close to your body always."

John gave me a brief hug, and then fastened the chain around my neck. As I dropped the small bag beneath my blouse, I felt a thrum that seemed to rumble through my body and move straight to my head. There was a sudden pain, and then for the first time in a long time, I felt a sense of clearness and awareness.

"Amanda, today you must watch for the weasel as you return to Antonio."

Just what does one say to sage advice from a sage?

"Okay, I will. Any particular weasel, or just your average run of the mill New Mexico weasel?"

He replied; "The kind that can cause great damage to the unguarded hen."

That gave me a chill, and for a moment I paused; but I knew

from dealing with John and other men of vision that asking a straight question would not get me a straight answer.

On that note, I left and made my way to the first hair salon I spotted. After all, my plan's guise would not be believable if I did not fulfill my stated purpose. Before entering, I stopped to telephone Antonio as promised. I knew he would yell at me, but still I needed to let him know I was alright.

I pulled out my cell phone and dialed Antonio's.

"Hello."

"Jose', why are you answering Antonio's phone?"

He hesitated. "Antonio handed me his phone, earlier."

"Well, are you going to hand him the phone so I can talk to him?"

"Amanda, I think he is angry that you left. He's worried about you."

I felt stunned, and angry, but mostly hurt. "Okay, thanks." I hung up the phone. This was not at all like Antonio. He seemed to sort of enjoy yelling at me when I upset him.

In my mind, my next task was a secondary necessary and I had not even made an appointment, but as luck would have it, a cancellation left the stylist with an opening. I was relieved, the last thing I wanted to do was drive around looking for a salon.

Although, it was nice to get seated and have the darling dark haired beauty pampering me, I had an awful lot on my mind. I explained, the trim and deep conditioning I wanted, and she went about her work.

Towards the end of my hair session, I felt a bit fidgety and angry. My mind began to spin, and I decided a trip to a couple of the shops in Santa Fe would not make Antonio less angry. So, I paid the girl for her services, and began walking the rustic sidewalks of the downtown area. I loved the Spanish inspired architecture and all the wonderful artisans that lined the streets. I fantasized about walking the same street on Antonio's arm enjoying the fabulous art.

I understood Antonio's love affair with Santa Fe. It was an interesting artsy city with an eclectic mix of people. Entering the darling boutique, I decided I felt like treating myself to something new and exciting to wear. Perhaps, something Antonio would appreciate after his anger subsided. It had been a while since I had taken a little time to shop for something new.

In a flash, I tried on and bought a very snug, bright red, short dress that I was sure would brighten Antonio's mood. With my eye on one more store I stepped out of the boutique and headed in the direction of a lovely little lingerie shop.

The warm sun felt sensational in contrast to the cool November breeze. I surveyed my surroundings as I strolled, then quickly slipped into the closest shop. I moseyed around inside the store, and tried to appear interested in the cheesy souvenir merchandise.

My stalker dressed in black, wore an earpiece and was speaking to seemingly no one at all. I recognized him from Las Vegas, it was the same man Antonio and I had fought while we were there.

Then it hit me; a weasel most dangerous to an unguarded hen –

I was the hen and the stalker was the weasel! Why could men not just say what was on their mind! Even a mystic can provide clarification on dangerous enemies being near!

Positioning myself among the merchandise for camouflage, I put the keys in one hand and situated my Barak/SP-21, in the other. Already happy with my purchase, I used the shopping bag with my new red dress to hide my hand.

A fleeting thought ran through my mind; Antonio would likely kill me himself if I did not come out on top of OPERA's jerk. A deep breath sent me through the door and out into the open streets. My pace was methodical and slow as I sauntered to the door of the Escalade.

Pressing the unlock button, I casually slid into the seat, and started the engine. I placed the Barak in my shopping bag in the seat next to me.

I shifted into drive and pulled away from the curb. Again, I chose to proceed at a slow pace. I wanted to make sure the thug did not lose me. I spoke to myself; it is a less lonely option when one is alone and in a precarious situation. 'Amanda do not give in to the urge, and speed up...this is your chance to nail the guy.'

I looked down at my cell, and brought Antonio's number up then placed it in my pocket. The man was now close behind me. I had to string him a long for a couple more miles. I grew tense waiting, but I had to be patient. If patience is a virtue, I missed out.

Finally, the landscape warned I was getting close to the gate of Antonio's estate. I switched the Escalade to manual shift, and began my game. Downshifting I feigned an engine problem. At first, the jerk nearly rear ended me, but soon he held back just enough to allow my plan to work.

I punched in the code and hoped I was close enough to activate the electronic gate. I continued to create the appearance of a sputtering engine. Just inside, I hit the button and the hood flew up. I grabbed the Barak, jumped out and watched from the slit at the bottom of the raised hood.

My perpetrator had abandoned his car on the road. With a pistol in hand he made his way in my direction. Just as he rounded to the front of the SUV, I gave him a swift kick. The weapon went flying as he landed on the ground in front of me.

Just as I pressed the button on my cell in my pocket, he lunged for his revolver and I fired hitting the ground right next to his knee cap.

Chapter 33

"I'm supposed to have a Ph.D. on the subject of women. But the truth is I've flunked more often than not. I'm very fond of women; I admire them. But, like all men, I don't understand them."
— Frank Sinatra

It was Amanda, she wasn't speaking to me, but I sure as hell heard her.

"Do not underestimate me...I will happily shoot you right between the eyes." Amanda's voice rang clearly through the phone; I had never known Amanda to speak in such a way.

You are on private property now you bastard...and this time you are not going to slither or whatever weasels do; away from justice."

I realized she was on the estate. Her shouts had me yelling for keys. I grabbed the keys...then snatched José. I heard her scream as we raced to the car.

"Lay down."

BLAST! A gun shot. "God, she's been shot, José!"

When we reached the edge of the driveway, I could see Ruger was standing behind Amanda. His pistol also pointed towards the enemy. Ruger moved closer to Amanda, and put his free arm around her.

"Amanda, are you okay?" He asked with a huge grin.

"I am great Ruger. What could be wrong?" Ruger laughed.

The relief, I felt was indescribable. She looked fine. About then anger began boiling my blood, José hugged me.

"She's fine. How in the hell did she manage this situation, José? I wanna kill her."

I left José laughing, and ran to her. I looked over my shoulder to the sound of my father's voice. Joe had driven my Pop to the gate.

José yelled back to him. "Pop, Amanda's fine. She kicked this slug's ass."

Pop showed obvious signs of relief. He asked José. "Did she kill him?"

"Not physically, Pop. She killed other parts of him. Look at the open hood. Amanda tricked the dumb son of a bitch."

I started bitching before I even reached her, "Amanda, how damn ridiculous are you?" I yelled. "You're killing me. Are you TRYING to kill me?"

She glared at me. "Shut up, Antonio, you would not take my call today. You hurt my feelings."

Everyone laughed. I took the gun out of her hand, grabbed her, and kissed her. "Amanda, he could've killed you."

"Antonio, I knew he would not kill me."

"Amanda, how the hell did you know?" My hug picked her up off the ground.

"You don't know a lot of things, Antonio. I have so much to teach you. This is not the first time I have stared at the face of danger. Besides, it is impossible to kill a woman who just had her hair done. Weapons cannot penetrate the force field." She smiled at me.

"You're going to kill me." She was incredible, I knew she could have killed the damn thug, but she didn't. She knew he was much more valuable to us alive. We needed information. Attempted murder charges just might get the man talking.

Pop and José came over to see her. Moving me aside, they hugged her, and Marc rooted his way into the group.

Amanda glanced down. "Antonio, where are your boots?" The question made everyone including me freeze. I didn't have any desire to have that conversation in public.

"Honey, I lost them." I said, shaking my head.

"Okay, I will help you find them. How would you lose your boots?"

I didn't answer. The red lights proved the Troopers had arrived. It was a timely distraction. I drew Amanda into me.

"Well, if it isn't the Doc, twice in one day." The Trooper commented. It was the same Trooper that had arrested me earlier in the day. Yes, I should have stayed in bed.
Amanda looked, "Antonio, what happened?"

"Oh, by the way, Doc, your boots are in my patrol car. They aren't my size so you can have them back. I'll get them out after we take care of our newest situation."
The Trooper was enjoying this entirely too much.

Her tone was fierce. "Antonio, you did not try to find me, did you? It will be a cold winter, if you did."

"No, I took my brother for a ride in Raven. José needs to

lighten up, and he has to get a new, more appropriate wardrobe for New Mexico." I looked at José. "Right, José?"

"Antonio said, I'm boring and he needs to take me shopping." José nodded to reinforce.

"Antonio, do not make your brother lie."

"Honey, it's true. See, you have no reason to punish me. You know, until after Valentine's Day. Amanda, that's too harsh. We've yet to celebrate Thanksgiving."

The Trooper tuned into the conversation, clearly, he was soaking up the details. He turned to remind Amanda. "Miss I'll need a statement from you."

He smiled at me. "You're welcome to go up to the house. I'll come up there to get your statement. In fact, I'll bring your boyfriends boots. Then he can explain why an Anthropologist needs to keep a weapon like the Desert Eagle Mark XIX-.50 AE in his vehicle. Don't get me wrong, it's a great little piece, which I admire, and have ever since I saw the Matrix for the first time; but not a weapon I would leave laying around."

'Bob' was wearing that expression again; the one that said; "not as dumb as I look am I?

After watching me try not to squirm, he turned once more to Amanda; "You are his girlfriend aren't you?" The Trooper enjoyed watching me squirm.

"Yes, I am Amanda Messenger." She informed in an alarmingly stern tone.

"We need to get you in the house," I told her. I started frog stepping her back to Raven.

Amanda insisted on asking; "But Antonio; what about the Escalade?"

"Someone will bring it when they're done."

"They need to know I switched it to manual shift. Can I get my things out of it, real quick?"

"José, will you get her things? Guys, did you hear that? The Escalade is in manual. Manual Amanda, what in the hell were you doing? Come on." Becoming increasingly perplexed, I put her in Raven, and took her up to the house.

My father and brother chose to oversee how the law enforcement handled the situation. Pop telephoned Michael Starr, who helped get the charges dropped against me earlier in the day. They wanted to increase our chances of gaining some information, having actually captured one of OPERA's men. They hoped Michael Starr's presence would help secure the possibility.

I assisted Amanda out of the car. She asked. "Antonio, why did you not put shoes on after you lost your boots?"

Oh brother, I thought. She was going to end up busting me over this deal. "Amanda, I'd just returned from losing my boots, and had not even made it upstairs to put another pair on when that rather urgent call came through my phone."

"I see. Antonio, did you have a bad day?"

I decided to humor her. "You were gone, were you not?"

Hell, she knew I was trying to distract her. I don't think she really cared to know, she loved a good game. I knew, I would tell her everything once the guilt ate at me long enough.

She responded, "Well… I am here now."

I smiled. "And you made one hell of an entrance, Amanda."

"It worked, Antonio you are not refusing to talk to me any longer." She kept talking. "Antonio, I almost felt guilty for leaving today, and in a way - I did. I don't want to feel guilty." Our eyes met when I spoke.

I felt like such a fool. "Amanda, you shouldn't feel guilty."

She held eye contact. "I want to do things, Antonio, some of those things I want to do with you. There are a couple things… I do not wish to do with you. I want the freedom to do both." She hugged me.

"Amanda, that's not too much to want." The woman has the damndest way of making me feel guilty. She had lacked freedom for so much of her life. Instead of freeing her, I repeated the imprisonment. How did I become so stupid? I started to think I deserved the slammer.

"Antonio, I fought back today. That jerk was following me. At first, I was scared, but not that he would hurt me. I was afraid for you. The longer he followed me, the more it annoyed me.

You see, right from the beginning, I decided to trick him. I drove slowly, I mean really slow. It made him crazy. I knew if he had the slightest chance to nab me, he would. More importantly, he pissed me off. Antonio he pissed me off more than you do."

"Amanda, that's unbelievable." My focus was locked on her, I knew she wasn't finished.

"You did give me some freedom, Antonio," she paused.

I was confused. "Amanda, I don't understand."

"For the first time since I became a mother, I wasn't worried about my boys having no one. I knew you would handle it, not that I wanted to die. Love and trust makes freedom. When I left this morning, I knew you would want to kill me when you discovered I was gone. Most importantly, I knew it would not last. That is freedom.

It was ugly for you not to talk to me. Nevertheless, I still knew you would forgive me. Please, do not think I wanted to take advantage of your forgiveness."

I understood, she was nuts, but I understood. She was also right.

"Amanda, I couldn't take your call. Honey, you knew that, didn't you? I would have taken the call if I could."

"Yes, I suspect, mostly because you would prefer to yell at me. That was out of character."

"Amanda, please don't make me explain now, I'll tell you everything later. I was in the slammer. They don't allow such calls from women in the slammer." My own confession made me want to laugh.

"You mean, prison?"

"Jail, not prison, the charges were dropped. For God's sake,

I wasn't convicted." She was sure to make the event monumental.

"Oh my God, Antonio, OPERA…"

"No, Amanda. It had nothing to do with OPERA." She never ceased to entertain me.

"Antonio you would be quite the piece of meat in a jail. Thank God you did not have to spend the night." I felt insulted by her implication.

"Amanda, how could you think such a thing? I'm not some pretty boy. God, Amanda, do you think I'm weak?" Now, I was appalled.

"No, Antonio. You are hot and sexy. You know, appealing. Antonio, you are not one-bit pretty, or weak. You are really, really hot."

She paused, tapping one finger on her sexy little lips; "How long until they will question me, Antonio?"

I laughed. "I don't know. Why do you ask?"

"No reason, I want to get it over with."

"Amanda, you surprise me." I didn't want to pass up the opportunity.

"Antonio, what are you talking about?"

"You're turned on at the thought of me spending the day in jail."

"You wish." She started to walk away from me.

I called out as she started up the stairs. "I don't have to wish. It's true!" She was never dull, or boring.

Chapter 34

"Nothing is unbeatable, just harder to beat."
— *Ian Sutton*

While the authorities questioned Amanda about the day's incidents, I decided, rather than pacing the floors, I would review documents and lab results concerning the Chosen. The family law firm in Miami was a tremendous help in providing background information.

I smiled, believing we were getting closer to the end of this journey. Maybe I would get my reward. No doubt, if I did, it would be a better deal than Humanity's. I really thought, I might get the girl. I wasn't sure I would ever receive an answer from her. Amanda never answered, and always remained vague about the future.

Undoubtedly, I wasn't very good at the whole thing, but Amanda seemed to like that most. She would never admit to the concept, but she liked my disabilities the best. The screwy woman and I somehow clicked.

Marc came into my office. "Antonio, they said you need to answer some questions."

I smiled at my little brother, "No problem, Marc."

"Amanda was something else today, she was one pissed off babe." Marc laughed at his own words.

I joked with my brother. "Amanda? Marc, she's sweet, how

could you think such a thing?"

"Antonio, a woman who pulls out a revolver and shoots isn't sweet. Amanda is fantastic, not sweet." Marc qualified his reasoning. I laughed and patted my brother's back.

"Marc, she's a pain in the ass, and I'm the idiot sitting around thinking about how lucky I am to have that pain in the ass."

"Hey Marc, tomorrow we've got to take José to buy some clothes. He can't run around here looking like a Miami lawyer. Look, Italian leather shoes, no socks…he might as well get a tattoo and an earring."

"Well, if Amanda can go to the salon alone, between the three of us, maybe we can get our brother some clothes and manage to stay alive." Marc added.

I continued the pun. "We could always take Amanda as our bodyguard."

José caught up with us. "What are you two laughing about?"

Marc answered. "We're taking you shopping for clothes, with Amanda as our bodyguard."

José chuckled a little. "Amanda can't shoot anything else for at least three days. They're considering charging her for shooting the revolver without a license, or permit in New Mexico."

I was furious. "Bullshit, José."

José cut me off. "Antonio, shut up, we have it under control. These investigators are helpful. Since she pulled onto the private property before she fired, we don't see any roadblocks.

Obviously, the gun was in your Escalade, you have a weapons license. That could save our asses. We are contending you are a careless dumbass for leaving the Desert Eagle in the Escalade, luckily she used your gun, not hers."

I shook my head. "That damn Trooper will have no problem thinking I'm an idiot. He's still calling me 'Doc' with sarcasm."

José agreed. "He didn't like you much, Antonio."

Amanda emerged from questioning. She smiled at the three of us talking. "Antonio it is contagious, I almost had to take a trip to the slammer." Her voice noted sarcasm.

"Yeah, José told me. Amanda - that would be over my dead body. Has anyone seen Pop?"

José answered. "He talked his way into sitting with Michael Starr during the questioning. Always the Judge, he wanted to make sure this guy did it right. Michael is a great attorney, Pop is just the Judge." We all agreed.

Right then, Michael entered. "Antonio, could I speak with you?"

"Sure."

"Antonio, is there some place we could speak in private?" Michael clarified.

"We can go up to my office."

Upstairs, I shut the office door, and directed him to sit in one of the club chairs. "Michael, is there a problem? They're not going to charge Amanda, are they?"

"No, that's not the problem, but Antonio; I realized listening to Amanda answer questions that I'm coming in on something in its eleventh hour. It's clear your incident earlier today wasn't the result of some middle-aged regression. In other words, you weren't chasing a woman out of some libido-driven stupidity. You thought she was in real danger, clearly that's true." He waited for a response.

"You're correct, Michael. I assume this creates a concern on your part. Please, be frank."

"Exactly, I don't feel right about you answering questions down there tonight, unless I know what's going on. Now, you can tell me, or not that's up to you. Regardless, even with your dad present, I can't protect someone, or something I know nothing about.

We have two choices. One, I can go down and tell the investigators we'll talk with them tomorrow, so we may consult. Meaning, you tell me just what in the hell is going on with all of you. Two, I just refute myself, you get somebody else, or go without. I know Amanda was walking a line in there that made her uncomfortable. Maybe I'm afraid of crossing the line.

That concerns me, and leaves me afraid of being unable to protect her. Ruger's not here for nothing. Not to mention, your family of lawyers from Miami, aren't vacationing. You're a world-renowned anthropologist, there's something huge going on here. I'm willing to help, if I can. If you aren't comfortable with that - Hey, I understand. I'm a professional, relying on information, but I can't handle dealing with something hidden from me." He was direct. I liked that.

"Michael, I apologize, you're absolutely correct. In my own defense, earlier it didn't seem necessary to explain. Of course, I didn't know that Amanda would capture and shoot at someone today. If you'll listen, we need your help.

Understand, it's complicated, Michael, and you may want to stall them until tomorrow afternoon. Believe me; you've got to give yourself some time to digest."

"I will tell Maria you'll stay here for dinner, if you will agree to join us."

Michael agreed. "Truthfully, Antonio, I'm baffled. It will relieve my curiosity."

"Michael, get ready. You're about to take a trip that will make you feel like you're in the middle of a movie." I opened the door so Michael could handle the waiting investigators. I followed him hoping to check on Amanda. I sauntered out by the pool, knowing she would be there.

"Amanda?"

"Yes?"

"I had a conversation with Michael. He sensed we had something going on here. I agreed to go over this situation with him. Is that ok?"

She grinned at my question. "That is a wise decision for a jailbird."

"Thanks, how long will I hear about that?"

"It depends on how long you want me around."

"Then I will hear about it for the rest of my life."

I bent over, my face close. My lips just short of hers, my tongue traced there lines. I spoke allowing my breath to tickle her lips.

"Tonight I'm going to do things to you, wild things. Think about it." I lifted my head enough to gain eye contact, and winked at her.

"Every time I do that, Amanda, you'll think about all the erotic things I'm going to do to you…how it will feel…how long until you will feel me doing them to you."

I winked again.

"See, it works. You're longing for me to play with you already." I stood to walk away.

She scolded me. "Antonio, that is mean."

I turned towards her, grinning, and winking, then left.

I caught sight of Michael. "Michael, give me a few minutes, I'm getting everything organized so we can be productive."

"Go ahead, Antonio, I understand."

I needed to find Pop and my brothers. On my way to locate them, I crossed paths with Amanda. She looked at me. I winked, and continued to walk past her.

I found Pop. "Pop, I think we need Michael Starr. He's waiting for me to give him some details and information." I paused for his reply.

"I think that's a wise decision, Son."

Chapter 35

"A woman's heart should be so hidden in God that a man has to seek Him just to find her."
— *Max Lucado*

After dinner, I wanted to make sure there weren't any gaps in the information I provided to Michael Starr, so I invited him up to my office for a drink. On my way up the stairs, I called out to Amanda, and winked. She tried to pretend she was annoyed. Michael and I enjoyed a brandy. He seemed trustworthy, and ready to assist us in reaching our goals. I felt secure knowing he was on our side.

Soon, we joined the others downstairs to call it a night. I was happy when I had successfully sent everyone on their perspective way. I sent another wink to Amanda before detouring.

Earlier, Pop said he wanted to see me in private. This was an unusual request as an adult I could only remember a couple of times I had actually been alone with my father. I walked back, tapped on my father's door, and went in.

"Pop."

My father's demeanor seemed oddly soft. "You make me very proud, Antonio. I'm your father, and I see your heart is good. Amanda is blessed and lucky to be loved by my beautiful son."

I was speechless. My father's kindness, so out of character, it frightened me. We had spent a lifetime of disagreeing. It was unnatural.

"Pop."

My father shook his head, not wanting me to speak. "Antonio, I brought a gift for you."

I couldn't imagine. My Dad was not actually a gift giver. I watched as he lifted the pillow on the bed uncovering a box. He handed it to me.

"You give this to your Amanda, but only when you know the time is right."

Flabbergasted, I opened the box containing my Grandmother's ring. My eyes filled as I stared at my father. I knew, in my Father's soul, this was the quintessential gift. The ring held monumental importance in my family. Through the years I heard the story many times. In 1960 when my family left Cuba, they had to hide the ring from Castro's thugs to get it out of the country.   Emotion overwhelmed me.

"Pop, I know how special this is to you. I know how special your Mama was to you. Despite all that's happened between us, Pop, I feel that same love and respect for you. We'll always love and respect this gift for what it represents."

I embraced my father. I couldn't tell him that I wasn't sure Amanda and I would ever marry.

I put the box in my pocket, smiled and left my father. After, the lights were off, and the alarm set, I stopped off at my office to hide the ring.

I entered the bedroom and shut the door. With my back against the door, I stood staring at Amanda. She came to me. Our eyes transfixed on one another. Without words we undressed. Amanda was so close. I could feel her eyelids open and close.

In an awkward passionate move, we made our way to the bed. I threw back the bed cover, and gently coaxed her to lie back. With her body flattened into a vulnerable position, I whispered. "Amanda, it's your turn."

She placed her fingers in the waves of my hair. In a brisk motion, I clutched her wrist. Her eyes stared into me.

"Submit to me, this time let me love you."

She sounded delirious. "Antonio, what if I can't?"

Uninhibited, I observed before me, her beautiful unprotected body. After a moment, I transferred my focus to my path. My mouth bathed her lips until they became succulent and swollen. Her shimmering eyes mesmerized me.

Above her, my movements suspended, her eyes hypnotized me as I inhaled her breath. In an erotic rhythm, her exhales became my inhales. The psychedelic glisten of her eyes was a narcotic that made me high. Even in the absence of her touch, it heightened my desire.

In spite of my delirium, my odyssey continued with the slide of my hand behind her neck. Her delicious neck became an offering. I raised her as if I were a vampire preparing to feed on her mesmerizing flavor. My fingers explored the lines, and my mind designed the blueprint.

Breathing against her neck, I evoked a blanket of goose bumps to cover her. My teeth skimmed the sensitive spot just below her ear, causing a sweet sound to escape her lips. Maneuvering her earlobe into my mouth, she moaned, turning, wanting more from me. I placed my lips at the opening of her ear. "Amanda, tell me you want me."

She spoke with more breath than sound. "Please, Antonio."

My breath became more difficult. "Amanda, I want to love you."

I gently returned her neck to a resting position. On the journey to maneuver her hills and valleys, my mouth became the chariot travelling through her body's terrain. Charming her softly, I played her skin as an instrument to evoke her ascension.

Reaching, arching, silently, she begged me for more. I touched her skin and fondled her breasts. Breaking the silence, her heavy breaths held me captivated in a state of delirium. The glisten from her peaks caused my mouth to moisten.

Both hands cupped one of her luscious breasts, slowly, with a gentle caress, I opened passion's door. Amanda's heart, I wanted most. In this place, I hoped my love would vibrate into physical waves that penetrated her heart.

The sound of her, surrendered an intense song, my head rose to witness. Transferring as my song, my fingers strummed her body. On fire, she squirmed from beneath my soft touches.

"Talk to me, honey."

Drunk, she fell into the covers, without respite my mouth caressed along her length. She belted to a sitting position, and grabbed my head. In a quick reaction, I gently gripped her waist to place her back where I could have her.

"Antonio." She could barely speak.

"Come on, talk to me sweetheart. Tell me."

I looked into her now heavy eyes.

"Antonio, I need to touch you."

"No, I'm making love to you."

I resumed my journey of her body; my fingertips like feathers tickled her skin. She trembled from my touches. Ascending her body, I paused above her, holding my weight with my hands, my back relaxed and straight. With muscles taut, I balanced over her quivering body.

My mouth consumed hers…her noises echoed through my cheeks. Her body begged for me, as I covered her face with kisses. Unable to contain her yearning need, she pleaded.

"Antonio, please."

I rose, as my body swayed above. Lightly, I brushed her with my tickling torment. She squirmed beneath to deepen the touch.

"Amanda, trust me." Kissing her, my lips absorbed the vibrations from her neck. Understanding my journey must continue, I accepted that a part of my Enchantress would remain veiled from me for now.

Her gasp matched by mine. Positioned, I groaned her name.

The beautiful temptress, wild beneath me, trembled and shook. As I loved her, her pulses rolled across me. I felt her love. The magnitude of her modulation caught me off guard as shockwaves rippled through me.

"Amanda, stay with me."

Chapter 36

"A wise man can see more from the bottom of a well than a fool can from a mountain top."
— Unknown

Marc had worked hard to keep up with OPERA's financial progress. As a financial broker and fund manager, Marc possessed great insight into the numbers that supported OPERA"s ascension. He was on a mission to discover where their unlimited funding was rooted.

Through the years, Marc and I often consulted one another on financial, and investment matters. From a distance, Marc advised me. Likewise, Marc respected my sense for the market and investments. We habitually shared our financial knowledge, and it was lucrative for both of us.

I enjoyed being around Marc. He was the younger brother most like me. Where I was somewhat of a rebel, Marc was a more of a modern traditionalist who, unlike me, chose to stay in Miami, near the family and to be close to a financial center. Miami boasted at being one of the best places in the world for finance. The only other logical choice for Marc would be New York, which hardly appealed to him.

I always suspected Marc might eventually take a walk on the wild side, and leave Miami. His wife, Elisabeth, played the determining role. I didn't know how the birth of baby Cecelia would influence their future decisions.

"Marc, go ahead, take a seat."

"How are Elisabeth, and Cecelia? Are you in trouble for staying here on the Project?"

"Elisabeth and Cecelia are fine. I hope you don't mind, but I promised her she could come out here when the situation became safe."

"Mind, are you kidding? I would love it! I've wanted to have my family visit for years. Having Cecelia here would be a blast, without the side effects."

Marc laughed at me. "Antonio, you're nuts."

"Yeah, so I'm told, daily. You have some numbers for me, little brother?"

"Yeah, you won't want to laugh at these numbers though. Amanda's correct. Financially, OPERA is strong, and has practically taken control of all property.

The government owns the mortgage market. The two brother and sister mortgage companies they acquired, now have unlimited funding status from the Federal Government. The two are now proud owners of 78% of the country's mortgages, with 148 billion tax payer dollars in the pot."

I was amazed, and it showed; "Marc…no shit…78%?"

"Really, there's more. It's bleak."

Feeling ill, I insisted he continue.

"There appears to have been a mass seizure of land. José is checking out several court cases involving the government's acquisition of land. I've run across an unprecedented amount.

Separate from the mortgages, and named seizures, they own 27.1% of all land, and 81% of the state of Nevada.

The mortgage siblings - the Government presented its involvement through the couple to the American people, as a way to reduce foreclosures with the prospect that both would soon survive on their own. Instead, it's the means of a giant property takeover by the government.

During the past six months, the two have foreclosed on a property every thirty seconds. In March, the foreclosures were equal to the sum of all the homes in Seattle, Washington. This does not even begin to touch on all of the imminent domain cases that we dug up. You will have to wait for those astonishing numbers"

"Damn…Marc, do you know how much property they have secured?"

"No, Antonio, I'm trying to obtain those figures. They are delaying the release of statistics, strategically."

Marc continued. "Over the past few weeks income from the private sector has shown signs of sinking. We're at an all-time low of only 42% coming from the private sector. As you can see, 58% is coming from the public payrolls. It is damn bleak, Antonio, and job loss is on the rise again. By definition this imbalance constitutes a socialist state"

"No kidding, I was not aware of that fact. The oil rigs, what's going to happen there?"

"They're still shut down. I'm unclear about the future status, but it's directly impacting a minimum of 20,000 jobs, and who knows how many indirectly."

The hits just kept on coming; "Anything else?"

"Insurance companies are already dropping off in response to the health care amendment. Rates are skyrocketing over the four-year frontloading period. It's a mess. They're opportunists, selling a rosy picture, without the facts. They are also discussing a mass amnesty for illegal immigrants as we speak."

"Thanks Marc."

After Marc left I noticed the office seemed to be in a state of disarray. Before starting work on my speech for the University, I attempted to organize the mess. I waded through the stacks, and filed documents that we weren't currently using.

A disc fell out of a stack of Press Releases. The words printed on the disk were, Amanda Messenger, MRI. I was stunned as I noticed the date coincided with Amanda's journey in the Escalade to get her hair done.

With the disk out of its case, my hands shaking, I slipped it in my computer's drive. My heart rate accelerated. The disk commands lit up on the screen. Positioning the mouse on the file, I opened to view what I feared most.

The summary reading, entered by the Radiologist, presented a serious set of circumstances. The one tumor had now grown to six compromising Amanda's brain, vision and facial nerves, in addition to her hearing. I certainly understood the Mossad's concern for her health. Her condition was worsening at a terrifying pace, leaving her vulnerable for an immediate emergency.

I opened the file to view the actual MRI, not an expert, but familiar. I needed Amanda's reading from the Doctor's visit. What could I do? After saving the file to my hard drive, I put the disk back in the case.

Deflated, and at a loss for answers, I sat comatose, in fear and contemplation. In a few short weeks, Amanda recreated my entire world into a whole new image. The implications, all the possibilities, were unimaginable, and left me with only one alternative. Saving her was the only choice. How, would become the focus…the only alternative. Funny, I should have known that getting her hair done was merely a decoy for a greater, more important reason to sneak out that day. It was not at all like her, and I should have known. I couldn't fail her. Saving her would become my new quest, a battle I would go straight back to hell for to win.

Chapter 37

"We are the mirror as well as the face in it."
-Rumi

Prior to the news about Amanda's condition, I was feeling pretty confident. We had kept OPERA at bay with weapons and clever manipulation. By anyone's definition, we had not backed down. We were a small force weakening their large attempts to gain control of us and The Scrolls. Unfortunately, none of these skills could save or protect Amanda from the enemy inside her head. All the weapons, ammunition, and intelligence in the world would not defeat her most prevalent enemy. The idea made me feel insignificant, and most of all helpless. With the brutal news fresh in my mind, I bolted down the stairs from the office with renewed dedication.

I looked around, and eventually found Joe outside tending to the landscape. "Joe, have you seen Amanda? I can't find her anywhere."

"Antonio, I saw her walking in the lavender. I didn't disturb her...the spirits surrounded her."

Even for a man of science like me, there are times when the word of the spirits is most important. Perhaps in the darkest of dark times every man is a believer. So I asked my native friend that, which I most wanted to know.

"Joe, she's not going..." I couldn't finish, but my old friend understood.

"It has not been decided, Antonio."

"What can I do? Joe, you know me. For 15 years, you and Maria…you're my family. Joe, you know I'm better with her."

Unusual for Joe, a soft, slight smile transformed his face.

"Antonio, to my wife, you are a son. To me, you are the son of the Ancestors. Amanda showed you the door. You opened the door. You can't be better because of her.
Antonio dig deeper you will understand. I have watched you grow these years. I could love no other man more than I do you my friend. You will see. Remember, the ancestors will show you. The Father's want you to succeed. They are the light."

My body trembled as I embraced, yet another of my favorite teachers. Struggling to make sense, but still not understanding, Joe's words gave me hope.

"Joe." The man, who was often my father, quieted me.

"Son, we do not always need words."

I nodded and began the reluctant path through the pungent lavender to Amanda. A glimpse between two branches in the breeze exposed her location to me. She appeared serene on the old platform that extended into the pond. Her feet hung over the edge. Obviously, she went there to find answers.

Like Joe, and the other Native wise men, Amanda sought her answers from Nature. God and the Ancestors spoke to her. I knew it with undaunted certainty. My greatest fear came from God, and the Ancestors. Afraid they wanted her on the Other

Side. I feared I would be powerless to make her survive.

My heart pounded in distress, waves of weakness, and helplessness flowed through my veins, and now my nerves. This feeling I held in a place beyond tears. The pain threatened to dissolve who I was…

Thrust into a state, nothing penetrated, not even the sweet smell of lavender Amanda once made me notice, not even the dynamic sensations our love making sent through my body, nothing could pierce my Wall of Dread. The power of trepidation paralyzed my reason.

In clear view, I saw the only love my life had known. I froze deciding to turn back. In fantasy, I saw myself drop to the ground, to hold my aching gut. Longing to roll on the ground, I yearned to succumb to the agony. Turning, I gave into my inner commands and positioned my feet to run away.

Her voice echoed from a distance, though she sat within sight. "Antonio, why are you leaving?"

The simple question she asked had an answer too complex to provide. Somehow, she understood.

"Antonio, what has you in so much pain?"

Knowing I needed to answer, I was mute, and without the mastery to overcome. It left me immobilized. Never had I fallen so hard, engulfed within the grips of the Demon of Anguish.

Her unselfish words were a knife, slicing my guts. "Antonio, I cannot breath if I am causing you pain."

Saturated with guilt, I fell to my knees, doubled over I cried.

Amanda didn't cry or touch me, her compassion had not escaped, but still her reason took center stage.

"Why are you defeated and giving up on my life? Why do you look for answers you do not want to find?"

The truth she spoke worsened my pain. The truth literally strangled me. I began to choke on the reality that clotted in my throat.

"Antonio, I am not dead, look at me, I breathe. What do you want to do? I can laugh and love. I can dance and make love with you. Don't bury me yet. Help me stay alive."

I clenched in pain. Of course, I wanted nothing more than to keep her alive and vibrant. Unfortunately, I was only a man, unable to defeat the Gods whom wanted her. They all believed me as a Prodigy, a Superman, The Personification of the Divine, but I was nothing more than a Man.

Without Amanda, I couldn't believe it mattered, not the Scrolls, not the '13' Chosen, not even the 13th Gate. Together, with her, it all mattered. Amanda gave me reason.

Like Solomon without Sheba, it would all fall apart. Solomon turned his back on God with the loss of his Sheba. Sure, he sent her home with unending love and glorious gifts. How could he be angry at his beautiful love, even when she left?

While she stayed with Solomon, Sheba's gifts were abundant, and meant only for him. When her kingdom needed her, he understood. Sheba didn't deserve his anger, for she did nothing wrong. Refusing to fight, he abandoned God, and pretended to replace him with lesser Deities.

Would King Solomon have changed the outcome, had he fought or even tried to keep his Sheba?

Does God make or bind all marriages? Maybe, God brings some together even joins them. Perhaps, marriage isn't even the same as being joined by God. He would, or could, and surely did bless marriage, but it just wasn't the same as God joining two souls.

God never interferes with man's 'will'. It remains 'Free Will'. Man chooses everything he manifests from the gifts and circumstances of God. Does God make the components available? Are the ingredients just lying about? I wasn't sure, but Amanda was right. She was alive, not dead. If I looked beyond my own pain, could I find the components to save her?

I glanced up at the most beautiful part of me, knowing I couldn't grieve for its loss. Instead, I must fight to keep it all whole. Her hand reached to me, all I had to do was accept it. This time grasping her hand was not enough. I knew my fingers must go between hers to intertwine, grip, and make a double-sided fist to lock hands with her, ready to fight.

The creation from the Ones couldn't make us strong enough as individuals. Joe understood. Hell, it didn't even make sense. The One we became when we were together - could 'Slay the Dragons'.

Reaching out to take her hand, I entwined my fingers with hers. Once weaved tightly together, our combined fist, created a connection between our souls.

The hand, the symbol of man's ability to connect the subconscious with the physical world, is the bond that bridges the gaps of all intrinsic beliefs. Our hands, now locked together, connected every fiber of Amanda's existence with every cell of my being.

Together, our individual worlds joined as one, and I saw into her beautiful depths. I knew what I needed to do.

Chapter 38

"The young man knows the rules, but the old man knows the exceptions."
— *Oliver Wendell Holmes Sr.*

I settled in to construct my speech. Addressing audiences, in particular the endowment, had gained me a great deal of recognition. However, this one was different. Professionally, this would be my defining moment. All the successes of the past would be forgotten, though the idea seemed oddly insignificant.

In the past, my professional persona remained light years away from my private self. At this juncture, I was unsure if I could keep them separate.

The words in my speech would live far beyond my years. The news would travel to the four corners of the earth. Every news agency on the planet would make The Scrolls the lead story. In the future, each time Solomon or The Scrolls appeared on the search engines, my words would appear. The pressure caused a great struggle within me. Where should I start? Where should I end?

The blank computer screen stared back at me. All these years I had distanced the two selves, and it was natural. Now, I had no clue, how I managed it before. No longer were the two separated. There was only one integrated man.

Standards dictated that I share my truth, a truth that would

likely be considered politically incorrect. The interpretation of
The Scrolls suggested the political correctness instituted by
society had kept us in a stalemate. Somewhere along the
timeline, we had failed to move forward. Real change quit
happening inside of us.

We no longer could use above to see below. The mirror we
once used to see what was hidden within us had become
clouded. Mother Nature kept changing in a forward motion, but
we the people did not. Could the speech be meaningful to the
journey?

I felt it arrogant to believe that it could be. Yet, what sort of
obligation did I have within its context? I had never presented a
personal public testimonial, and I wasn't sure the desire rested
within me.

I smiled, realizing Amanda would only share the experience
from a personal perspective. Otherwise, she wouldn't do it at
all. The harsh reality was the truth might end my career. Hell,
did I care? What was more important, my legacy as an
anthropologist or my legend as a man?

I let my head fall back against the chair. Closing my eyes, I
drifted back to the beginning of my quest. Soon, in my mind's
eye, an image began to emerge from the pieces. Why did
OPERA and even the right wing militia want to suppress the
information in The Scrolls? It suddenly made sense, to scare the
hell out of the people.

Scared people were easier to control. The changes, especially in the cosmos would be more frightening to an unsuspecting public. It would also open the door to the belief that the world shared a common enemy, thus producing the perfect recipe for one world government. Much of the information in The Scrolls was already in circulation. Many ancient cultures understood the cycles, but the Mayans, Hopi, and Egyptians did not have the impact that the words of King Solomon would. Solomon was recognized as the wisest of all men by all three monotheistic religions.

I realized, I had missed one important part of the translation, tomorrow. Today was once tomorrow, and tomorrow is always the next day. When does tomorrow become today? Does it become today the day after it is written or the day after it is read? In Hebrew the meaning seemed more perpetual. Shalom means until the next day. In Spanish, mañana, much like the English tomorrow, simply means the next day. It was ridiculous to believe, the next day would never come, despite its perpetual implications.

A tap on the door distracted me. Michael Starr and my father entered. Michael was carrying a folder. I sighed, wondering what new problem had surfaced. He handed me the documents.

"Your father has single handedly secured the Summit. I took care of the pertinent local law."

I opened the file, and looked up at Pop. He spoke first; "Son, I feared once the facts were made public, a fight for it could get fierce. The present ownership could have been annoyed by the escalating interest; I secured the deal with a nominal effort."

And to think Pop knew nothing of the treasure Amanda and I found.

Chapter 39

"Everything in the universe has a rhythm, everything dances."
— Maya Angelou

I caught a glimpse of Amanda sitting by the pool. Near the guesthouse I picked up the giant duffle bag I had hid, and threw it over my back. . I slipped around the back to the lab entrance, and entered the security system code. The door slammed behind me.

"You know I could have a gun in your back."

Startled, I shouted. "Damn, Amanda! What in the hell are you doing?"

"I'm following your awesomeness around."

I wasn't amused.

"Antonio, you said this place was not off-limits to me. Did you change your mind?"

Sounding huffy, I exclaimed; "Certainly not!"

"Perhaps you want to tell me what is going on?"

"No, perhaps I don't want to tell you."

"Okay, bye."

She walked to the door.

"Amanda, stop right there," I commanded. Saying she was aggravated would be an understatement.

"Antonio if you don't want me, I can take a hint."

"Amanda, the moment you open the door you'll set the

damn alarm off."

"Now, I am a prisoner with a captor who does not want me."

"Cut the drama, Amanda."

"There is no drama—when it is the truth! You are about to do something foolish. Let me out of here. Go ahead, do whatever you were planning."

What in the hell did she know? This one part of her annoyed the hell out of me.

"Amanda, why did you come out here?"

"I wanted to see you..."

Rolling my eyes, she had me frustrated. "You're getting hives."

"No, I am not."

"Prove it!"

"See."

"Amanda, you have hives."

Looking down at her chest, she saw that she did. "Sometimes...wanting you gives me hives."

"Have it your way."

"Open the door. Let me out of here. I hate it here anyway. That is probably why I have hives. I think it is moldy somewhere."

I guessed there were artifacts inside with mold. Walking to the door, I put in the security code.

"Antonio, you need a ventilation specialist here." She left

without as much as a glance.

A ventilation specialist; where did she come up with such things? Why in the hell did she hate this place so much?

Unzipping my duffle bag, I started to think, and wondered if Amanda's hives were from mold. Disarming the alarm, I realized she might have actually been having a reaction, and need an injection.

Damn her, I thought, as I looked upon her trail of clothing leading to my office. She expected me to come to her. Worse, she wanted me to know that she knew I would. I wanted to turn around and leave, but fat chance of that happening.

Inside the office door, I couldn't see her. Eventually, I surmised she was in one of the tall club chairs. I took a deep breath before moving in front of her, annoyed with myself, I folded my arms in front of me.

She ordered. "Sit down, Antonio."

Reluctantly I gave in and sat.

"My sweet Antonio, why are you so distraught?"

The audacity of the words could make a man burst. "Amanda, I'm whipped."

She continued the game. "Antonio, I cannot do the punishment torture thing, it does not suit me."

"Come on, you're torturing me now."

With her hand on my cheek, she spoke to me.

"Why did you come?"

"I feared you were having an allergic reaction."

With one determined tug on my shirt, she pulled it over my head. "Do not be cranky."

Unable to control my response, I grinned at the Temptress.

"I want to make you feel better, my love."

She was feeding me shit, and I didn't even care. Everything about it was insane. Standing between my legs, she removed her bra as I watched with eager eyes.

"Does that help your mood?" She waited, I didn't answer.

Her hands tickled the edges of her panties as she asked me. "Will this change your demeanor?"

I smiled, and she looked positively arrogant as she sat on my lap. "I am sorry I made you so cranky."

Closing my eyelids, I felt her body rub against mine. It felt warm and erotic. Mind, body, and soul, She was my playmate. The erotic pain was a perfect reward worth her torture. Truth is I wouldn't want my playmate any other way.

"Antonio, I am missing something." She made me laugh aloud. I nodded and stood.

"You knew."

"Damn, Amanda. Come on, you've got me."

Chapter 40

"To fear is one thing. To let fear grab you by the tail and swing you around is another."
— *Katherine Paterson, Jacob Have I Loved*

I returned to my lab with my legs still in a Jell-O like state from Amanda's seduction. Quickly, I picked up my duffle, and left. Normally, I would drive, but even the sound of the Gator would get attention, I didn't want to attract.

With brisk strides, I was determined to make it to the old Native ruins not far from the underground shelter at the back of my property. Once I reached the cistern and opened my duffle, I prepared to enter and retrieve the Scrolls from its top-secret hiding place. No one knew where I had hid them, not even Amanda. Although, I had tried to tell her, she didn't want to know.

Trying to remain completely covert, I removed a retractable camouflage umbrella, one of the very same I used many times on location in the desert. Unfolded, it not only provided ample shade, but also blocked the vision of any unwanted watchers. I doubted the likelihood, but was sure the Government, including OPERA, had the technology to watch me at all times. I just didn't understand how they would have somebody, sitting, watching, 24 hours a day.

There was no time, with the final stages in place, it was all or nothing, and I was no fool. With cloak and perfect reason, my ruse was in place.

I'm just enjoying the back edge of my property, underneath the comfort of a Giant Umbrella. Besides, the Estate was locked down like Fort Knox. No way was some bunch of fascists getting in without an Army. I didn't care what side of the political spectrum they claimed their allegiance stood.

My diving gear on, the safety line hooked into position, I anchored then stepped off the side, and descended into the cavity for the Scrolls. I plunged down several feet into the murky water. There was no room to swim in the confines of the narrow cemented walls. Descending about 20 feet down, I spotted the door to the chamber. I popped it open with the crowbar, and removed the waterproof safe box containing the Scrolls. Without hesitation, I allowed myself to surface.

I hoisted my body over the edge. Standing, I reached for the duffle and placed the armored box inside its depths. Out of nowhere, I felt a kick from behind. The punches came at me, and I shouted. "Amanda, what in the hell is wrong with you?"

I grabbed her wrists. Despite the restraint, she continued to punch me. In between right crosses I noticed her tears.

"What's wrong?"

"You scared me!" Her voice screamed.

"How in the hell did I scare you?"

"You were down there too long."

"Amanda, your imagination has run away with you. I'm fine. Look, please, don't kick my shins, it hurts…Calm down."

I wrapped my arms around her, and drew her close against my body. I tried to talk, but she went ballistic; kicking and screaming. Managing to free one hand, I threw back the mask that covered my face, with too much force. It fell back into the cistern. I tightened my hold around her.

Screaming into my chest, she shouted. "You are going to make sure you die. I wish I had never laid eyes on you!"

"You don't mean that. Amanda – how did you get this worked up?"

"See, you pretend to be stupid."

"Amanda, I'm not pretending anything. How long did you think I was in there?"

"Forever!"

It was wrong, but I couldn't help myself, the laughter escaped me. Sorry afterwards, I flinched from the brutal kick I took to the shin.

"Damn it, Amanda that hurt!"

"Well, then drown yourself, I don't care."

After wiggling away from me, she took off. I was, frustrated, but still, I chased her.

"Amanda, we need this area to stay private, if anyone knew about the things that are back here, well, it could be dangerous."

Turning, she glanced at me. "What about me, in case you got in trouble?"

"Honey, your sense of timing needs work. It's an abstract mess at best."

"Antonio, you are getting ugly." Secretly, I loved it when she said that to me.

"You could have provided me with a stopwatch, Einstein."

Laughing I said. "Who's talking ugly now?"

"I knew you were planning to do something stupid hours ago, you blew it in the lab. I hate that place, so I had to go to alternate plan B. Your escapade has taken the whole afternoon."

"Amanda, the hives came because you lied."

"No, I am allergic to the room you do that stuff in... Get a ventilation specialist, he will tell you."

"Why can't you feel happy? I'm fine." I wasn't sure, since there were now lumps and bruises, fresh from her attacks.

"Sometimes, I hate caring... I don't want to care."

"Well, just kick my damn shins over that bullshit, maybe you'll learn to like it."

Spinning around, she headed towards me with full-force. I caught her in my arms and picked her up off the ground. Crying, she buried her face in my neck.

"Amanda, come on, stop it."

"I am so ashamed."

"Why?"

"I have never hit or kicked anyone I cared about in my life out of pure anger."

"Listen; help me out of this wet suit. I'll put this stuff away and we'll go wash all this cistern mud off of us. You have it all over you. We'll take a bath." I used my most consoling voice, and added a hint of erotic hand movements to convince Amanda the bath was not only needed but was my way of apologizing for scaring her. Her immediate compliance was the answer I needed to know she forgave me.

Chapter 41

"A common mistake that people make when trying to design something completely foolproof is to underestimate the ingenuity of complete fools."
— *Douglas Adams*

At the University the next morning I ensured the area was prepared. Since I would lay the ancient Scrolls out on the table to be photographed as they arrived, the area had to be prepped and ready in order to minimize the Scrolls exposure to the ambient environment of the lab. The University's camera equipment was designed to expose ancient parchments to minimal damage; perfect for the Scrolls. The photographs would be part of my presentation. Anxious, I awaited the Scrolls arrival.

Kevin Collins walked in the room. A few moments earlier, I had called him to come down. "Antonio, what in the hell are you doing? Better yet, what in the hell is going on? You're making me so nervous, I can't sleep, my wife is upset with me...The endowment is due here in two hours. Antonio, I need some cooperation!"

I gave Kevin an arrogant smile with a pat on the back. "Kevin, calm down. I made you a promise, and I'm keeping it. What about you? I believe you agreed to do something for me. Are you going to be a man, and honor your word?"

"Antonio, how can you even mention that when I know nothing about what you're up to here? Damn it! I'm the Chair of the Department that means you're supposed to inform me."

"Kevin, calm down... Have I ever disappointed you?" Despite Kevin's chase, I calmly continued to prep the area.

"No, but lately you're not yourself. You're treating me as more of a joke than you usually do..."

"Kevin, you're right, I'm different, but I don't think you're a joke. Really...don't whine this is the best damn day you've ever had at the University. When you quit crying, maybe we can talk."

"Okay...Damn you! Antonio you've gone rogue. You've got me hanging over a cliff, so you win."

"Kevin, don't be so cranky. No wonder your wife is all upset."

I smiled raising my eyebrows, and then continued.

"Here's the deal. Kevin. In less than five minutes, armed security will walk through that door with a gift to this University. It is the archaeological find of a lifetime, one that has nearly put Amanda and me below ground, in a box, several times. So quit thinking about your own ass."

"Well..."

"Well what?"

"What is it, Antonio?"

"You'll see."

"Antonio, why do you hate me?"

Laughing, I responded. "I don't hate you Kevin. In fact, I'm the only one in this damn department that doesn't want your job. That makes you crazy! There's nothing they could attach to your job to make me want it. So calm down, buddy, I never wanted it. Now, my life has changed so much I don't know what the hell I'm going to do."

"You wouldn't leave the University, Antonio. You can't… Hell, they would blame me."

"God, Kevin, you're whiny. Listen, I love UNM. I prefer to be a part of it, but things have changed. The University now competes with other things in my life."

"Antonio, surely you aren't talking about leaving because of a woman. When I met Amanda, I distinctly got the impression she supported your position here."

"It's more complicated than that, but it would be a good time for you to start worrying… Maybe, lose a little sleep over your part of the bargain. Yeah…I'm a dumbass… Amanda would never ask me, or want me to leave UNM. For once, you're right about something Kevin, her. Put your teeth in this. I have fed my own damn ego with this career of mine. Tonight, I'm presenting what will be considered my career's defining moment.

This is going to shock the hell out of you. The rest of my career will be making hers, and saving Humanity from disaster. You pompous ass… I gave you first chance to help me with her work. It's your choice, but if you drop the ball, I won't think twice about finding help elsewhere. You're right…I would leave in a minute for this woman, and never be sorry. Got that?"

Kevin didn't respond. He stared at me. A text message sent me over to open the outside door. The Scrolls had arrived. I felt a huge sense of relief.

"Kevin, get on the phone. I arranged for the University security to assist in surrounding this area throughout the night. They should be here by now."

Ruger and two of his ex-military cronies entered carrying the Scrolls container. Kevin muttered something about 'hairless gorillas' under his breath; and Ruger gave a look of contempt to Kevin, and his buddies did a simultaneous growl back at Kevin; he jumped a foot, and I loved it! Ruger winked at me, and then he and his 'gorillas' took up position around the room. I took the box with the Scrolls over to the table to take the photos I needed for the presentation.

"The security is in place. The guards you asked for are here, they are placing guards in the hallway even as we speak."

"Thanks, Kevin. Where is Bart?"

Kevin was eyeing the massive skull with a dagger through it tattooed on one arm of the guard standing near him, when he heard my question he looked bewildered, and he was getting on my last nerve. He stupidly asked; "Who?"

"Kevin, get your head in the game! The Museum Curator, I told him to prepare a place for the Scrolls. Now, where in the hell is he? I need to take a presentation photograph of these, and then Bart needs to take them to their display for safe keeping."

"Okay, but I don't even know what the hell they are, Antonio." God, he was sounding petulant now!

"Oh yeah...It's just a couple of Scrolls authored by King Solomon."

"What the F...?"

"Watch it Kevin... We don't say those words here. Better review your employee handbook... Now, find Bart!"

Kevin looked a nervous wreck as he dialed Bart again.

"Antonio, he isn't answering."

"Damn it. Ruger, stay with the Scrolls. I'm going to find him."

"Antonio, let me go find him." Ruger didn't seem to like the arrangement.

"No Ruger, he doesn't know you, and the Scrolls must be protected... Ruger, I'll be fine."

I headed down the corridor that led to the Museum offices. Uneasy about Bart, my senses were on a high alert. I reached around my side to retrieve the Desert Eagle.

God, I prayed Bart wasn't in danger. Bart was a great guy who worked hard for the University, and the Museum. He didn't deserve any trouble. Hell, Bart had a wife and kids at home. I would never forgive myself if anything happened to him. Something slithered behind me; in a flash, I spun around; the Desert Eagle in my hand was poised to fire.

"Damn it, Kevin! I could've shot your dumb face off. What are you doing?"

Kevin was frozen; eyes crossed staring down the barrel of the Desert Eagle in his face.

"Kevin, Go Back… Bart could be in big trouble."

"Antonio, what are you doing with that?"

"Kevin, this is Dangerous Business! Besides, I have a damn permit. Go on… Get out of here…Kevin; I don't have time for a Suit!" I knew Kevin hated the reference of being a Suit; he wanted to be known as a Field Man!

Suddenly, Kevin became defensive. "I'm not a Suit! Antonio, you have to let me come… I'm the Department Chair."

I threw back my head in frustration. "Kevin, if you get your ass shot off…it's not going to be on my shoulders… Here!"

Reluctantly, I raised up my pant leg and pulled out the Glock and handed it to Kevin

"Shit, Antonio. You're armed to the proverbial teeth."

"Kevin… Shut Up!"

Kevin sheepishly gazed at the weapon in his hand.

"Antonio, is the safety on?"

"No, you dumbass…you could die… Get your stupid self-ready to shoot. The guys after the Scrolls are part of a fascist militia protected by the government."

"What…?"

"Shut UP… I'll tell you later. Damn it.…Bart of all people doesn't deserve to die… You, on the other hand, are really beginning to piss me off… I'd reserved that spot for Amanda, and my Pop. There's no room for another one…"

Prepared to open the door that led to the short corridor housing the museum offices, I paused to assess.

"Antonio, does Amanda know about these weapons? My wife would croak." Kevin had really started to grate on my nerves. I couldn't believe I felt compelled to respond.

"Kevin, think about this, Amanda thinks I'm a man. As long as I don't shoot off my baculum, she's okay. Your wife probably thinks you would blow your damn head off. Sandy is a smart woman."

"Antonio, that wasn't necessary... What's a baculum?"

"Kevin - something you shouldn't worry about, because you don't know what to do with it."

"Oh, I get it... I'll have you know...I'm a great lover."

I rubbed my hand over my head. "I'm sure you are...all by yourself! Now, Shut Up. Unlike yours, Bart's wife likes him. She wouldn't appreciate us out here talking about our dicks, while her husband is in danger."

I thought for a minute.

"Kevin, get down... and watch this door. Don't stand up, there's a window. Do you understand?"

"Yeah!"

"By the way, Kevin, never look at Amanda again the way you did the first day I brought her here. You wanted to lay her on the floor... She'd never even give you a second look." With that off my chest, I went through the doors to the other side of the hallway.

Before a holiday and without a specific purpose, the rest of the staff was gone.

Keeping my back against the wall, I made my way to the door of Bart Lambert, PhD, Curator. With slow precision, I made a 360 degree turn in precaution. I tried to turn the knob...locked... Damn! Bart had to be in there.

God, I thought of his wife Sere, he called her Little Dove at home; she was a native with no one to depend on but Bart.

How could I get in there? Grabbing the knob again, I shook it. Unlike the new doors in the other building, here they still had a keyed entry knob. Placing the Desert Eagle back in its holster, I removed a credit card... Hell...I'd never done this before, didn't even know if it was a real trick.

I slid it in and fiddled with it. The moisture from my brow began stinging my eyes. The card slipped. Securing it, I wiped my forehead. Returning to the lock, I made another attempt. BINGO!

I, opened the door...panic enveloped me. Only the back of Bart's head was visible, and he hadn't turned with the sound of my entrance. I kicked the door shut and rushed to face my fear.

Bart, bound and gagged, had a note attached to his chest. There in huge capital letters was a personal message for me...

DR. DOMINGUEZ - OPEN.

I thought to free Bart first, but immediately feared that it might be a trick.

"Bart, man...I'm not taking any chances. I'm opening this

first."

Bart seemed a little out of it.

Dear Dr. Dominguez,

Do not give the scrolls to the University! You have a choice:

The MONEY-

or the Alliance shadows you for the rest of your life. By the way, you would miss those expeditions.

Where is she, Doc?

Get them to us, in the South lot.

We'll be waiting.

Don't be an idiot and make that presentation.

With Love,

The Alliance

88

I shoved my hand in my pocket, took out my knife, and freed Bart. How did they know about 88?

"Damn, Bart, I'm sorry. Are you okay?"

Bart shook his head, yes. I went to the door.

"Bart, I'm sorry to do this to you, but I have to make sure they don't have Amanda." I yelled out the door. "Kevin, Get Your Dumbass in here and watch out for Bart!"

Kevin rushed in, waving the Glock about like an idiot as he scampered around the corner.

"Kevin, stand next to Bart and watch the door. I'll send help, so…" I paused. "Bart, can you take the damn gun."

"Yeah, go, Antonio… They're crazy sons-a-bitches!"

"Thanks, Bart!"

I belted out the door, and raced back to the room where I left Ruger guarding the Scrolls. I tried to process as I ran. A call to check on Amanda might alert them, and could put Amanda in more danger. Damn, I should've let them take the Scrolls right from the start.

I busted in through the doors of the photography room. Ripping the note out of my pocket, I shoved it into Ruger's chest.

"Antonio, what is it?"

"Read it… They tied Bart up, and left it on his chest…someone go get Bart and Kevin from Bart's office. Be careful I left them a weapon."

"Calm down, Antonio!"

"Damn it…Ruger. They've got her. What can we do?"

My demeanor clearly pushed Ruger to the brink. He grabbed my shirt, got in my face, and in short words, told me.

"Go to your office…I'll take care of Amanda…Stay put - until Showtime!"

Unsure why, I did exactly as Ruger ordered concerned as to why in the hell Ruger went ballistic. Ruger was on a radio, he spoke quickly then disconnected. He ordered his companions to stay, and he did it without saying a word; he just pointed with his hands made a few signs and moved out with a purpose.

The two guards suddenly looked a great deal like the gorillas Kevin had called them. They seemed tense, and were almost sniffing the air with their extreme diligence. Time to go…

When I reached my office, I was surprised to find two armed guards already posted at my door. I acknowledged them and slipped the key card in the slot, entered, closed the door, and locked it. I then, walked through the waiting area, back to my actual office, and shut the door.

"What took you so long to get here, Antonio? You know, I thought the books in your office would be interesting, but they are all stiff, horrible, and out-of-date. Can I redo your office book selection?"

Speechless, I stood and stared in a daze as I listened to the Enchantress flap her mouth about the damn books.

"Antonio, what is wrong with you? Ruger said you would be

right here. Two hours later, I am sitting here with a bunch of boring books. Now, you walk in, and you just stare at me?"

"Damn it... Amanda, you're killing me, I thought OPERA kidnapped you!"

"Do I look kidnapped? Hello, kidnapped means missing!"

"Now, Antonio, your imagination is getting a bit wild. I am more secure today, than the Queen of England. I rode to this place in an armored truck for God's Sakes. Do you know how toasty it gets in the back of an armored truck?"

Laughing, I stood in front of the prettiest sight on God's Green Earth!

"No, but I'm sure I'll find out."

"You bet you will. I felt claustrophobic and clammy for an hour. Why did you make such a ludicrous, overreaching arrangement for me? Personally, I'm a bit miffed about it, it was awful hot."

"Amanda...Shut Up!"

"Antonio, do not get ugly."

I smiled at her. "I can't kiss you when you won't shut...the...hell...up!"

"Oh... "

My mouth covered my Sorceress' lips, quieting her rants, and lingered for a while. Having quenched my need for her, I released as my thirst turned to hunger.

"Amanda, let me say you have all the facts wrong this time. Yes, you may do whatever you wish about my books. I'm sorry they don't suit your taste. Sweetheart, if I had known you were going to be here for an extended visit I would have been much more accommodating with some good reads, especially for you. Guess what?"

"What?"

"I had no idea you were here, or that you rode here in the back of a damn hot truck."

"Oh…I'm sorry… Are you going to stay angry with me long?"

"No, that's the problem. I'm not at all angry!"

"Antonio, what is wrong with you?"

"Nothing now, you should've seen me five minutes ago!!" I was swinging her around in happiness when I heard a voice.

"Excuse me sir." Looking over my shoulder I saw one of the guards from the Scrolls Team, standing there with Kevin. Well, not with Kevin…more like holding Kevin up by a hold on the back of his suit collar. Must have been a tight hold, Kevin's face was turning blue.

"Maybe you should drop him, and then tell me why you are holding him in the first place, when you are supposed to be guarding the Scrolls?"

The mammoth man dropped Kevin like bag of flour. Kevin went down wheezing.

"The scrolls are safe sir. I fortified the area before coming here. This man came to the lab and said he was authorized to handle the scrolls." He looked down at Kevin- literally.

"We disagreed on the subject Sir. So I brought him to you to clarify."

I cleared my throat, and waved my hand in a 'that's okay manner'. "No, you did right; he does not have the authority to handle the scrolls."

"Then it will be okay to inform the team, that the next time he interferes we can shoot him." With that remark said with a wink Kevin could not see. The soldier walked away.

I took Amanda's hand and we walked out of the room, stepping over Kevin in the process. We had someplace to be, and we would be there together.

Chapter 42

"We are made wise not by the recollection of our past, but by the responsibility for our future."
— *George Bernard Shaw*

The auditorium was packed. I looked out over the watchful crowd. They were in tune with me, savoring every word and every movement I made. I watched Amanda, Her face flushed. She looked as if she was nauseated. I assumed she was just nervous until I saw that she was glancing over at Cynthia.

In spite of Amanda's behavior, I sweetly continued seducing the audience in anticipation of their big prize. I could tell Cynthia's demeanor was causing Amanda distress. Unfortunately, a recent call from Cynthia in Amanda's presence revealed that Cynthia and I had shared a long time relationship of nothing more than rendezvous'. Our meetings were spread over long periods of time, but fit both our needs. It was a matter, I would have preferred she never find out about.

Yes, Cynthia looked sophisticated, blonde, with long, very strong legs, and nothing out-of-place. She enjoyed the upper crust. The woman evoked superiority, wearing high-society with a capital 'H'. Amanda was graceful with a classic beauty. She was reserved and strong without wearing it in public. I could only imagine what was developing in her mind.

Up on the stage, the curtain opened, uncovering the screen. Amanda now, looked tuned in. She knew I was revealing the gift to the University. The spectators gasped, blinding flashes emerged from every direction when I officially announced the Scrolls would have a new home at UNM's Maxwell Museum in Anthropology.

After the audience regained their composure, I resumed my address, except, in front of everyone; I did a one-hundred and eighty degree turn.

"The Scrolls are much more than merely an artifact, it is an instruction manual authored by the Wise King Solomon. It will rest here at the University of New Mexico where everyone can view and study it. The Scrolls belong to God's people, to the Grandsons of Abraham, and the Sons of Jacob.

I want to share a little about the meaning revealed within the Scrolls text… They offer us a warning from the King."

I could tell by their faces, Amanda and my family was astounded that I would offer the warning in this venue. Watching them, I moved the crowd from euphoria to immediate emergency alert. Amanda was very nervous; I could see she grasped her skirt in her fists.
Soon, I offered my testimony in the defense of King Solomon's, far past mutual, inspiration.

"We are told King Solomon was the wisest King ever. I have learned King Solomon's wisdom emerged as his greatest asset. It also became his worst liability.
His wisdom wasn't completely positive. Much of what he knew disturbed him, to say the least."

The text within the Scrolls reinforces the ideas and prophecies of many cultures. The earth and the cosmos are constantly changing. In science this is well established fact. When change ceases death is the ultimate result. This is true of every living thing.

The most perplexing question is: Does Mother Nature adapt or react to us, and does our survival depend upon our reaction to her?

The greatest differences between ancient man and modern man lie in this concept. Ancient people had remarkable reverence for nature. Modern humans seek to manipulate and deny refusing to accept their subordinate position.

Continued renewal or life itself depends upon this constant change. By design or accident, cycles exist. Many events we label as catastrophes are in fact life. They are part of the renewal process. There is no amount of debate that can change this fact.

Perhaps, our behavior can add speed to the process, but it cannot slow it down. In other words, it is not politicians or overzealous leaders that truly control us. It is Nature. Regardless of your religious beliefs or affiliations, Nature and the Cosmos are the true dictators.

Our reaction to change is purely dependent upon intelligence, and our interaction with one another. Oppression is the most dangerous of all. It is the result of misused power. Power requires control. Control cannot take place without suppression.

The Tribes were sent out of The Holy Land to create diversity as a means of survival. The Tribes were unique. Each had different strengths, and weaknesses, thus different goals.

The Tribes were sent out to inhabit the four corners of the earth. Even our ancestors knew one day the population would converge, and The Tribes would once again, be joined together.

Mother Nature's cycles will continue. She will remain in constant change through a renewal process we call disasters. The inhabitants will not adapt if they are suppressed, and forced to fight corruption. These same people will die, if they do not continue to further their intellectual abilities.

Except for the recent boom in technology, for the first, the masses are losing intellectual ground. This can only be a result of suppression. The only mechanism for moving forward is problem-solving. We must embrace problems not manipulate their existence.

Hypothetically, in the very near future, Mother Nature may require that we grow rice instead of corn in Nebraska. We must have the ability, and intellect to institute this change in a timely manner.

Resistance in nature is dangerous. We must not try to suppress these cycles. We cannot win a battle against Mother Nature. Simply put, praying for rain is a better alternative, than injecting the atmosphere to provoke rain. The masses will adapt if the knowledge is available. Thousands of years of history are proof positive.

Anger and intellectual diversity can be astonishingly productive. Racial and religious adversities are never productive. Nevertheless, race, and religion provide us with important beliefs, and social connections. These contribute to the diversity. Most religions unexploited provide a basis for socially responsible interaction and charity.

The God of Moses displayed a greater degree of concern over our social interaction, health, and respect for Mother Nature than for Himself. We must freely as individuals heed the advice of our ancestors, especially those whom cared enough to leave the message. Cognitive dissonance and arrogance are the deadly extremes.

"The Scrolls provide many lessons and answers many profound questions. The secret is to abandon everything you thought you knew, open up your heart, and mind to the Truth. Find someone open, and beautiful to share the experience with…I did."

I then weaved the Science behind the processing of metals into my tale, wanting to add some scientific credence to the process.

Again, I paused and took a drink of water. Afterwards, I picked up the stool, carried it to the other side of the stage, and sat it directly in line with Amanda.

"At the exact same time the Scrolls came to me, I received a Messenger. Serendipitous! One might even say 'Divine

Intervention'. I can't argue with that. My Messenger was connected with the Divine, and I could never have understood without her Wisdom, and knowledge.

The lessons from King Solomon are far-reaching, as they offer answers about every level of Humanity. Perhaps more importantly, they speak to Man's individual struggles.

The teachings can enable each of us to become better partners, and ultimately, better members of the larger group. No longer can we hide behind Sunday school stories. The Scrolls command for survival. Only those, whom bother to understand, and practice their lessons, will survive into the next Era."

I casually stepped off the stage and handed a piece of paper to Amanda, and went back up on the stage. I proceeded as if nothing unusual had happened. Amanda unfolded the paper.

Dear Amanda,

I was hoping you would be so kind as to allow me to escort you for an evening on the town.

Tomorrow night, I could pick you up at 7:00 p.m. and then we could go to Geronimo's for a nice chemical-free dinner.

Afterwards, who knows?

If the answer is yes, and you'll be my date, please place your right hand on your heart.

Awaiting your answer,
Love,
Antonio
88

Amanda smiled as soon as she read it. Immediately, her hand

went over her heart. I winked at her without missing a word.

With a flash, the auditorium went black. The next thing I knew, I felt a smack and I fell back onto the stage floor.

At the same time – Pffft –Pffft…two waves flew passed our heads.

Amanda lay sprawled across me on the stage floor, unable to move. Suddenly, the lights came back on. I tried nudging her as flickered light came from the cameras' flashes.

Amanda, frozen, wasn't moving at all.

"Amanda!"

By then, my entire family had reached the stage in a panic. Ruger was right behind them, and lifted her off me. She couldn't stand.

"Ruger, is she hit?"

"No, she's got a concussion or is in shock."

I surveyed the area. Two bullet holes were in the presentation screen that now stood alone on the stage, directly behind where I had been standing. I scooped Amanda away from Ruger, and yelled as I took off with her. "They're in the ventilation!" Guests were already stampeding to the exits. Above, one of the vent covers was hanging open.

I ran backstage, carrying Amanda. Kevin crouched in a corner, hiding. I traveled the back way, running down the hall to my private office.

Balancing Amanda's limp body, I slid the key card, and rushed inside. Worried, I placed Amanda on the sofa and pulled the Glock from my boot.

I couldn't understand why she looked conscious, but remained frozen.

"Amanda...Honey... We're fine.

Amanda...You saved my dumbass again. Sweetheart, I'm fine."

Damn, her trance-like state began to scare me. Then, she spoke. "Antonio, what happened? Where are we?"

My head fell onto her stomach.

"Do you remember, Amanda?"

"You gave me a note, it was so sweet."

I leaned over and kissed her.

Amanda returned my kiss, and then said; "I was sitting there so pleased to share this moment with you, and I suddenly felt a wave of anxiety, and what felt like a push that lifted me out of my chair...that is all I remember."

Could our lives get anymore unreal...mythical legends, Biblical Scrolls, and now phantom body tossing! "Our days are getting stranger by the minute...but whatever it was, it saved my life through you"

"Wow, did I miss the end of your speech?"

"Everybody missed it, there was no end, after you jumped on the stage and knocked me down."

She laughed; "Once more I have saved you; and managed to get out of a public appearance!"

Ruger interrupted my reply when he came in and told us they had cleared the building without finding anyone. "It is like they disappeared into thin air, most of the exits require a remote access code, so they must have one and can blend in with the crowd when needed."

Ruger paused and glanced between me and Amanda. "Antonio, there is something else, and at least it is good news. Can you step outside for a moment?" At that moment Amanda's phone rang, so she waved me away.

I followed Ruger into the hallway, and closed the door behind me.

Ruger spoke in a soft voice; "I got a message a little while ago, and it is not the only one. It seems your "13" have their own way of knowing they are needed. They are all aware of what is going on, and a few of these names on the messages are for your eyes only." He handed me a stack of emails, and walked away.

Glancing at the names on the messages, I was floored, and confused. Then again, after the last few days, nothing about any of this should surprise me. Whistling the tune to the Twilight Zone under my breath, I leaned against the wall and read the messages from the "13".

Chapter 43

"Time you enjoy wasting, was not wasted."
— John Lennon

While in Miami, Amanda and I had compiled a list of candidates to serve as the Thirteen Chosen. In a matter of days, my family's law firm worked diligently to perform background checks to narrow the list, and assure us of each individual's particular character. We could have saved our time. The "13" knew who they were and were on their way. But we were going to continue with the DNA test just to be sure.

We then, arranged for blood to be drawn from each of the arriving "13". Each sample was secured and transported to the University of Arizona, where the team of experts responsible for the science tested the specimens. Once at the lab, the DNA was extracted and tested. Then, each was matched against known specimens of data from the Thirteen Tribes. No surprise there, they all matched.

The night before the Summit gathering we had arranged a reception at my home for the Chosen. Soon, Ruger would be arriving with the Thirteen and the entourage of security surrounding them. I used my time to reflect on the King's Journey. It was a moment when I thought I should be asking myself if I was crazy to be instituting an outrageously public plan by an ancient man that might very well have been insane, but I wasn't.

Because, regardless of whether the thirteenth nexus opened protecting the human race from cosmic annihilation or not, the thirteen represented the true reality of the Tribes' equality and diversity. Scientific DNA proved it. Codes within the text of the Torah substantiated the science. Without the help of many brilliant minds ahead of me this would never have unfolded, and the mystery would have remained veiled. I was proud to be the coordinator of the remarkable project.

I rolled my chair back away from the desk, and stretched out my legs as I began to wonder. How had the other twelve energy points around the World been activated in the past?

The Temple Mount in Jerusalem was surely activated by none other than Solomon himself as architect and builder. The Temple was a powerful structure that at one time housed the Ark of the Covent, the most powerful of all, once believed to be the place where God lived on Earth. Even without the Temple it remains to be considered the most powerful nexus of all.

Stonehenge with its circular architecture and dynamic acoustics was surely activated through sound. Perhaps, specific music or chants from builders or was it their descendants? The structures meticulous alignment with the Cosmos added to the ingenuity and potential synergistic event.

Quasi archeologists and their mainstream counterparts alike agreed that evidence exists supporting the idea that the

Pyramids at Giza had a fiery past. The King's Chamber constructed from rose granite provided the unique firebox. With the capstones in place they became a furnace with raging fire reaching into the Heavens, maybe even producing transmutated gold as white manna. Even today, test have proven that time slows down near the Pyramids.

Delphi near Mount Parnassus was surely charged from the famous Oracle retold as a tale of the mighty Apollo defeating Python the dragon. Later, this site featured the all-important Pythian and Pan-Hellenic games, and eventually inspired the first Olympics and the eternal flame.

The Mayan pyramids at Chechen Itza shoots energy beams from within into the Heavens. The photographs are proof of the long history of a directed protruding force that attracts fierce unexplained lightening.

In the Tibetan Gangdise Mountains lies Mount Kailash a sacred site for many Buddhists it is home to Buddha himself, and Hindus claim Lord Shiva resides upon the Summit. Perhaps, one or both of the holy men opened the door. The rich stories paint an otherworldly glow. The amazing landscape is home to the fabulous nexus with a vast history of open doors to the outer-dimensions. I thought despite Amanda's distaste for the cold she would love Mount Kailash.

The area in South Africa considered to be the cradle of humanity, an energy nexus spoke of by King Solomon, had only recently revealed more than 20,000 circular building structures dating back 7,500 years, a place with long lived legends of supernatural episodes a point in common with all of the energy strongholds. A place so rich in artifacts it can boast ownership of the little understood 100, 000 year old Adam's Calendar.

Creating the border between Turkey and Iran, Mount Ararat the highest peak in the Armenian Mountains with an abundance of Biblical legends, the site believed to be the location where Noah struck land and abandoned ship.

Adding to the idea of Mother Nature's renewal often manifests as man's destruction, yet perhaps, the most perplexing to me was Krakatau the massive volcano in Indonesia predicted to be suppressing an eruption that will destroy massive amounts of the eastern United States. Experts warn when Krakatau erupts a tsunami will hit the United Sates within 8 hours changing everything.

The Dead Sea, a body of water, and the lowest point on Earth surprised me the most. Although it is not short of a powerful history, it seemed unlikely. I came to believe that it provides the penetrating connection to Earth's Core in the synergistic chain.

The 3,000 stones at Carnac at Brittany France was the resting place of what I consider Solomon's calm energy. It rests in a lazy communal area of the country virtually unnoticed and unstudied for years. A series of carefully placed stones aligning with the Cosmos, a structure likely built during King Solomon's reign.

Machu Picchu was said to have originally been built as home to the Inca emperor Pachacuti around 1438 has often been called the "Lost City of the Incas." A place they abandoned after the Spanish Conquest. The landscape held significant spiritual meaning to the Incas. Today word of its properties has spread igniting interest from people from all walks of life.

Hidden Mountain certainly lived up to its name for it was the most inconspicuous site of all. I guess it was fitting as it resided in America, considered the New Land, home to the final nexus.

These events, in a chain reaction with Earth's Poles would create a force field of protection for the planet. A concept explored in great detail by modern science fiction authors. The weaker parts or areas where holes had already penetrated the atmosphere of the magnetic veil could, according to the King's instruction be protected by carefully designed Para-magnetic obelisks.

The sound of the gates alarm system blared through the house, and disrupted my musings. As I jumped to my feet, Maria came through the door wring her hands in her apron and exclaimed; "Antonio, you have to stop Amanda! I tried to keep the paper from her like Joseph said, but she saw the picture and the headline; they are comparing your finding Solon's Scrolls to that stink about Hitler's Diaries! She is furious and has gone down the drive to confront the media outside the gates."

Great! I had hoped to prevent Amanda's reaction to that bit of stupidity! Kevin had released the news about my endowing the University with the Scrolls, and now the press was either praising them as the find of a lifetime or delegating them to fake status. Amanda had read the negative press!

Rushing through the house I reached the door in time to see Ruger running down the drive after Amanda, who had opened the gate.

We both slid to a stop in time to here the first reporter's question.

"Ms. Messenger, while we were all thrilled to see the photos of your dramatic saving of Mr. Dominguez, it is apparent from our research that the picture did not do you justice, our research also brings into the light, a certain lack of credentials on your part as an expert involved in what has been claimed to be 'the find of the century... Do you believe your appearance will help convince the world of the authority and validity of your claims in regard to the scrolls actually belonging to King Solomon?"

Amanda stood there for a moment and looked at each of the reporters with their microphones and cameras aimed at her. I knew she hated publicity, and this must be a nightmare for her. I started to take a step and Ruger stopped me. "If you pull her back now, they will eat her alive from now on." He whispered harshly.

Amanda's voice rang out clear and firm. "Hopefully amongst the throng gathered here, there is a voice of reason. Also, I hope that this idiot is not the only one who will be reporting on this matter. For if he is; then we are lost before we even begin."

Dozens of voices rang out assuring her they were not idiots, and willing to hear her out.

"I will speak, and you will listen. I will not answer questions, and I will not stand for a single insult to myself or Doctor Antonio Dominguez."

Amanda turned to face the first reporter. "You sir, your first mistake here today was your belief that you could flatter me with words on my physical appearance. Your second and even graver mistake was not referring to Doctor Dominguez accurately. He is an extremely reliable source on all things connected with King Solomon; as your 'research' should have confirmed.

I will wager a bet that your newspaper is one that has either started or perpetrated this absolute trash that compares the uncovering of King Solomon's Scrolls to that farce surrounding Hitler's Diaries." With that said, she flung down the offending newspaper in front of the press assemblage.

"Now then, let us set the record straight. It is a known fact that a fleet was sent out by King Solomon. It is a known fact that over the years certain artifacts such as the Decalogue Stone, have been found on the American Continent, dating back to biblical times and have even been debated in judicial settings, and they are all connected to the Hebrews. It is a known fact that as a solid connection, the ancient beliefs, customs and traditions of North, Central and South America can be traced directly back to the Hebrews.

I suggest that each of you complete a fact finding mission, search out the truth and do not rely on as President Roosevelt described it; 'Muckraking' to sell your news. For while the sensationalizing of facts and fiction always grabs attention, the bare truth supports a long held belief in this country, that the people have a right to know and judge for themselves."

With that my flame haired virago, turned, walked back to the house with a dirty look at me and Ruger. I walked to the gate, smiled at the look of astonishment on their faces, and closed it firmly but quietly.

As I walked away, I heard one reporter say; "Did she just compare us to the muckrakers of 1912?" And another reporter responded; "Yes, and I am not so sure we did not deserve it."

Ruger stepped in beside me, and casually said; "I think she's mad at us."

"At us, why would she be mad at us?"

"Because in her eyes, I did not protect your reputation, and you did not address the issue of your validity for the articles in the news."

"Well damn. I guess I have to go apologize and them I will try to save your bacon."

"I like your Amanda; I wasn't sure at first, but she's growing on me. Ruger finished with a laugh and wandered off towards the guest house.

***

Later that evening, Amanda and I descended the stairs to greet the Thirteen Chosen. Our gathering would be the last prior to our public address and introduction at Hidden Mountain.

Quickly, upon our arrival, Amanda released my hand, and rushed towards Brad Humphrey. I watched as she embraced her friend, a former geophysicist, and current public speaker. Brad was one of only three people Amanda suggested as worthy enough to receive her endorsement. After reviewing Brad's work, I agreed with her. His ability to explore and correlate mathematics with the unseen world was not only uncanny, but remarkable.

Distracting me, my friend and teacher John Bear affectionately patted my back. "Antonio, my son, you found the way. The ancestors are with you."

I nodded at the man; I had met fifteen years prior, upon my arrival in Santa Fe, the place I now called home. During my early days as a teaching professor at the University of New Mexico, I studied the Native culture, and local archeology at great lengths. As an expert on Native American diversity and ancient cultures, John Bear had contributed a great deal of time, and knowledge into helping me fully understand the lesser obvious aspects of the Native Peoples.

While John and I were reminiscing Amanda joined us. She and John had bonded right from the beginning. They seem to share an understanding that truthfully, I couldn't quite grasp.

That night, Amanda had a peaceful presence as she floated through the exemplary group of individuals. While I was conversing with Jacob Leeds, the only medical doctor among the Chosen, I saw Amanda approach Rabbi Daniel Apter. The Rabbi and scholar from Los Angeles was quite possibly one of Amanda's favorite people in the Universe. Rabbi Apter was an advisor Amanda often consulted both personally and spiritually.

The energy among the group was powerful, yet calming. The chemistry from the members was evident. As I observed, I made eye contact with my caretaker Joe. Joseph Whetstone, now a member of the elite group. A constant in my life, I felt proud to endorse the man and his abilities as an electronics expert made his inclusion that much smarter. I nodded at Joe and made my way through the crowd.

After a few short steps, I stopped to talk with Isaac Lederman, a longtime friend of my brother Jose. Isaac was one of the most charitable guys I knew, and one of the most brilliant and successful players in the world of International Banking. He had dedicated his life to promoting youth charities in greater Miami and inThird World countries around the globe. His work had changed the lives of a multitude of kids, and no-one, outside of a select few, even knew his name. Isaac and I shook hands and I scanned the room for Amanda.

You see there were only twelve of the 13 present in the great room. One special member of the Chosen was hidden from

Amanda's sight. I waved to Marc as I stepped over to her.

Once I reached her, I wrapped my hand around her arm at the elbow, and guided her across the room. Within seconds my brother Marc, also a member of the Chosen appeared with Amanda's brother Andrew. Amanda turned white at the sight of her brother. I knew it was a walk out on the proverbial limb, but I had taken the chance.

As a brilliant structural engineer, I knew Andrew would be a valuable addition to the Thirteen. Eventually, the nexus would need a Hall. His expertise would provide valuable knowledge.

After the cool reception to her brother, Amanda nearly danced across the room to welcome author Jeff Goldin. He and Amanda had a lot in common, both read, researched, and wrote to the point of near obsession. His skills as historian would be an important addition.

It was in those moments, watching Amanda, I really became concerned about my decision to include her brother. I wondered if I should have consulted her as I was unaware of the details. The fact is, it is not my choice, but that of Destiny.

Luckily, Paul Simmel approached me from behind. We shook hands and exchanged some pleasant conversation. Paul was a former military specialist. His duties had landed him in the Middle East on several tours. Paul had an amazing talent for cartography, and could read the most ancient of maps like I could read pictographs, and no doubt, his combat training was a plus.

As I was finishing my conversation with Paul, an archaeologist, and fellow colleague on several digs, Eric Nachman caught my attention. He now, held a position as curator with the museum at the University of Texas.

Standing with Eric, I was happy to admit that having George, the young Yuchee Priest join us, felt like we were closing a circle that had been left open on the floor of that hotel room when his grandfather bled to death in my arms. I smiled in satisfaction as Amanda spotted George and made straight for him! I watched as she took his arm in hers, and took him over to be introduced to John Bear.

With one more hand to shake, I headed across the room to join Jason Weil, a soft spoken Quantum Physicist. Jason and I had met several times over the course of my career, and often enjoyed long debates over his thoughts on raising human consciousness. His peers had often compared his work to that of Einstein and Bohr. His inclusion as one of the Chosen was a puzzle I had to think on.

I stepped back and watched the Thirteen Chosen and gave a sigh of relief. Despite Amanda's moments of uneasiness, the evening was a brilliant success. Searching for Amanda I saw her wave, and mime that she was going to change out of her gorgeous dress before leaving for the Summit. I waved back and continued to circle the room; eavesdropping on the myriad of conversations that were rolling around me.

Amanda came out of my office bathroom with her clothes

changed for the trip. She was slowly returning to a normal demeanor.

I grabbed her arm; "Come on, they're ready for us."

"Antonio, what about my boots…?"

I scooped them up as I pulled her along. Outside my office, I led her to a service door where we hopped into a limo with tinted windows. Ruger was inside.

The drive to the Mountain wasn't long. After her boots were on, Amanda gazed out the window, and commented on our entourage.

"Antonio, what are all those cars doing?"

"Well, let's see. The '13' Chosen, followed by the Media, gads of other interested people, and, of course, almost my entire damn family came to town."

I slipped my arm around her. "Amanda, are you okay?"

"Yeah, I think so."

We remained quiet for a few moments. The Sun stretched across the horizon in an even more stunning display than normal.

"Look, Antonio, it's like the Aurora Borealis, except it's a curtain…it looks like it is enveloping the Summit. Streams from the Heavens are circling Hidden Mountain. Colors…there are so many hues…" Her jaw hung from her mouth.

"My God…" It astonished me. The upper atmosphere, charged with electricity, created the anomaly around our destination.

"Antonio, what does Aurora mean?"

I smiled, knowing full well Amanda knew what it meant.

"Dawn, Honey… Dawn means beginning - the first light of day. As a verb, it means to be realized, or understood."

"Antonio, I think it's Serendipitous."

"It is Serendipity with a Capital 'S', Amanda!"

"Antonio, could Leonids Meteor shower be responsible for this Aurora curtain?"

"I don't' think so, this must be a separate event."

"Do we have time for you to explain it to me?"

"Amanda, are you asking about Leonids coming from the constellation Leo?"

"Yes, of course."

"Well, sometimes you're a bit vague, Leonids Meteor Shower occurs within the constellation of Leo. Coming from the east, the cycle peaks every 33 years, Christians value this, because it coincides with the maturation of Jesus.

The brightest star within the constellation of Leo is Regulus. The word Regulus means, 'Ruler' - The 'Star of Kings'. Beginning with King David, the King of Judah, thus making Leo the sign of Judah, and the Lion the representative for the tribe of Judah."

"Antonio, it started when Reuben defiled his father, and the Sons of Joseph, Manasseh and Ephraim received their split birthright. Chronicles I, 5:2 explains.

Judah is the hidden power until the 13th sign arrives during the

Galactic Alignment 12/21/2012.

At that time, Judah will come into power, perhaps as the Messiah. Joseph's sons are the birthright, preparing the path from the House of David. Antonio, you are the hidden Judah."

"Good, God Amanda… Honey, please, it doesn't make sense to keep trying to turn me into something prophetic and Biblical! I just want to do the right thing, and be a man."

Ruger, always so silent, stepped out of his comfort zone.

"Come on man; get your head out of the clouds. All these years, all the things that have happened to you… And you still don't get it. I've seen men in their element – I've seen the eyes of men before they knowingly walked into the jaws of Death.

You, my old friend, are walking into Life. I can see it, I've only seen a few things like it, but damn it, Antonio – Right now, you're the man. And I'm damn proud to be a part of it. I just hope we have enough civilians out there to keep us from getting nuked."

Amanda continued with prophecy. "Antonio, you don't have a choice. You are the Bull, the Taurus that devours the Nations from Numbers, 24:8. The Nations are the Racial Barriers. You are ripping them to shreds as we prepare for the Lion to take over. The Lion is the King of Judah."

I stared at her with amazement. It was all too far-fetched for me. Then I looked back at Ruger. They both had grins the size of watermelon slices.

"Amanda…Stop, I want to be a Man, a man that loves you.

Isn't that enough for you?"

"Of course, but it is not about me. How can we deny the parallels of your existence? We are not – You are."

"I don't know how, but let's deny them. Okay, Honey?

Amanda, let's go out tomorrow night and pretend we're ordinary. Saturday we will put my family on a plane back home. Saturday night we'll be alone for the first time in quite a while.

We can do 'wild things'. Sunday, we'll fly to the Midwest for the week of Thanksgiving. I'll scare the hell out of everyone, again, being the only Cuban and all.

There, we can shop for some free-range organic stuff, cook organic turkey… whatever you people eat in Organic Land.

Think about this, let's leave your home after the holiday, fly some place exotic all alone and just make love for two weeks without getting all Biblical. Then, after all of that is over, we'll reassess. Okay? For me, please?"

"Okay." She said okay, but the look in her eyes said something different.

"That was too easy, Amanda, you're scaring me."

Chapter 44

"There is a mysterious cycle in human events. To some generations much is given. Of other generations much is expected. This generation of Americans has a rendezvous with destiny."
Franklin D. Roosevelt

Up on the Summit, surrounded by the rainbow of the Aurora, meteors lit up the sky. Curious observers, and media personnel, found their vantage points. This moment represented a huge victory against OPERA. No, we had not yet defeated, or even curtailed the enemy, but we had won a couple big rounds.

The '13' Chosen slowly made their way up to the Summit to officially dedicate their lives to King Solomon's cause. Watching them, we reveled with pride at their diversity. God's children truly did come in all sizes and colors. I had used science to prove it and a mystical element had pulled it all together. I found it hard to believe I had been a part of something so Divinely Inspired.

I squeezed Amanda's hand and smiled at her. We shared the excitement of our victories. When the '13' reached their designated place on the Summit, I once again took over the microphone, appealing to my audience.

I glanced at Amanda as her cue. She had no idea what to expect, as I had purposely failed to share my plans and my speeches.

I recited Aaron's Prayer. First in Hebrew, and then translated in English

"As someone once praised me on an important day - Today you portray monumental strength and courage.

רוֹמָא :לְאַרְשִׁי יֶּנְב-תֶּא·וּכְרָבְת הֹכ ,רֹמאֵל וְיָנָב-לֶאו זְהַא-לֶא הֵּבַד גכ
.םֶהָל

.וְרֹמְשִׁיו ,הָוהְי ,רְכֶרָבְי דכ

.וָּנֶחִיו ,רָיֵלֵא וְיָנָפ הָוהְי רֵאָי הכ

.סוֹלָשׁ רְל םֵשָׂיו ,רָיֵלֵא וְיָנָפ הָוהְי אָשִׂי וכ

.סֶכְרָבָא ,יִנֲאו ;לְאַרְשִׂי יֶּנְב-לַע ,יְמָש-תֶּא·וּמָשׂו זכ

'Speak unto Aaron and unto his sons, saying: On this wise ye shall bless the children of Israel; ye shall say unto them:
The LORD bless thee, and keep thee;
The LORD make His face to shine upon thee, and be gracious unto thee;
The LORD lift up His countenance upon thee, and give thee peace.
So shall they put My name upon the children of Israel, and I will bless them.'
You have my deepest gratitude, and admiration, for the task you are about to undertake."

Suddenly, an unheard noise grabbed everyone's attention, spinning them around to the East.

Directly at the blessing's conclusion, an orb shaped light

with a tail like a comet came down from the Heavens. The circle of its contact engulfed Amanda, I and the 13. The brilliant light appeared as a solid. The brilliance penetrated us, driving into the Earth beneath our feet.

I drew Amanda's body into me, in an act of protection. I held her so tight I doubt, she could hardly breathe. Somehow, she managed to squeeze out the words that ran through her mind from Numbers, 24:17.

"Antonio… 'I see him, but not now; I behold him, but not nigh; there shall step forth a star out of Jacob, and a scepter shall rise out of Israel, and shall smite through the corners of Moab, and breakdown all the sons of Seth'."
Genesis 49:9

"Judah is a lion's whelp; from the prey, my son, thou art gone up. He stooped down, he couched as a lion, and as a lioness; who shall rouse him up?"

I smiled at her. "Amanda, the mike was on - you just told everyone."

"Oh my God…Antonio, I don't do that, I hate speaking publicly."

"You just did, and actually, it was awesome."

A little shaken, I felt compelled to begin my planned address. "I am going to recite a beautiful piece written by My Beautiful Messenger. The meaning is fitting of our task ahead.

"America, by design, was a mother, a gigantic womb prepared to give birth to the new. As her contractions increased, the labor was not easy, and she experienced great pain.

A Nation born from love, her likeness stood in the harbor as a reminder of that unconditional love."

Amanda turned as red as I have ever seen a human being turn. I was reciting an oratory she had written, one she had never shown me. I smiled and winked at her.

"America was not a brother vulnerable to sibling rivalry and competition. America was a mother, a loving mother, who loves her children, and respects the children of other mothers. Her children misbehave, yet she still loves them.

She could control her children's lives, but biting her bottom lip, she holds her breath, knowing they must be free to find their own way. Mother America could provide for her children, and their necessities, but she does not.

Sometimes it causes her pain, since she cannot deny them their journey. Sometimes forced to watch her children suffer in pain and agony, she's always there to love, and comfort. Her primary goal exists to allow her children's journey without her interference.

She must walk a fine line with her children, loving them all equally. As a child's battles may cause a Mother's pain, she knows she must only help without paralyzing, or demeaning the child's own abilities. After the battle, the child must once again go out alone.

Misbehaved, as children tend to be, their punishment must

be swiftly appropriate. Once punished, their adventure must continue, free to journey once again.

America, the great mother, often finds great sadness within her children's rivalries. One of her toughest jobs, yet, she loves each child unconditionally. However, her required fairness does not allow a set of wavered rules.

More importantly, she understands that her children must learn, and grow. Therefore, she must often remain quiet.

The greatest mother knows some will succeed beyond her expectations. She will beam with pride and respect. Some of her children will struggle and fail. Knowing she must push them, ultimately she must allow their freedom.

In the past, some of her children toiled with failure, daunting, and seemingly insurmountable even in her old age. Somehow, someway, these children persevere. Her struggling children have risen from the depths of their own souls, and slain their Dragon of Defeat, by striving to succeed.

The mother understands her ceaseless job, the only one that must remain the same. Despite unending anguish, that pelts her like the seasons, she knows her children's maturation depends upon her consistent lack of interference.

The mother is wise, her unconditional love undaunted. Her children are her own. With the ability to alleviate so many of their struggles, and mediate all of their disagreements, she could with ease, deliver their necessities in a pretty package.

She could force her children to consult, and inform her

much more often. Perhaps, institute more rules and decide career paths for them. Controlling what they eat, she could name the doctor's that would treat them.

Maybe she could control the treatment, and the doctors, that remedy diseases. She could run the companies where her children work, or own their home loans, and their homes.

The Great Mother often struggles with questions of herself along these lists of issues. She loves her children deeply, longing for the day they will emerge from adolescence, becoming mature and loving adults.

Her children have long teetered on the verge of true maturation. Adolescence, an ugly stage, is the least of her favorite phases. The schizoid nature undermines development, and unnerves her daily with their petty behavior.

Bullying, fighting, cheating, identity crises, and abundant tragedy, she must be strong. Selfless, stable, her wisdom vast, she understands how to alleviate their struggle.

By increasing her control she'd quiet adolescents, and make things seem so easy, but ultimately, she knows this would be a selfish act. Any act providing her with more power, or control, could make her life more easy, and her heartburn would be healed. However, her children would suffer more, forever stuck, un-grown, or worse - regressed.

No, she is well aware her job must be maintained, as she must raise her children free from domination as best she can. They must find their answers, constantly change, and solve their own dilemmas. She must only encourage, and serve as a role model, acceptant without restraint.

The Great Mother knows by changing, she would cease to be what she always was - America the Great unconditionally loving mother.

"My own immigrant family is an example of the relationship, and love, our Great Mother affords those whom choose to strive.

In the 1950's, my Pop came to law school in the US, he returned to Cuba to marry my mom and start their life. My brother José, and sister Nydia, were both born in Cuba. Pop practiced law there and bought a home, with the intention of living his life, and raising his family in the beautiful island country.

Instead, things began to change, and became communistic, as Fidel Castro, Che Guevara, Raúl Castro, Camilo Cienfuegos, and others began a revolution to take over the government. Pop, along with several others, organized against the rebels, but the movement became too bloody. During the years he spent getting an education in the States, he became very familiar with America, the Great Mother.

In 1960, Maurice Dominguez brought his mother, wife, and two children from Cuba into the arms of our America. They left everything behind in Cuba.

At the checkpoint, almost free from Cuba, they were stripped of all their family heirlooms and jewelry, except for my

Grandmother's wedding rings. Pop had hidden the rings in my brother José's diaper. He couldn't bear my Grandmother's loss of the one physical reminder that remained of my Grandfather.

My Pop came to the United States with less than a thousand dollars. He began practicing law in Miami, representing the indigent. Pop allowed them to pay what they could for their legal services, and helped a lot of people in dire situations. Later, he made contact with some old schoolmates, and quickly had a hugely successful law firm in Miami.

My Father soon purchased our wonderful family home near South Beach. The Dominguez Law Firm and the Dominguez family home are still the center of my family's lives.

None of this would be possible without Mother America being who she was, and hopefully, who she'll remain. My own family is a testament of the Great Mother's Beauty in the Land of Possibility."

I looked out over the silent crowd, unsure of why their reception to my speech was not the one I had thought it would be. Uncertainly I looked at Amanda and saw in her face her unease as well. Had we both been so wrong about those gathered here and the sense of camaraderie we had built and been so sure of?

The next moment we were both knocked back by the wave of sound that thundered across the mountain. The crowd was crying and clapping and the Heavens seemed to join in with thunder from a cloudless sky!

Amanda took my hand and pressed it too her cheek, and together we walked down through the large crowd and finally made our way to join the others, my family, her family, our friends, colleagues; the Chosen. We were finally ready to take the next step on King Solomon's prophesized path…

Chapter 45

"Success is not final, failure is not fatal: it is the courage to continue that counts."
— Winston S. Churchill

When we were finally able to leave Hidden Mountain after the media finished with us, and the family had departed; Amanda and I drove back together, still holding hands across the console. There was no need for conversation—the feeling of contentment was all we needed.

On the day before Thanksgiving, Amanda and I were standing outside watching the sunrise. I watched her staring into the direction of the garage where the Harley rested in its shiny glory. She moved next to me and began rubbing her body against mine.

"Antonio, it is a beautiful morning."

I wrapped my arms around her knowing full well she had something in mind, and it wasn't the obvious indoors activity I constantly found myself hoping for.

"It is a wonderful day Amanda."

"I would not be at all opposed to taking a ride. You know, sometimes a girl likes to let hair flow wildly in the wind. Especially, in the presence of a man she has her eyes on."

I chuckled and whispered in her ear; "In biker leather?"

She giggled. "Of course, in leather, after all, is it not the entire experience that makes it a worthwhile adventure?"

330

"That it is my love."

Before I knew it, we were decked out in riding gear and boots armed, confident and mounted atop the beautiful bike headed to Hidden Mountain. Amanda's arms wrapped around my middle I drove through the leisurely mountainous back roads to the Mountain.

Against my back I could feel Amanda's positive energy flowing into my veins. Racing down the sloped highways I felt the gentle tap of her giggles against my spine. It was truly fun to play with her.

By the time we reached the Mountain, we were both delirious with laughter. I guessed I had never spent a more enjoyable two hours with another human being. Oh, and did I mention how incredible she looked that day? Irresistible, that's it...the tight black leather molded perfectly against her lean, yet muscular body. Her flaming hair blowing in contrast with the sleek black, well, to a professor like me it was tantalizing.

I thought I was going to lose it while fastening the repelling gear onto her. Prior to meeting Amanda, I had hoped one day to meet a compatible companion, and had never achieved even a sliver of that hope. Never in my wildest dreams had I ventured to fantasize about sharing even a portion of my life with a gorgeous sensual woman whose passion rivaled my own about the things I love.

Again, I let myself fall behind her as we hiked to the top. Watching her trek up the trail amused me. It was a grand day and soon, again, we would be repelling into the throat of the ancient volcano.

We uncovered the private entrance into our treasure trove. A secret, which still only the two of us shared. As had become customary, I repelled down into the chamber first. Acting as Amanda's coach, I talked her down. Of course, by this time she no longer needed my guidance, but this did not hinder me.

She didn't even complain when I caught her in my arms as she glided to the bottom. It was just that kind of day. We were happy to be there together sharing a moment that for a short time was completely ours.

Knowing the magnitude of what we were about to do, our lips locked sealing our allegiance in an affirming pact. In silence, I let her legs drop onto the ground and freed her from the constraints of the repel cord.   I stopped for a moment to stare into the same dancing kaleidoscope eyes that had first cast their spell upon me. Her soft smile told me it was time.

I picked up my pack and unzipped the pocket containing the prize, but instead of reaching for it, I nodded to my beautiful companion to do the honors. She licked her lips and smiled up at me, her white teeth shined through the dim light of the cavern. With gentle grace, her hand slipped inside and pulled out the soft pouch.

Again, our eyes locked as she loosened the drawstring bag. Holding it open she held it out to me. I smiled and reached inside to reveal one of King Solomon's most sought after treasures. Unwrapped it seemed to stare back at us as we stood for a few moments paralyzed by its power.

Amanda took my free hand and twined her fingers between mine. Together with the King's key we approached the locked entrance into the unknown.

∞

Made in the USA
Charleston, SC
27 July 2012